The Secret Book Of Sacred Things

TORSTEN KROL

This trade paperback edition first
published in Great Britain in 2012 by Corvus,
an imprint of Atlantic Books Ltd.

Copyright © Trosten Krol, 2012

5 7 9 10 9 8 6 4

A CIP catalogue record for this book is available from
the British Library.

Trade Paperback ISBN: 978-1-84354-579-8
eBook ISBN: 978-0-85789-660-5

Printed and bound by CPI Group (UK) Ltd, Croydon, CR0 4YY

Corvus
An imprint of Atlantic Books Ltd
Ormond House
26-27 Boswell Street
London WC1N 3JZ

www.corvus-books.co.uk

1

Today the sea traders came again. Last year they could not get through because a moonquake made the mountain pass they have always used collapse, blocking the trail. That was a bad year for all concerned. We got no salt fish and salt for preserving our beef, and the traders got no beef to take back to their home by the sea. We could not give salt to our herds and had to let them find natural salt licks in the forest, which we do not like to do because of the wolves. We lost two cows and three calves, and we missed eating fish, which is always a nice change from beef and goat. And that same moonquake that destroyed the trail also made the weather go strange again, with too much rain that washed away some of the corn crop, and the wheat yield was the worst anyone could remember. There was plenty of nightblaze at the same time, what they used to call aurora. I know that old word because I was called after it, but everyone calls me Rory, which used to be a boy's name sister Luka told me, but there are no boys in our valley called that. I am the only one.

That was a very bad year with all those things happening at once, but when the traders came today there was a celebration that made everyone come running even from the furthest farms to welcome them and their horses. We have less beef to trade because of the wolves, and did not slaughter as many as usual when the air turned cold because nobody knew if the traders would come this year, but then they did and now everyone is happy. I had to leave the trading field and come do my words for the day, but I rushed through that without sacrificing penmanship which is always important with the words, and then did something I have been thinking about for a little while now. What I was thinking was how nice it would be to write down something apart from the usual, something just for me, so what I did after I finished my words was take the oldest book with the yellowest pages that has got half of them missing and use that to write in.

We have got many many of these in the room of names. The one I have been writing in for the last year or so has got 'Accounts' on the front. Sister Luka told me this was something that mattered in the old world farbackaway but nobody knows what it means now. So I took another Accounts book with half of it missing to write other things in it that do not have anything to do with the important task of writing down the name of Selene, which protects us ever and always against calamity and tribulation. I write her name again and again until my hand gets too tired to go on and I have to sit awhile till I can pick up my eagle feather quill again to write some more. Only this time I am not writing the name of Selene, I am writing other things. It was the coming of the traders again after all this time that made me so excited I did what I did and started a secret book with my own words inside of it.

These words are not written from sacred duty like the rest, only for me. If the traders had not come today I would have been too scared to do what I did and would not be writing these words now. At the end of the day I have to take my book of names to sister Ursula so she can count how many times I have written down the name of our lady Selene and write down a number in her own book of numbers, which gets added to the list of numbers sister Ursula is responsible for. She has got books of numbers, piles and piles of them going back forever to the beginning. All the books of names are kept in the room of names, where I do my work, and all the books of numbers keeping a strict count of all the names are kept together in the room of numbers. Both rooms are on either side of the hospice. There are some who say that a dying person taken to the hospice can feel the power of the names coming through from the room of names to ease the pain of their dying. Sometimes sister Luka lets a dying person hold one of the books of names for comfort, which makes things easier for them. I have seen this for myself so I know. When my time comes to die I will ask for one of the books of names, maybe one of my own that I wrote as a girl, and I will hold that book to my breast like they do and go easy into the place that is death. If the moon does not come crashing down and destroy us all meantime. But that will not happen and is a bad thing to be thinking, because all the namewriting of Selene is the very thing that will keep our moon sailing around and around the earth, sometimes near and sometimes far, but always she returns, and that is when the moonquakes come, when Selene fills the sky.

I feel guilty as I write because I have not asked permission to do this secret writing, but today I have already written the name of Selene as many times as I usually do, so sister Ursula will not suspect anything. I expect the guilt will go away after a while and I do not get caught. The secret book must be hidden in the room of names, not taken away somewhere else and be at risk of someone finding it. I will just slip it under another pile of empty name books and nobody will ever know. Sister Luka would most likely punish me lightly because I am the Scribe. Only one person can be that, and it is me until my death and then they will choose someone else to write the name of Selene over and over and keep our moon in the sky where she belongs. So being the Scribe is important work, and the ones who do important work get treated just a little bit different to the rest. And there is no harm done in writing down what I think. I know all the words there are to be known, so writing down some of them apart from the name of Selene is not a bad thing in my opinion, but I will keep my opinion to myself. Being the Scribe will be even more important when I start my bleeding and become a woman. There is nothing more important than that, and everyone at the church will celebrate, all the women there, and I will be one of them at last. To be a woman is the best thing in all the world and this will happen soon.

The trading field is in the village, too far away for me to hear. There is such excitement now that we have fish and salt again. Nobody here has ever been to the sea, which is a longlongway and hard travelling, the traders tell us. They have never found another place to trade with among the mountains, nor along the edge of the great water, what they call the seacoast, so there are just these two places where people live and all those mountains in between. Sister Briony told me there were more people and places in the old world but they were all destroyed because they worshipped things not meant to be worshipped, unimportant things that have no existence now and good riddance, sister Briony says. Now we only have those things that are important, like growing food and sending our prayers to Selene, which is why we were spared here in our valley. I asked her why the fish and salt traders were also spared in their village by the sea, and she explained they were also spared so they could bring us fish and salt. We could live without the fish, but not without the salt. Fish is something extra, just as our beef is something extra for the sea people, but they do not send their prayers to Selene, they offer them to a giant fish, sister Briony says, that comes swimming along past their village every year at the same time, a fish so big it would crush our village beneath it. The sea people are not bad, just ignorant, and we must not look down on them, because they come a long way each year to bring us what we need. But I am never to discuss with them anything to do with Selene and our important work here because they would not understand, and might even be angry that we do not worship their giant fish. So we are always friendly with the traders but we do not talk to them about anything but beef and fish and salt. The same wooden casks go back and forth between us every year except last year, and it will always be that way for as long as our prayers keep Selene in the sky. The traders are beholden to us for this without even knowing it, and that is as it should be.

Women have little to do with them because the traders are all menfolk. Our own men do the trading, salt fish for salt beef, and share jugs of cider from our apple orchard so everyone is happy with the trades. It has been this way from the time of our grandfathers' grandfathers' grandfathers. If it was not the right way to be doing things we would have been punished for it like the people in the old world were all punished for turning away from the simple things, the important things. We will never make the same mistake they made, and because we do what we do here at the church of our lady Selene, the traders are made safe also from calamity, although they do not know this as I said. We women are responsible for all the world, which is Selene above and earth below. We are between the things that would crush us to powder if they came together, so we keep them apart. All this is simple to explain among ourselves, and simple is best.

I will dedicate these pages to Selene. This way I know that what I do will be a good thing, as all things done in the name of our lady are. I can hear some of the little sisters running past my window, which has three panes of glass and one pane of wood, actually a shingle cut to size and fitted when the pane broke before I was even born. We have no way of knowing how they made glass in the old world, so we must be careful of all the panes we have left, even if they are all turning yellow like the pages in our old empty Accounts books. Most rooms have wooden window shutters that are opened in the morning and closed at night, even in the warm season. There was a farmer who kept his window open one hot night and a cougar came inside and took his baby child, but it was only a boy. Even so, nobody fails to close their shutters now when the sun goes to rest. The men have taken Sol to be their own 'object of worship' as sister Luka says, because they must have something of their own to be kept apart from the important business of we women, just like the traders with their giant fish that visits once a year, which they have named Fluke. The trader men have Fluke and the valley men have Sol, who warms the seeds in the earth to make them grow so we have grain for our bread and apples and berries and so forth.

I have heard that the men believe Sol is the one we should be sending our prayers to, since he stays farfaraway and does not threaten to crush us here below like Selene, but Sol has his own ways about him that are puzzling, by which I mean his path across the daysky has been known to shift sideways a little, especially after a moonquake has set the earth to trembling when Selene returns in the closest part of her journey. The traders say that Selene when close makes the sea lift itself out of its own water and overrun the land, so their village has been built back from the shore a ways, and when the sea rises up so too do the mountains shake and groan, which the traders say is the waters beneath the earth shifting their mighty weight, and each time Selene passes closest to the earth, which is the seventh night of Selene, the earth itself turns a little further away from Sol, so his path runs a different course and one day he may never rise again to warm the earth, which would be the fault of Selene for causing this, the traders say. Our own men would not say this terrible thing out loud even if they have it in their minds. We know they agree with the traders because sometimes their wives report to sister Luka what they say, but only when their husband has been rough with them, so this keeps the men from mistreating their wives. No man would want to come up against sister Luka, who has a way of looking at them that lets them know they are close to big trouble or even banishment if they keep it up. That is what happened to my father, who killed my mother for no reason other than he was a bad man, and so he was banished from our valley and never seen again. I did ask just once when the traders were here before if my father had gone to live among them, but they said no, so the wolves and the cougars must have taken him as they rightly should for his sin against a woman.

The traders usually stay just a few days in the trading field, then go away. We will see them again next year unless there is another landslide or even a volcano to make their path perilous. The last volcano around here poured out smoke and fire when I was very small, but I do remember it pouring all that blackness and flame into the sky way off among those other valleys where nobody lives, just wild things. Our prayers to Selene kept the wind from blowing all that terrible ash in our direction, and the Scribe before me, who was an old woman even then, wrote the sacred name over and over, more times every day than usual just to keep the wind blowing that way so all our fields and orchards stayed green and were not turned grey, which is how the volcanoes killed the old world and everyone in it. Sister Luka told all of us little sisters how everything longagofaraway was burned to cinders to remove it from the face of the earth where it did not belong. So now we have only the simple things that are important and the volcanoes have gone silent, even when Selene comes close to us on seventh night. She still makes the earth tremble, though, making landslides like the one that kept the traders away for a whole year until they found another way. They are very determined about trading with us and will not be kept at a distance. They do not know this, but our lady Selene is the one who makes them brave enough to keep finding a way through to us, because our work here is so important.

This time the traders will stay longer than usual while our men slaughter some cattle for them and pack the flesh in the new salt that has come at last. Here at the church we keep ourselves separate from them until they leave, but we are always polite to them even if they worship a silly fish, because they do not know any better. And sometimes the traders leave with more than salt beef. Sometimes they leave with a young man who wants to see what there is outside the valley, which is called adventuring. Only young men and boys feel this peculiar need to be seeing what there is between here and the sea, even if it is just more mountains and valleys and places where wildfires have come and gone over the years leaving everything behind them black and ugly until Sol makes the land green again, but that takes a very long time.

There was one boy called John who went away with the traders rather than live with his father who he did not like because of fighting in their home, and he has gone back and forth with them between the valley and the sea all his life until this time when he did not come, so I will need to ask why not when I am done writing today. John has said out loud he does not like to be in a place run by women, meaning we sisters of Selene, and he has been known to try persuading young boys to leave here and go live with the fisherfolk where men say what to do. Every time he comes back to our valley with the traders he and sister Luka have words with each other about that, but I do not think she really cares all that much so long as he does not tell girls to go away also. A boy that wants to go adventuring is best left alone to do that if he wants, because this is better than staying here where he does not want to be and making trouble for others. Sister Luka says all it takes to keep men less troublesome is to let them have what they think they want and then they take away their discontentment with them, which we do not want here. Life is hard enough with Selene tearing at the earth on seventh night, so we do not need other difficulties to do with men. Let them go where they want and take their bad temper and discontent along with them. That is the sensible way to handle them. And that is why sister Luka is our leader here, because she is the most sensible and has been alive a long time so she knows everything. I am her favourite.

And now I will tell how I came to be the Scribe, which can only be a girl because boys are not taught their letters unless they want to be in a class with the girls, which they never do want so there are no boys that read and write. Why would they need letters if they devote their lives to growing things and not to prayer? So the Scribe is always a girl, then a woman, then an old woman like the one before me. Her name is Belinda and she could not be the Scribe any more when her eyes turned milky white with age and she could not see her pages and bottle of ink or find her quill even she was so blind. Usually the Scribe keeps on until death, but Belinda was given special permission to stop because of her eyes, but then someone else had to be chosen quickly or else Selene might not have been kept in the sky for want of her name being written down as it is supposed to be. There were three girls ready to be chosen from, myself and Irma and Eunice, and sister Luka had to make a decision before the end of the day because seventh night was just two nights away and the names had to be added to the book very soon or else we would risk calamity.

Sister Luka took us all to the creek where it opens out to make a pond, and pointed to the little insects there that are called water boatmen because they skim along the surface of the water without sinking into it. 'Now then,' she said, 'who can make a water boatman carry a leaf across to the other side?' Irma and Eunice did silly things like finding a small leaf and dropping it onto the back of a boatman, but the leaf slid off every time and the boatman went on his way without it. I knew I was much cleverer than those two so I did not bother doing what they did. Instead, I pulled a hair from my head and tied it around a leaf stem, then I captured a boatman and very carefully tied the other end of my hair around one of his tiny scrabbling legs, then put him back in the water. He dragged the leaf behind him but would not go across the creek, so I had to take off my moccasins and go into the water, which was only shallow, and direct him across to the other bank by holding my hands either side of him until he went where I wanted. When he went all the way across sister Luka clapped her hands and told me I would be the new Scribe, which is the most important job of work in the church, more important than the herb garden or the beehives or the bakery, more important even than the reading classes.

Irma gave me such a look that I knew she hated me for winning, but Eunice did not care even if I was much younger than them both and showed them up for stupids. Later on Irma chose to be a spinner and weaver and Eunice is being taught to look after the beehives by sister Frieda. That is also important to do, but being Scribe is best. Most likely those two will both leave the church when they are sixteen and take a husband. I just have that feeling about them, because not every girl can stay with the sisters forever the way I will choose to do. I do not want some man sleeping in my bed and putting babies inside me to care for while he goes outside to look after the cattle and goats and crops, doing the men things while I make meals and clothing with a baby on my breast. I do not want that, being some farmer's wife. I would look at my husband and think him a fool for not being able to read and write. Irma and Eunice will forget how to do that once they become wives, because men do not think much of such things as churchwork and none of them like sister Luka very much. But it was men that made the old world the way it was by being in charge of it, and look what happened, so now women will make things right and help keep those things that belong in the sky to stay there and not come crashing down onto our heads like before.

And now my wrist is tired from writing.

2

I did go to the trading field yesterday to ask about John who left our valley, but the traders told me he was dead. He had got sick in the lungs in the year they could not get to us and died with his fisherwife looking on and crying because they had a new baby as well as a grown-up son and daughter, so we will see John no more. I did not feel sad about him, since it was his choice to leave here and live with other people faraway. But I did get a surprise when the trader pointed to a boy among them and told me, 'That's his, that one there belongs to John. She come with us to see where her father come from.' So it was not a boy at all, it was a girl with short hair and boy's clothing. I stared at her until she noticed and stared back. It was not a stare from curiosity as you might expect, it was a hard stare without blinking, her eyes looking directly into mine. People from the valley know not to stare at me that way because I am the Scribe and worthy of respect, but this one from outside was no respecter of things she did not understand, and kept right on staring at me, at my smock, so unlike her crude outfit made from leather and very filthy besides.

She kept staring until a man came between us with a cask of salt, and when I saw her again she was looking at something else going on across the field, some kind of wrestling match, a farmer and a trader with too much cider in them, but it was a friendly fight with lots of shouting and laughter from their friends, just exactly the kind of thing men do with each other when they have nothing better to occupy themselves with. The girl who looked like a boy had turned her back on me to watch them. No girl from the valley would do any such thing or the men would think her a hussy. There are some like that here, and they are forever causing disruption among the men and their wives. There was one girl sister Briony told me about who was ordered to find a husband before murder was committed because of her arousing jealous passions among the unmarried men. That one had been a poor learner and was taken from the reading and prayer classes because it was clear she had no mind for higher things, the matters of importance that concern our lady. She has four young children now and is not often away from them and her hearth.

This fishergirl appeared to be just a year or two older than me. I could not tell if she was a hussy, with her eyes staring at the wrestlers, or if she was maybe different some other way. After all, what kind of girl would want to go journeying with traders like this? But it is no matter to me what kind she might be since she will be leaving with the men who brought her. The fisherfolk must be without rules to have allowed her to come with them so far from home, as if she was the boy she so much wanted to seem like with her pants and jerkin and wide-footed way of standing there, hands on hips to watch the men wrestle, all the while keeping her back turned to me. It was enough to make me want to slap her, although that is forbidden by Selene, whose desire it is to witness no acts of disorder among us.

I walked away from the field and went to my duties in the room of names, where I spent all morning writing down the name of our lady, covering page after page with *Selene Selene Selene Selene Selene* until I grew tired of that and have brought out from hiding my secret book to set down the things that happened at the trading field. It was a good thing the traders came back to visit us, but I know I will be wanting them to leave again. They are not like us, can never be like us. When I am head of the church, after sister Luka has gone to the sacred gardens of the moon to walk with Selene and look down upon the earth, I will not allow the traders to come into our village. No, they must wait by the mountain pass and send one man to tell us they have arrived, and then we will take our trade goods to them there. They only come to trade, so there is no need for them to be among us so much as today. That trader girl has been raised in ignorance like all from outside the valley, unless her father John told her about our way of life here.

Life almost stopped in the farbackaway because men could not control their appetite for dominance and slaughter, all those kings and presidents and ministers directing their armies to kill and destroy so they could take what other people had instead of cooperating and exchanging things peacefully like we do with the traders. They will take away beef and honey and hides from the tannery and we will have their salt and fish and shells that some of our women like to wear as a necklace, but only one strand, anything more is hussiness in the making and not allowed for that reason.

Men and women must live together so there will be more people to populate our valley and continue our good work, but they must be married by sister Luka. In time it will be me who conducts the ceremony, binding the hands of the man and woman with grass and instructing them to walk together in the name of Selene who wishes them happiness and fruitfulness. That is when the male surrenders his family name for that of the female as proof of his love. I will be calm and serious like sister Luka to make the binding meaningful for the bride and groom, so they stay together for the children that will come. When a girl reaches sixteen she can marry and have children, but I will become a sister instead, like sister Briony and sister Ursula and sister Mattie who teaches prayer. And after a long time I will be the High Sister like sister Luka and be responsible for everything until I die. I will be sister Rory, easier to say than sister Aurora. It all seems so far away still, years and years, but I must be patient. There will be more people in the valley then, so my duties will be greater than those of sister Luka.

And by then our moon Selene may be closer, more deadly than now. We do not know if the wide swing she takes away from the earth goes further out than before, which makes it come back closer than ever on seventh night, or if that makes no difference. What makes the difference, of course, are our prayers, which can move the spirit of Selene to spare us. It was Selene after all who placed herself between the earth and the great stone flung at us from the stars as punishment for the violence and selfishness of men throughout those longwaygone centuries of misrule. It came from outer darkness like a plunging hawk and struck a glancing blow upon our poor moon that sacrificed a part of herself to spare us below. Then the stone continued on, slower than before and broken into pieces by contact with Selene, and fell down with a terrible roaring that was heard by all the thousands and thousands of people that lived on the earth then, and struck us mightily for the sins of men. All the lands of the earth erupted with smoke and fire, and those parts of the great rock that fell into the sea made waves high as mountains to sweep away villages along the coast as a wind will sweep away chaff and dead leaves. The earth was in tumult and disorder, sister Mattie says, for years and years. The sky was filled with smoke as the forests burned and the ground shook as the waters beneath the earth sloshed and spilled like water from a dropped bucket and mountainsides slid down to cover villages forever. It was the end of everything that ever had been, and the only reason it could have happened was the god of the stars was not pleased by the evil done to everyone by men. So the time of rule by men was ended, and the time of rule by women began, right here in our valley that was spared because one woman called sister

Winona had been granted a vision by Selene and took all her fellow sisters with her to a place of safety before the great stone came to destroy ninety-nine of the earth's one hundred parts, blessed be the name of sister Winona.

We are taught that Selene sent men to the valley for the creation of more people and to establish the new way of doing things. These men came to the sisters and wanted to tell them what to do. They carried the ancient weapons that have always been the cause of murder and outrage upon women, and sister Winona would only let the men stay if they would destroy their weapons and agree to be led by her. Their leader was called Ranger and he did not want to do that, so sister Winona took him to the end of the valley where the badlands begin and ordered him to leave, and he did. He left all his men behind. When they were told Ranger had gone they did not know what to do until sister Winona told them they had to live without weapons foreverafter, and if they did this they would be presented to the sisters for selection as husbands. The men agreed to this rather than follow Ranger into the badlands, and they set their weapons down and did not pick them up again. They were not allowed to choose wives from among the women because the sisters would be doing the choosing from now on, to set things straight with no more nonsense about men being the leaders. That was all over and done with, and good riddance. And that is how life in the valley was started in the name of Selene who saved us all. I will be taught more later on.

And now I will say the most important thing of all. Because the moon may be coming closer than before and filling us with fear, and because the sun has been changing his path across the sky for reasons we do not know, something new has to happen to make us understand all of this. Sister Luka has said this to sister Briony who told it to sister Mattie who whispered it to me as a secret thing because I have been helping her in the evenings with preparing her lessons for the next day. The new thing that must happen is a mystery even to sister Luka, but she has been praying for guidance to keep us all from calamity. 'This is our time of peril,' sister Mattie said to me, 'and the answer will be revealed by our lady Selene at exactly the right time, so we must all pray hard like never before.' It is known that the Scribe is spared regular prayers because her writing is itself a prayer made with a quill and written words instead of spoken words, so this new thing will not make any difference to me except one way, which is my own secret to keep, except for writing it down here, like talking to myself about all of this. It is so hard to explain, but the very moment sister Mattie told me about the new mystery and peril I knew it had something to do with me. Yes, I knew this in such a strong way it made the blood hum in my ears as sister Mattie's words poured into them. Somehow I will make it happen, this new mysterious answer. I do not know how and I do not know when, but it will be me who makes the difference and saves all of us. If it was not true I would not feel this way. My blood runs faster as I write this, remembering the feeling. I am certain sure. It is the biggest secret in the world and even I only know a small part of it, the part about me. It is like I know ahead of all the rest that I will be the one, but it must not be spoken of or there will be envy and spite because the answer can only be revealed to just one person, not to everyone, not even to sister Luka. Only to me. So now I am waiting.

This morning before I came to the room of names I went to the long meadow called the field of Selene, which is where we keep the sacred herd. When sister Winona came here with her friends she brought chickens with her for their eggs and flesh, and seven llamas with her to make clothing from their wool. The herd grew larger over time, but not too large for our needs. We do not eat their flesh because they are the special creatures of Selene, not like the cattle that came wandering into our valley after the coming of the stone, and goats came too from somewhere and were bred for eating. I am especially fond of the llamas and love to touch their woolly sides and stroke their soft noses and watch them chew their cud. They are gentle but they will spit in your face if you annoy them, but none has ever spat in mine because they know I love them. Even when they die from old age the llamas are not eaten. They would be too tough in the flesh by then anyway, so they are burned like we are. I have one special favourite among them, called Brindle on account of her brown and grey coat. She saw me by the fence and came over to have her nose rubbed and her long shapely ears stroked. I am allowed to give her a carrot from the kitchen garden because I am the Scribe.

Watching Brindle eat, I saw Chad coming along the road into the village with his bow over his shoulder and dragging a dead wolf by the tail so everyone could see he has killed another one. Chad is our wolfkiller and allowed to carry a weapon to do his duty. Twice he has killed cougars, which are more ferocious than wolves. When he brings in a kill he has it skinned at the tannery and when the skins are ready he makes clothing from them with the hair still on. That makes him look like an animal himself, but I think he likes that. Chad has been without a wife since his own died in childbirth despite everything sister Rose could do for her. Sister Rose is the birthing sister that has brought most of us younger ones into the world, but with Chad's wife and baby she failed. He did not ask sister Luka for permission to marry again and did not care for his farm properly, so that was taken from him and given to another. All of our land that is good for growing things must be worked for the benefit of all, so nobody was surprised when Chad's portion was taken away, and he did not seem to mind about that anyway, going off into the forest by himself for a long time, gone peculiar in the head by sorrow over his wife and baby, which was a girl. We did not see him for the longest time, then he came back to the village with his first wolf and he has not stopped killing them since then.

They say he has a special gift for hunting wild things because he has become a wild thing himself all covered in fur and his hair uncut and filled with twigs. They say he has not spoken a single word since his wife and child left him, and most likely never will again. After he has been given some supplies he will go back into the silence of the forest to hunt down the beasts of prey there. Chad moves amongst us like a ghost and the small children fear him because he is so strange, but he does good work for the benefit of all so he is allowed to go his own way. Sister Luka told me the valley can hold all kinds and not everyone is the same as his neighbour. The one thing not allowed is for someone to do nothing, not contribute to the village somehow.

My own contribution is the opposite of Chad's or any of the farmers or the blacksmith. What I do is more important than just feeding people or making things for us to use like the potter does. As sister Ursula said, the Scribe spends her time scratching away with her quill 'to keep the sky off our backs'. What she meant was, keeping Selene off our backs, but she will not say it that way because some might see that as disrespect for our lady. She can be very outspoken sometimes but does not go too far. One time sister Ursula tripped over her own feet and fell onto the healing herbs she had just planted next to the sundial and swore very loud with all the old words, fuck and shit that sister Luka does not like to hear. Of course I said nothing because it is a small thing and nobody should fuss over those. I did notice that sister Ursula gave me a look after she fell and realized I had heard the bad words, so I gave her a smile to let her know I would not say anything, but then she got angry and asked me if I thought an old woman falling over was funny, which I did not. So it goes to show that the way you think people see you is not really the way they see you. I was very hurt that she said that to me, getting it all wrong, but I did take away a lesson from that, and the lesson is, you can keep people from seeing who you really are just by not telling them. They will think they know you but they do not, and this is an interesting thing to know. Most surely they do not know me here because I do not tell them what I know about myself. We are supposed to share everything, but I do not think this is wise or even possible. For example, nobody knows that I know I have a special task to perform soon, or that I know I will take over from sister Luka when she dies, which will not be a long time because she is old like sister Ursula. Sometimes secret things are more real than real things. But nothing is secret from our lady.

And now I have to take my pages to sister Ursula to have her count up the names of Selene and enter them in her book of numbers. I asked her once how many times the name of our lady had been written down now since the beginning, but she would not tell me. Only sister Ursula and sister Luka know how many times.

3

That fishergirl. Yesterday evening when I went to our dining hall she was seated at the table for the little sisters like me, the ones who have not taken their vows of full sisterhood yet, just sitting there like all the rest in her leather clothes that stink of fish. I could not think of a reason why she should eat with the sisters of Selene instead of with her own people at the trading field. They have campfires there and cook their own food, some of our beef we have traded with them, so why should she need to be at the church? I asked sister Kath who was dishing out the soup why she was there, and she told me, 'Sister Luka said,' and ladled soup into my bowl. There are only twenty-three of us little sisters and the tables are not large, so I had to sit opposite the fishergirl to eat, even if seeing her there made me lose my appetite. She was already done with her bowl and was rolling it around and around, making a very annoying sound, until sister Nell, who was the big sister in charge of our table, told her, 'That's for eating out of, not playing with, girlie.'

'My name's Willa,' she said.

'Put it down anyway.'

So she did, arranging the bowl very carefully in front of her as if it was made from glass not clay. That was to make fun of sister Nell, who ignored her but I could not. Her face was smirking under the skin as she let her eyes wander along the table, then they came back to me and stayed locked on my own in that same rude stare I saw her use at the trading field. So I asked her, 'Why are you looking at me?' And she said, 'I thought *you* were looking at *me*,' which was an answer I had no answer to, so I stared at my bowl while I ate, all the while hating her for being there where she had no right to be. She should have been with her own kind around their campfires, not with the sisters, little or big. The church is for the sisters, not for anyone else.

Sister Marion brought around the bread and this Willa creature grabbed the nearest loaf before anyone else could and tore a large piece of it off with her long brown fingers that had filth under the nails like a farmer, then crammed it into her mouth and chewed with her eyes closed. Then, with her mouth full of food, she said, 'Good bread,' as if complimenting sister Marion's baking was an excuse for poor table manners. I told myself she was from a backward people and did not know better, but when she said, 'The best I ever tasted,' it only made me angrier, especially when sister Frieda at the next table told her, 'We know, it's the best in the whole world,' and laughed. The fishergirl laughed back at her as if she was a sister worthy of making conversation with us, and said, 'Maybe I'll stay here then,' which got sister Frieda laughing again, as if the notion of this girl staying with us beyond mealtime was not itself laughable. I have always thought sister Frieda something of a fool, but everyone tolerates her because she can coax the finest honey from her bees. Once I heard her laughing with the carpenter who makes our hives, as if he had said something clever, but I have spoken with that man, his name is Roy Poulson, and he is not clever at all.

The Willa thing tore off more bread and crammed it into her face, rolling her eyes and playacting like a silly child trying to make its parents laugh just by being an idiot, and some of the little sisters laughed at her, encouraging her to be even more stupid until sister

Nell told them to be quiet because talk and carrying on during a meal made for bad digestion. And that made the idiot girl put on a fake look of shame with her mouth turned down at the corners, which made the other little sisters laugh all over again, especially those nitwits Irma and Eunice, until sister Nell, who is big and meaty, banged her soup bowl on the table to make them stop, only she did it too hard and it broke. The look on her face when that happened made everyone who wasn't already laughing start up, even sister Nell, who took up the broken pieces and shook her head over them, laughing even if breaking things is frowned upon here because of the extra work it makes replacing them, so I was surprised that she did that. I was surprised at all of them. The Willa girl had made everyone behave stupidly without even trying very hard. Everyone but me.

I finished my soup while they all had their mouths open showing their food, then I picked up a loaf – not the one Willa had touched – and tore off a small amount suitable for holding, not a big chunk like only a greedy person would have done. Yes it was good bread, but I could not chew it properly or swallow it down, and ended up coughing bits of it onto the table before I could bring my hand up to stop that. And Willa said, 'Hey, don't waste it,' which started the laughter again. I was so furious my face turned red, I could feel it burning clear down my neck into my smock. I wanted to throw my bread into her stupid laughing face or say something clever about how the bread where she came from probably tasted like fish, but I know she would have agreed with that in a way that would make everyone start laughing all over again, so I said nothing and concentrated on my cough, making it stop.

By then sister Marion had begun serving up corn cobs, hot and steaming and dripping with butter from our own small herd. Willa picked one of the biggest from the serving bowl and studied it from one end to the other with a look of mock seriousness on her face, then she said in a voice that could carry to all the other tables, 'I hear you don't allow men in here. I can see why you don't need them.' There was a moment's silence, then the whole room erupted with the most idiotic cackling and howling. When I understood what they were all laughing about I was shocked. Even the big sisters were joining in, with sister Nell holding her fat sides as if to keep herself from cracking open like a ripe seed pod.

And then sister Luka came into the hall. We do not see her at mealtimes, she takes her food alone in her room, so she must have come through to the dining hall to find out why there was so much noise. This was such a surprise it made everyone stop laughing, with Eunice the last one to bring her silly tittering under control. Sister Luka tipped her head a little way to one side and lifted her left eyebrow, which is her way of saying, What's going on here? without saying anything. Sister Nell held up her broken soup bowl and told her, 'I broke it.' Sister Luka said nothing, and now everyone was embarrassed. She turned and went away again, and sister Nell was not in a funny mood now. 'It's getting cold,' she told us, meaning the corn, and everyone began eating in silence. It was good to see them all looking shamefaced that way, all except one of course. Willa sniffed her corn and began attacking it with her teeth. She ate like a man, tearing off kernels and chomping like a horse. It was revolting to see that and I could barely nibble at my own. Even the smell of sister Kim's wonderful butter could not make me eat another bite. Sister Marion had made a rhubarb pie that is usually my favourite, but I did not take a wedge, just sat staring at my plate with my stomach turned to stone. That Willa had ruined everything.

Later I could not sleep and went to the window of the dormitory I share with little sisters Sarah and Cicely and Janet. None of these will ever become a big sister, maybe Sarah but not the other two, they are not right and will choose to be farmwives when they are sixteen. The ones who stay on will choose a thing they are good at – baking and cooking, tending the herb garden – and will be big sisters from that day on. Sarah is very quiet and will probably stay with the church because she is so thin and mousey and fearful no man would want her anyway except as a servant, so she will be better off staying here where at least she will not have to do things against her will and can earn her keep helping out with small tasks, although it is hard for me to see her as a big sister someday. I think she is simple myself, but do not hold this sad thing against her because she did not choose to be that way. They were all asleep as I stared out at the stars through our tiny glass window pane. Outside there was fire in the sky, so much of it I could not bear to see it through so small a thing and tiptoed downstairs to watch it outdoors.

The nightblaze was green and blue with just a little yellow and pink here and there, all of it glowing silently in the sky like windblown curtains of light, billowing and fluttering and disappearing only to come back somewhere else above the horizon, endlessly shifting and shining down through the darkness. I have always loved the nightblaze, even when I was little. I am told I would stare at it for hours until sent to bed by my mother who was murdered. She chose rightly for my name, Aurora. I truly feel that Selene is comforting me for my loss with this display so beautiful.

'Real pretty like,' said a voice in the dark, and I turned to see whose but already knew from her voice. She was just a little way off but hard to see with her dark boy's clothing. I tried to think of a reply but could not. She had no right to be where I wanted to be, alone watching the green light shimmer and swirl above. 'We call it cold fire,' she said. 'What do you call it here?'

I told her, 'Nightblaze.'

'Know what it is?'

'Yes.'

'Well, what?'

'The magnetical shield of Selene that protects us from the sky.'

'We say it's dead souls gone to heaven, but that's not there any more so they just flit around looking for someplace to land, but there's nothing so they just keep flying around.'

'That's stupid.'

'Why?'

I wanted to tell her it was stupid because we do not teach that here, and the sisters of Selene would be the ones to know about such things. The flying souls were like their fish god Fluke, just silly childish things to believe. Our souls go directly to the gardens of the moon to walk with Selene, the women do. The souls of men go somewhere else, if they even have souls, maybe to Sol that they secretly think we should be sending our prayers to.

'Stupid why?' she asked again. She even came closer to me although we could hear each other perfectly well and there was no need for her to be doing that, or even be there in the first place. I did not invite her and would like to know why sister Luka said she could stay. She is not like us, more like a boy with her loud voice and staring.

'Because.'

I saw the white of her teeth. She was laughing at me, or grinning, but the reason was the same – she did not believe in the glory of Selene or the teachings of the sisters, like all the rest of those traders with their giant fish and souls in the air.

'You're the scribbler, aren't you?'

'No, the Scribe.'

Someone must have told her the crossed feathers embroidered on the breast of my smock are to tell the world who I am, but she was showing no respect.

'My father told me about you. There was an old one before.'

'She went blind, but she can still do things.'

'We had one old man go blind, last year when everything went bad. The fish didn't come, not even Fluke. We thought the world was ending. Cold fire all the time and nothing to eat, lots of starving, so he had to go so there's more for the young ones.'

'Go where?'

'Oh, back in the hills a little ways, just far enough so we won't smell him when he dies. You've got to be hard or it's bad for everyone when there's not enough food. You don't do that?'

'We have a hospice.'

'Horse piss?'

'Where you go to die peaceful and calm. It's really just the infirmary, the same room, but if someone's dying then it's the hospice. We look after them and don't send them away. The laws of Selene forbid cruelty like that.'

'You've got more food here. When the fish don't come it's bad. We just have to.'

Of course that was just an excuse for cruelty, but I did not want to say so. The fisherfolk are not like us and it was not worthwhile to argue with this one.

'Want to see something?' she asked me.

'What thing?'

She dug inside her jerkin and brought out something on a leather thong that shone white in the dark. 'Whale's tooth.' She came closer, offering it even though I did not ask to touch it. 'Not a big one like Fluke, the smaller ones, the black and whites. Touch it, see how heavy.'

She was so close I raised my hand to keep her away, and she thought I was reaching for the tooth and put it directly into my hand. The tooth was smooth and warm from her skin, and heavy like she said it would be. I tried to picture how big a mouth it must have come from and was frightened. If wolves had teeth this big we would all be eaten. I dropped it and the tooth swung back to her. 'It's for luck,' she said.

'Why are you here?'

'The High Sister said, that one with the funny eye.'

Sister Luka could not help having an eye that looked sideways a little. It was so rude of this one to talk about that. She tucked the tooth away.

'I mean why did you come here? Traders are men.'

'So what? I asked and they brung me along. I'm good with horses. My father came from here. When he died I wanted to see where he's from. He told me some things.'

'Are you leaving tomorrow?'

'Not till we get more meat salted away. So you're the one writes down Selene's name all the time. What for?'

'Didn't your father tell you?'

'He said to keep the moon from falling down. Is it true?'

'Yes.'

'Well, what kept it from falling down before, if nobody was writing down Selene all the time?'

'There was no need in the old world. She went around and around just far enough away you could cover her face with a fingertip. Before the stone came and hit her. Now she wants to go away but can't because we need protecting from more stones, so she goes away off yonder for three nights and then changes her mind and comes back for three nights, only when she gets here she comes too close and then there's moonquakes when the earth reaches out for the moon.'

I could have explained about the power of prayer but there was no reason, not for this one who would not understand anyway. She made a sissing sound with her mouth to let me know she did not believe it was only me keeping Selene in the sky on seventh night. I could have explained until morning and she would still not have understood. I could smell her sweat she was so close. One of the big sisters must have put her in the kitchen or maybe the store room to sleep, not with any of the little sisters, or the barn with our milking cows, that would be suitable. Her face was green then blue under the nightblaze, which always gets brighter before Selene returns. That would be two nights away now. Everyone is more afraid when she is coming back towards us than going away again.

'We say Fluke flips her back to the stars with his tail before she can fall in the sea.'

'Well, that is just wrong, but we never make anyone believe against their will.'

'I guess you couldn't if they don't want to.'

She made it plain nobody could make her do anything she did not want to. It was not in my mind to tell her any different, so let her keep her giant fish with his tail big enough to swat the moon, only a child would believe that kind of stupidness. Her face was raised to the sky and she said, 'Well, those souls are sure beautiful anyway.'

She did not think I am anything special even if I am the Scribe. There is no talking away that kind of ignorance, which would be like talking to cows or apples. I was getting tired of her anyway.

'I'm going back to bed now.'

'Is it big enough I could lie down next to you? The fat sister put me in with all those sacks of flour that are hard to lie down on.'

'No.'

'I could breathe out all my air and be skinnier.'

'No, we have our own beds. We're not allowed to share.'

'I heard different from that.'

Now it is true that sometimes the little sisters will share a bed, especially on seventh night when the ground shakes and Selene rides close above us like a blinding white eye and the littlest are afraid. And it is also true that after we begin to bleed we are allowed to sleep together and there is sexual instruction from the older ones to the younger ones so we do not grow up thinking we must be some man's wife to find pleasure. That is all to give us a choice, to leave and be married or stay and be a big sister with the others.

Thinking about this made me remember Willa's joke about the corn cob, which was not even funny, just rude. It made me shiver to think about putting something like that inside me, then even a little bit sick. And she smelled very bad, like someone after working all day in the fields. Sister Nell should have made her take a bath before letting her into the store room even. She just should not have been anywhere near our church. Most likely it was sympathy for a girl all alone with those men that made sister Luka allow her to join us, but that was misguided because she does not belong here. Sister Luka is too generous sometimes with people not deserving this, but as High Sister she has to make all kinds of decisions so some of them are bound to be not so good.

'So I can't?'

The way she kept on asking made me like her even less. She was trying to make me change my mind just because she is older than me. She was talking to me like a big sister, which she is not, and I made a plan to stay away from her until the traders leave. Maybe they will leave before seventh night, but probably will stay in the field where there is no mountain to shake down upon their heads, and leave afterwards for a safe journey back through the passes to the sea. So I will have to keep away from her for two days and not let her find me.

'Goodnight,' I said and turned away before she could start talking again. All the way across the churchyard I was expecting her to shout something or else trail along behind me, asking still, but she did not do those things, so she is not such a bully as I thought, or else she is one of those silent haters that think evil but say nothing.

4

This morning sister Luka took me aside after breakfast and asked something strange. She said, 'Have you spoken with the trader girl?' It is not against the rules what I did last night, going out to look at the sky all shimmering. I have seen others do this especially when the night is warm and Selene is coming, pushing all that green fire before her to let us know, so right off I told her yes, and sister Luka said to me, 'What is your opinion of her?'

'She's just a fishergirl.'

'But what type of person?'

To be honest, I thought that was a silly question. She is not like us so what did it matter what type. I said, 'Very rude.'

'That seems to be the general opinion.'

So she has been asking others what they think. Why would she be doing that?

'She has asked to remain here with us when the traders leave.'

That made me almost fall over. 'What for?' I asked, feeling sick. 'Kitchen help?'

'To receive instruction in the habits and customs of the sisters of Selene. To live among us and be one of us.'

'But she isn't one of us.'

'Well, of course, but her wish is to make that right.'

I stared at the moon pendant hanging between sister Luka's breasts, not daring to stare into her face. Willa here among us? That cannot be. She is not suitable, not not not. I could think of nothing to say that would not come out as a shout, which you cannot do to sister Luka, she is the High Sister. She put her hand on my shoulder. She has done that once or twice before, actually more, because she knows I am different to the rest. She has never put her hand on some other little sister's shoulder that I ever saw and the reason is plain. I am her favourite because she knows I will wear the moon pendant someday just like her, and the shoulder touching is to let me know she knows. I have always been aware of this.

'We are not a closed society, Aurora. We are prepared to take in a girl from the outside who wishes to learn. She has never been taught to read or write, poor thing. I hate to think of the life those seacoast women lead under the thumb of their men. We must rescue her from that fate, don't you think? We are a sisterhood. How could it be right to deny one of our own?'

Sister Luka hardly ever uses my full name, so she was making a serious point, wanting me to agree with her, but how could I? Just the thought of something as boyish as Willa living here with us every day forever made my head spin. She would never fit in and be one of us, never never. I could feel tears prickling my eyes but held them back rather than let sister Luka know I did not agree with her and never can about this. She gave my shoulder a gentle shake to make me look up into her face and told me, 'We must do what we know is right. Knowing what is right is what defines us and separates us from those who do not know. If they wish to know, we have the obligation of teaching them. Willa has come to me and asked to learn the mysteries of Selene. We will all help her to sisterhood, as we must.'

'Yes, sister, only…'

'And you will be her special sister until she learns how to behave correctly.'

I think I gasped at that. If the Willa thing wants to learn, she can sit with the littlest of the little sisters and take her lessons that way like the rest. Why should she be treated any different than any other new girl? I could feel the blood humming in my ears as sister Luka released me, saying, 'This is a special task. No one has come to us before, so there is no set way to do what we must. I've decided that Willa must have a friend here to put her at ease among us. All girls want to be friends, our hearts make us that way. To deny friendship to her would not be sisterly, now, would it?'

'No, sister.'

'Willa will take her instruction with the beginners' class, but she will feel unhappy being with girls so much younger. For that reason she must have a special friend closer to her own age.'

'But she's older than me, lots older…'

'But you are very mature for your years, Aurora. You know this is the reason I chose you to be Scribe above girls who were older than you. I sensed a specialness about you, and that specialness is called upon here.'

'Yes, sister.'

'To make her feel at home among us Willa will share a room with you, just the two of you, like real sisters. I know this is the proper way to begin setting her on the path to sisterhood.'

'But… she thinks a giant fish makes Selene go away after seventh night.'

'Willa is not responsible for the nonsense her people have told her. It's our responsibility now to drive out everything she thought was real and true, and instruct her in genuine truth. Who knows, she might even take our belief back to her own people one day, and allow them to hear the truth also. Just think, she might become our very first pilgrim!'

It was the silliest thing I ever heard, these plans for Willa. She is not clever enough to do special things. I think sister Luka is being too kind to this newcomer, is overcome by her generous heart and making herself think Willa is something more than I know she is, but you cannot say this to the High Sister, so I said nothing. Sister Luka could look a man in the eye and tell him what to do and he would, because she is High Sister and the valley is beholden to her for keeping Selene in the sky and not crushing our fields, but she has always been very soft with females, as you would expect. Only this time she has picked the wrong female to be soft over. It will never work, I will see to that, and sister Luka will allow her plans for Willa to drift away as she learns what kind she really is – the wrong kind. Willa could no more be a pilgrim spreading our faith to outsiders than little sister Sarah the mouse. But that is for me to know and nobody else. I will make sister Luka think I want to do what she wants me to do, but really I will do something else and will do this so cleverly nobody will know what I am truly doing. Another secret. I am getting good at these.

'You'll share the little room behind the stores. I know you find her bad mannered, but that is just poor upbringing. Make a little of you rub off on her and she'll be someone we can all be proud of. This is a new thing for us, so it must be made to work.'

'Yes, sister.'

'Already you're being responsible and mature. Move your things now before you begin writing, that way you'll both be ready to share later on.'

'Sister?'

'Yes?'

'Can she have a bath first?'

Sister Luka tried to hide a smile, but I was serious – Willa stinks, and not just of fish.

'That has all been arranged. Sister Briony will teach her our way of cleanliness.'

'Good.'

I could not help saying that. Sister Luka walked away towards the bakery with her head held high as usual. Watching her, I felt guilty for my feelings about all this. It is going to be very hard doing what she wants and keeping my true thoughts hidden, but I will do that because I know I can.

I did what sister Luka told me to do, moved my few things to the small room, where sister Nell and Irma and Cicely and Janet were struggling to fit my bed from the old room through the door. There was already another bed in there for Willa but she was not there herself, which she should have been seeing as all this is being done for her sake. I wondered if she slept on a bed in her fisher village or on a pile of animal skins on the floor. Then I went to the room of names and have done my daily quillwork – *Selene Selene Selene Selene Selene* – and have set down in the secret book what happened.

5

Yesterday afternoon after I finished my duties at the room of names I delivered my work to sister Ursula for counting and recording in the book of numbers, then went to my new room to see if Willa was there but she was not, maybe getting that bath she needed. I was about to leave when she came in looking very different than before, with a clean smock but not a new one which she did not deserve, just an old one with repair patches. All our clothing is spun from llama wool by sister Loren and sister Amanda, who really are sisters, the only ones here from the same mother and father and they have always worked together doing this. Willa's hair stood out from her head in wet hanks and her face was clean, also smiling very wide with happiness I think, so she must appreciate what it means to be clean like us, her first lesson you might say.

She said, 'I'll take this one,' and went and sat on the other bed, like she had chosen it for herself, but really she had to because my things were on my bed so that was mine. The way she moved her behind around on the mattress stuffed with goat hair and corn husks made it plain she was not used to anything so nice. She would not stop smiling. She said to me, 'Now we're sisters,' but I did not agree with that. Then she said, 'Soon we'll love each other,' which made me want to hit her across her smiling mouth, but what I did was smile just like she was doing.

'Yes,' I said, and her smile got wider so she believed me.

She pulled at her smock. 'This tickles.' Her leather clothes must have been so greasy with sweat they slid across her skin easily, but now she would have to get used to being clean and washing out her smock once a month like the rest of us because I would not share a room with someone smelly. 'Sister Luka told me I start my lessons tomorrow.'

'You'll be with all the littlest sisters, learning to read.'

I wanted to see her face fall but it did not. She said, 'When I've learned how, I'll write down the name of Selene like you've been doing.'

My mouth fell open at that. Really, she understood nothing. 'That's a special task,' I told her, 'so you won't be doing any such thing. I am the Scribe.'

'But not forever.'

'Yes, forever until I die.'

'But there was another one who didn't die,' she insisted, like a truly stupid person.

'Belinda went blind, so she was excused. I won't go blind.'

'You don't know that. Nobody knows what might happen tomorrow.'

'Yes I do. You'll be doing the same thing as the others, helping out with all of them until you pick the thing you like best, weaving or baking or… anything useful. We all have our place and stay there.'

She was ignoring me. 'I'm so happy,' she said, beaming at me in a way that made me very annoyed with her for thinking she could be my friend and tell me things a friend would say.

'Did you have a bed in your village?'

'Not like this one, and everything is always covered in salt. We say how lucky we are to be covered in salt all the time because that means we'll be well preserved and not get old. That's a joke we say, but everyone hates the salt.' She went on to describe the salt pools beside the sea, a flat place that used to be a valley something like ours, but when the great stone fell from the sky the land disappeared and seawater came rushing in to cover everything, so the people that used to be farmers became fishermen instead and built walls around the pools to capture seawater at high tide when Selene raises it up, then it evaporates in the sun and they gather up the salt for trade.

She talked very fast and I pretended to be interested, then asked her, 'Won't your people be sad if you don't go home?'

'Why would they be? It's one less mouth to feed. Anyway, some of your people have come to stay with us, like my father did, so this is fair exchange.'

It sounded like a very poor trade to me, even if she is female.

She asked, 'What do you do when you aren't writing down the name of Selene?'

'Sometimes I get asked to help out with whatever needs doing, but mostly it's the names.'

'So you get to sit down all day while everyone else is working?'

I had to keep my voice under control when she said that stupid thing. 'No, the Scribe has to make every word of every line a prayer. Every time I write the name of Selene I send a prayer to her for all of us. Sister Luka says it's the most important work we do, because if I don't send those prayers when I write, the moon might fall, and the moon is bigger than the great stone, so that would be the end of everything.'

'What about the prayers everyone else sends? Don't you all have to pray every morning and every night? Are they just extra?'

'All prayers are heard by Selene, but the prayers sent while her name is being written are more powerful. Sister Mattie will teach you all of this, all the things you have to know.'

'So you really pray every time you write down her name? How many times a day would that be?'

'I don't keep count, Sister Ursula does that. But don't ask her because the number is a secret. Only sister Ursula and sister Luka know how many times going back to when the great stone fell.'

She frowned a little. 'Why don't you say some better prayers that'll make Selene go away to where she used to be all the time? That way she wouldn't come so close and make the ground shake and the mountains slide down into the passes.'

'There aren't any prayers like that.'

'How do you know if you don't try?'

'Because if there were prayers like that we would know, sister Luka would, because she's the High Sister. And she doesn't or she'd tell me about them. So there aren't any.'

It was useless trying to make her see anything, she was too stupid with all her questions. Someone like her could never understand how hard it is to be sending prayers to Selene all day long while I write her name over and over. I really do send a prayer, just a short one, for every time I write her name. That means I have to concentrate very hard while moving my quill tip across the page in little scratchy movements, again and again. *Selene our mother spare us your daughters below. Selene our mother spare us your daughters below. Selene our mother spare us your daughters below.* I do not ask our mother to spare her sons, since we do not think men are important, because it is women who give birth to both sons and daughters. In the old world it was men who thought they were the most important thing, which was wrong of them and made the great stone come. It is the female who nurtures, not the male, so men are something we must have to make more babies, but it is the girls who matter. The men are protected by our prayers only because they are here with us and so are kept from harm as well, what sister Mattie would explain to Willa as the Proximity Principle. Sister Mattie will have to explain what proximity means, and principle too because Willa knows nothing. This plan of sister Luka's to educate her to be one of us is a waste of time. I just know from the way she was watching those men wrestle in the trading field that she will leave us and marry. Anyway I would not want her here when I am High Sister so that will be a good thing.

Just then the gong rang for evening prayers before supper. 'We have to go to the prayer room now,' I said, standing up. I was glad I wouldn't have to look at her across the room any more and listen to her questions. And we are not allowed to burn candles after bedtime because that is a waste, so I would not have to look at her in the dark either.

All the sisters were gathered there when we arrived, big and little, also sister Luka, who always starts us off. The prayer is the same one I say when I write the name of our lady, so Willa picked it up directly and bowed her head like all the rest while we chanted over and over *Selene our mother spare us your daughters below* until sister Luka rang her gong, then we all went to the dining hall and ate salt fish, the first in more than a year. Willa was quiet, which was surprising, so I think she was trying to fit in by being like us.

And later on when bedtime came she surprised me again by falling asleep even before I did, so I did not have to hear her voice. Lying there in the dark I made myself forgive sister Luka for having done this foolish thing she has done, taking Willa among us, because she did that in the name of Selene, for whom all females are holy. Even Willa.

6

The face of Selene on seventh night is beautiful and terrible because she blots out the stars she is so close, her mighty strength reaching out to the earth, drawing us nearer in her loving embrace. In the old world Selene showed only one side of herself, so slowly did she turn, but since being struck by the great stone that has changed. Now she spins so fast you can see her turning, bringing into view the mountains and plains from her far side, showing us every part of herself while she grinds across the sky, even the long scar of her sacrifice left behind when she was struck that glancing blow that saved us from calamity.

When a sister begins her bleeding she is given a privilege, which is to see the face of Selene very close through sister Briony's instrument, which she says is older than a tortoise but younger than the stars and came from the old world. This is the only thing we have from waybackwhen and is precious so it is not used except when a girl is ready to look through it at our lady Selene. I am still waiting my turn. Willa is older than me and has told sister Luka she began bleeding a year ago, so on seventh night sister Briony took her up to the tower at the corner of our church so she could see for herself and look for the gardens of Selene. Everyone who uses the instrument looks for this but so far the gardens have not been revealed. Irma said she saw it but was not believed because she is a fool and because she said the gardens were filled with purple birds and pathways for walking with Selene when we are dead. She said the gardens were at the edge of the awful wound that stretches across the face of Selene, but nobody else has seen this and she was given a talking-to by sister Luka for lying about something so important. Sister Briony looked where Irma said but told us there was nothing there, only the yellow-white plain with its little circles and pockmarks. You could not see birds on the moon even through the instrument, even if they were bright purple. Whenever Irma says something silly now she gets asked if she has seen any purple birds lately, which makes her shut up and go away to cry because nobody believes her, but that is her own fault for fibbing. Sister Luka has said the gardens may be invisible to human eyes to spare us something so enchanting we would want to be there ahead of our natural time, meaning someone might kill herself to be there among such beauty as we do not have here on earth, and I think this may be true. If it is in the power of Selene to turn aside a mighty rock that would have broken the earth in half if it struck head-on, then it makes perfect sense that she would be able to make her gardens invisible. So the gardens could be anywhere among those pale grey mountains turning above us in the nightsky.

All the while Willa was in the tower with sister Briony I was not happy. She has only just come among us and cannot read or write and knows almost nothing apart from the prayer, which is easy to remember, so I do not think she should have been allowed to see Selene through the instrument so soon. On seventh night it is not unusual to see almost everybody outside, staring up at the moon. Sister Belinda told me this was partly out of curiosity to see the sacred gardens of Selene with or without the instrument, and partly out of fear that we would be struck by a moonquake while Selene rides above us and the church roof might fall in and crush anyone inside, even though our church has stood for a very long time and was even here before the great rock came. We are told that sister Winona who came here first with her followers made this her place of refuge from the world of men just because it was so big a place and made from stone and very suitable, which shows how wise she was to do that because now we are many and there is still room for all, blessed be the name of sister Winona.

Selene is so big she cannot be blocked out by both your hands held together at arm's reach, that is how close she rides to the earth on seventh night, pulling at our waters as if to draw them up to her own dry lands. She is so close you expect to hear a faint roaring sound from her path across the stars as she turns, but Selene is silent as death, and I have noticed that on seventh night the owls do not hoot and the crickets do not talk as they watch in fear that mighty circle above. When Sol is directly on the far side of the earth and blasting his light onto the face of Selene it show us every little thing there, all the peaks and ridges and valleys and plains but no oceans or seas at all and no rivers. Selene is a world without water except in the hidden gardens where fountains are. Everyone was waiting to see if this time there would be moonquakes as the waters of the earth were tugged and pulled at. Sometimes we hear rumblings back among the mountains, but this night we heard nothing, so Selene has chosen to be merciful. Her strength is such that if you place a tub of water under the moon on seventh night it will raise itself just a little in the middle. Sister Rose says she has seen this but I have not.

We watched the shadow of our world passing across the face of Selene, the curve of a mighty black circle with edges that ripple a little bit as they pass over rough ground or sail up mountain slopes and down the other side and on again across a flat plain where no human foot has ever walked. Sister Briony says that during the time of the old world some people did sail to the moon in a skyboat to see if the gardens really are there, but they could not find them and did not go back to search again. I do not believe this story and sister Luka says we do not have to. Selene would never let anyone set foot on her except when dead, so that is just one of the stories from long ago when people did not understand the truth and made things up to pretend they did, just so they would feel better.

I watched with all the other sisters and could not help but see how the mouths of the littlest hung open in wonderment at what they saw, even if we have seen this time and again, because now the edge of earth's shadow was entering the wound of Selene, the terrible gash opened in her side by the great stone from the distant stars. It is always special to see this and does not happen every seventh night. Sister Briony says in the old world the people knew in advance exactly how the moon would look on a particular night even in the months and years to come, because backthenaway the earth was fixed in its path around Sol and Selene was fixed in her path around the earth and there were no surprises, but now there is no way to know when the shadow of the earth will touch the wound. Now we are not sure from one year to the next, or even one month to the next if Sol will follow the path he always took across our daysky. Sister Briony says our world may be tipping over on its side a little bit more all the time, only she does not know if this is because Selene comes so close or whether there is some other reason. Sister Briony knows about things away from the earth, but only Selene can know the entire truth about what is really happening. Anyway we do not need to worry if we are tipping over because even then Selene will be held up in the sky by our prayers and especially by the names without number I write down in the Accounts book every day *SeleneSeleneSeleneSeleneSelene* until my wrist is tired, but the work must go on or I will be to blame if we are crushed. Sometimes I am frightened to be the one holding back calamity on behalf of us all here below, but that is also my strength and the thing that will make me be High Sister someday. I know this in my heart.

The edge of the shadow was travelling along the wound, but not for very far because its path was not true and it left the wound to race along flat ground and then over a little mountain standing alone, then on again toward the curving edge of one of the big circles that are like the ripples in a pond if you throw a rock in. On and on it went, speeding across the face of Selene.

I looked up at the tower but could not see sister Briony or the instrument or Willa, who could see our earthshadow through the instrument much better than me, even though I am the Scribe. It should not be this way. When I am High Sister I will let anyone, even the newest little sister, look through the instrument at Selene even before they can read and write. But no men. They do not have the right. If a man was to look through the instrument bad things would follow. Men need to be looking at the earth beneath their feet and concerning themselves with breeding cattle and planting crops, which they do well, and not wondering about important matters taking place in the air because that is not for them. In the old world men looked up and wondered and invited calamity down upon our heads, so this is not allowed any more. Sister Winona knew this before anyone else and took her friends away from men so they could not be made to do what men wanted, blessed be the name of sister Winona.

I watched Selene passing above until our mighty earthshadow ran off her edge and into the night. The great wound was turning away from us also, and sister Kim began gathering up the little sisters to send them to bed. I waited by the stairway to the tower but Willa and sister Briony did not come down for a long time. They must have been looking very closely for the invisible gardens together. I kept waiting but then got very angry about all this and went to bed. When Willa came in I was going to pretend to be asleep so I would not have to listen to her talking about the thing I am not allowed to do yet because I have not begun my bleeding. That has always been the rule here but I will change it. I wish my blood would come so I do not have to think about this any more. There are many other things to think about, but because Willa went up into the tower to stare at Selene through the instrument I can only think about this, which only makes me more angry. Sister Luka says we must be women even before we are women, meaning we must not allow ourselves to be petty about small difficulties, but this is hard for me.

At last she came in with a candle to light her way and sat down on the edge of my bed. She should have gone to her own bed because I was pretending to be asleep, but she sat on mine instead, as if we were friends, and shook me and shook me until I pretended to wake up. Her face was smiling with joy, which must have come from seeing Selene so close.

'I could see everything!' she said. 'There are mountains and valleys and flatlands... and the place where it was bashed by the great stone... and the shadow! I watched it flying like a bird!'

If sister Luka could just hear her talking about Selene as 'it' and the sacred wound of sacrifice as the place where Selene was 'bashed' she would stop thinking about Willa as suitable for being one of us and send her home with the traders. I hated her smile. Her teeth are straight, not a little bit crooked like mine.

'Wait till you see it,' she went on, 'it's not like seeing from down here, more like being so high in the sky you're halfway to the moon and everything is twice as big... Why are you looking at me like that?'

'You woke me up.'

'You'll have all night to sleep. Listen, what do you think Selene looks like?'

What a stupid question. 'You were just looking at her.'

'Not the moon, I mean Selene herself. I asked sister Briony and she says Selene is so beautiful you mustn't look at her or you'll be blinded. Her clothes are woven by silver moon spiders so she shines even when she's standing in the shadows, and her skin and hair are the colour of moonlight when the sky is clear. Do you think she shines in the dark?'

'I haven't seen her,' I said. 'Nobody has.'

'Well, someone must have or how would sister Briony know about the silver spiders?'

'You're not supposed to burn candles after bedtime, it's wasteful.'

She blew it out and set the candleholder down beside my bed. I smelled the sour smoke coming from it. Then she lay down beside me! How dare she do that! Our beds are narrow and there is no room for comfort.

'I was wondering if I did the right thing coming here. My father told me about this place and I just wanted to see if it's like he said. I was going to go home again, but then I had this thought. It came into my head like a bird through the window and flapped around in there trying to get out, but it couldn't because it was supposed to be there, because Selene put it there.'

'She did not.'

'What I was thinking is how I should stay here and be the sister of Selene I would've been if my father stayed here and never went to the sea. It's like putting something back the way it should have been all along, see? See what I'm saying?'

'Yes.'

'So I went to sister Luka and told her Selene put this thing in my head, this thought, and she told me it's most likely a sign. It might not be, but most likely it is, because if it wasn't I would've stopped thinking it, but Selene made me keep on thinking it, so that means it's really from Selene, that's what sister Luka says. But then after she said I can stay I got to wondering about it anyway, is it the right thing and will my ma be angry I didn't come home… until tonight. When I saw the moon so close like that I knew it was a true sign, the bird through the window, so now I can stop wondering and be happy here.'

I have been waiting for a sign from Selene, a message so powerful it could only come from her, but it has never come. I know I will be High Sister and I know I will be part of the new strange thing that will be happening soon, but those things, even if I am very sure about them, did not come from Selene. A sign from Selene should be like a voice whispering in your ear, an invisible voice telling you things you did not know before or were wondering about. But there was no voice, just a feeling that I am special and so these strange new things will be happening because of me. If only it could have been a voice I would know it came from Selene, but no, it was something like Willa was telling me about, this bird through the window and suddenly you know something you did not know before. Stupid Willa has not been told by Selene to come here, it was just a bird, but now because sister Luka said it *might* be a sign, Willa has made herself think it truly is, but it is not, it is like what I had only not so important. I know that if Selene is going to whisper in anyone's ear it will be mine. Willa has had a false sign and it is the fault of sister Luka for encouraging her to think it is real. This is very upsetting to me because I never before heard sister Luka say anything silly like this. But that can only mean she is not so close to Selene any more and is not thinking clearly the way she usually does. I am too young still to be High Sister, but sister Luka must be losing her specialness to be talking this way and putting false hopes into Willa like she has. This is a new thought but it is just a thought, not a sign, so I will not do what Willa has done and start thinking Selene has told me this. Selene will tell me everything in time, but I am young still and must wait. And the important thing is, knowing that Willa has had a false sign and sister Luka was also fooled makes me more powerful. To know the truth when everyone else is thinking something false is a wonderful secret to have for my own, so I will not speak about this and the secret will be more powerful because of that.

'And another thing that makes me happy is having a new friend.'

I was wondering if the new friend was sister Briony when Willa put her arms around me and kissed me on the cheek. My mouth opened I was so surprised, but no sound came out, so Willa must have thought I agreed about being friends even if I did not kiss her back. I felt like a stick of wood as she squeezed my shoulders. Willa believes all kinds of things that are not real, so I should feel sorry for her like I feel sorry for Sarah the mouse for being slow. But I will not show any of this.

Willa suddenly let me go and rolled off the bed. Her foot kicked over the candlestick but she did not notice. She told me goodnight and I think I said the same to her as she got into her own bed where she should have gone in the first place. She gave out a silly noise like a big sigh, and after wondering about that I knew it was the sound of someone who is very happy. Happy about nothing! I listened to her breathing in the darkness and asked myself if it was possible that I could be wrong about all this that has happened just recently, more things at once than I am used to, but then I knew I was not wrong at all. It did not take Selene to tell me that.

7

More strangeness! Chad the wolfhunter has killed a deer and left it in front of the room of names. I was working like always when I heard something bump against the door. I waited but there was nothing more, so I left my desk and opened the door. There was the deer, a young doe with an arrow wound in her neck, and there was Chad walking away across the yard to our gates that always stand open, which lead to the road to the village. Why has he done this? Now I had to go and tell someone, which would mean less writing. No one is supposed to disturb me when I am in the room of names, that is the rule. But I suppose Chad does not know this, not being a sister. But why not take the deer to the kitchen if he wants us to have it? He has never given us meat before, just takes everything to the village and they cut it up to share among themselves with a chunk set aside for Chad, then the meat is hung in the smokehouse and the hide is taken to the tannery to make shoes and winter clothing from. But then I knew why he put it where he did. The deer is a gift for me, just me, because everyone knows the Scribe is the only one allowed into the room of names. Even in the village they know this, so he would not have put the deer outside my door if it was not for me. So then I had to abandon my work and tell sister Kath, so she could cook it. She was not happy that Chad did this because now she has to skin it and gut it herself without really knowing how, because we get our meat from the village butcher already sectioned and ready to cook. I left her grumbling about Chad and his craziness that makes him live like a wolf himself and went back to my work. But how strange that he did this. Now I am wondering if Chad has seen something about me that is showing him that I am favoured by Selene, some sign or other nobody else can see, but Chad can on account of being different than the rest. This might be true, I am thinking.

And about all this thinking. I seem to be doing it all the time now. My holy work is to write down the name of Selene and send my prayers into the air while I do that, but behind the prayers is all this thinking about everything. When I look at the other sisters I see no signs of thinking. I know sister Luka must be thinking because she has so much to take care of here, being in charge like she is, but the others just seem to milk the cows and weed the herb garden and bake the bread without thinking at all. Even when they pray they are not thinking, I can tell. So this is most likely the reason I will be High Sister someday, all the thinking that I do from the moment I wake up in the morning to the moment I finally fall asleep. So much thinking but I do not want to share any of it, not even with sister Luka, not since she started showing an interest in Willa. And this is why my secret book is so important. If I did not write down my thoughts they would fill up my head and make it burst.

By the time I had finished enough pages with *SeleneSeleneSelene* and took them to sister Ursula for counting it was late in the afternoon, and she told me I had to go to the infirmary to see sister Belinda who has been asking for me. The infirmary is not just for the sisters but also for any villagers who are feeling poorly, but they hardly ever come. Sister Rose is in charge there, giving out herbal medicines for this and that ailment, but there was just one patient there. Sister Belinda went blind a year ago and that was sad, but now it seems she is sick too, which is not fair. Bad enough to be blind and helpless like she has been since I was made Scribe in her place, but to be sick on top of that is cruel punishment for nothing, because sister Belinda has always been very nice to everyone, especially to me. It was her that told sister Luka I should be considered for taking over her scribal duties, and sister Luka agreed to give me a chance. So I have a soft spot in my heart for sister Belinda.

She was sitting up in bed with a shawl around her shoulders even though the day was still warm, and looking into the middle of the room, but her head turned when she heard me come in. I sat on the stool beside her bed and asked her why she wanted to see me. Her face is like a dried apple with two white stones pressed into it, which I did not like to look at so I looked to one side of her.

'Have you completed your names?' she asked.

'Sister Ursula is counting them up right now.'

'I wonder if sister Ursula has enough room in her head for all those numbers.'

'She doesn't have to keep them in her head, there are books and books just holding the numbers of the numbers of the names.'

'I know that, child. I was Scribe for forty-three years before my eyes were taken. I used to wonder which would give out first, my eyes that were dimmer by the day or my poor wrist and fingers that had to keep scratching away even when they hurt. Does your hand give you pain?'

'Sometimes, a little bit.'

'When that happens, just think of Selene. She knows the pain that comes from worship of her name, and it's the name, the thinking of the name in prayer, that lends a powerful healing.'

'I know. I do that.'

She nodded her head a few times. Her head had turned to face me when I sat down, but now she turned away to face the middle of the room again. I waited for her to say why she wanted to see me, but she said nothing. I was hungry and wanted to go to the kitchen. I am not allowed to eat while I write the name of Selene, but am allowed to go to the kitchen afterward and be given a biscuit or some cheese to quiet my stomach growls until suppertime. She was not saying what she wanted to say and my innards were poking at me to be fed, but the old sisters have to be respected so I waited, pressing my hands into my stomach to make it settle. I would not have done that in front of someone who could see me doing it.

Finally I asked her, 'Is it your eyes that made you sick?'

'No, that is a separate ailment. My insides don't like me any more.'

She said this with a smile that showed how many of her teeth were missing. Sister Nell is our tooth extractor because she is strong, but I do not need her to be taking any of my teeth yet awhile. Sister Belinda looked so sad with her missing teeth I felt guilty for not looking at her directly. And she still had not said why I was there.

'You know the saying, child – from the infirmary to the hospice is just a hop and a step. I think I may be ready for the hop, and the step will follow soon after.'

'Are you dying?'

'I'm shuffling slowly towards death's door. Nobody does that quickly or willingly.'

'The arms of our lady will open for you.'

'So they say. They aren't open yet, though.'

That sounded a little bit disrespectful to our lady, but when someone is so sick that they think they are dying you must overlook such things.

'Are you content?' she asked me suddenly.

It was not a question I was ready for. No, I was not content, not about anything except being High Sister, and that was farfaraway still.

'Yes, sister.'

'You are very young. Your discontents are yet to come.'

'Yes, sister. Will they be very bad?'

She pursed her lips so much she made grooves around her mouth. 'That depends.'

'Oh.'

'Has your blood come yet?'

'No, sister.'

'Do you want to be a big sister when you reach sixteen?'

'Yes, sister.'

'And maybe High Sister someday?' She was smiling again. I counted eight teeth.

'If I'm found worthy.'

'I'm sure you will be. I see you with the moon pendant on your breast. But with authority comes the burden of the highmost. Will you be ready for that, I wonder.'

'Yes, I will.'

She laughed, but not unkindly, more like she was expecting me to say that.

'Are you able to keep a secret?' she asked, and that made me smile, what with all the secrets I have been setting down in my secret book.

'Yes, sister.'

'Because the higher you rise, the more secrets you must keep.'

'What kind of secrets?'

'The kind that will test your faith.'

'Why will they do that?'

'Because that is the nature of secrets. There are always things that are not for the ears of those below.'

I wanted to hear one of these, or more, just from curiosity, but she would not tell me. I wondered how many secrets sister Luka had in her mind. More than mine? That did not seem possible, unless the true reason she allowed an unsuitable girl like Willa to join us was some kind of secret. I would give anything to know the reason.

'Do you have secrets, sister?'

This time I counted nine teeth but she would not give out any secrets, would only say, 'Before I die I'll share one with you, but you can tell no one, it must stay a secret.'

'Thank you, sister.'

'Just one, and the rest I'll tell to Selene.'

'But she already knows them,' I said. 'There are no secrets from Selene.'

'That'll save some time then,' she said, showing eleven teeth now. Somehow sister Belinda was finding my visit very funny, which was annoying. Then she suddenly bent forward and gasped out loud, grabbing at her belly. Her mouth stayed open, making an awful sound. I watched a long drool come out slowly and begin dangling down towards the bedcover, then she pushed out sister Rose's name and I hurried off to fetch her back. Sister Rose told me to go away then while she gave some special sickness broth to sister Belinda.

I went to the bakery very upset about all this. What would the secret be, and would she remember to tell me in time before she died? Sister Marion gave me a biscuit and I ate it while walking through the corridor to the teaching room. I peeked inside and saw Willa and the littlest sisters getting instruction in their ABCs. The older ones at that time of day would be finishing up their lessons in the weaving room and the bakery and so on and would all be thinking about supper, but of course all these sisters had lunch while I was writing and would be nowhere near as hungry as I was before sister Marion gave me the biscuit.

Then I went to the kitchen to see what sister Kath had done with the deer, and what a mess! She had made no attempt to skin it, not knowing how, and had gone and cut off a hind leg so there would just be a little bit of skinning to do, but that had not got very far either and she was standing there red-faced and angry about Chad's gift with a bowl under the deer's butchered flank to catch the blood dripping out. 'Rory,' she said, 'go tell Franklin Lee about this and have him come with his cart and take this darn thing away for proper cutting up.'

I told her, 'My duties are done for today,' which was true.

'It's a favour, not a duty. There'll be good meat off this and the best cut for you if you go get him now.'

I said I would and set out for the village, which is not far away and covers more land than the church, although the houses are not made from stone, about twenty of them and the blacksmith's forge standing a little way off from the rest. Franklin Lee's house is also his place of work and the meatstore is in front. I went in and smelled the meat and the sawdust that he gets from carpenter Roy Poulson to soak up the blood. He was talking with two other men and ignored me until I pushed past them and told him we needed his cart to come fetch a deer Chad left with us. Franklin Lee looked at me a long time then said, 'Why'd he do that?'

'I didn't ask him,' I said, 'he just left it. Sister Kath says to come right now.'

'She does, does she?'

'Yes.'

'Well, then I guess I'll be along directly.'

Having said that, he made no move to shift himself, just kept staring at me with a look on his face that was supposed to put me in my place, I could tell. I do not like Franklin Lee. Just because he does a job of work that makes everyone come to him for butchered meat he thinks he is important, which is such a joke, him thinking that way about himself. One time I heard sister Mattie say about him and Grover Styles the miller who grinds everyone's wheat and rye that they are big fish in a small pond and that makes them think they are bigger than they really are. The other two men were looking at me the same way, without respect even though they knew who I am – the Scribe. What I do is so different to what they do they cannot understand its importance, and so they think they are better, that is clear from their faces when they see me coming. They do not like me just as much as I do not like them. I know what they think of me because a stupid boy told me what they say behind my back, the name they call me to themselves. They call me Spooky Clamphole, all the men and even some of their wives who have been a long time away from the influence of Selene after they left the church to get married and bear children. Even them. But I can never let them think they have offended me with this childish namecalling or it will give them power over me, which no man can have. Let them call me whatever they like, they are ignorant and without merit.

On the way back to our church I saw Chad loping along in that peculiar way of his and waved at him. He was on the far side of a field of wheat, so I could only see the top half of him, but it was Chad with all that hair long and unbound trailing behind him. He saw me waving but did not wave back, even turned his face away. He is so strange I do not know what to make of him. He is like a shy suitor bringing me gifts but too bashful to talk. The trading field was empty now, of course. The traders had left with their beef packed in their own salt. My deer that Chad left would not be salted and stored, it would be eaten quickly because deer meat is a treat for us. In the old world there were lots of deer, they say, but after the great stone made all the forests burn their numbers dwindled away to almost nothing. Now they are coming back, so not only will there be more deer meat for us to eat, the wolves will eat them too, and the cougars, so they will not be bothering our herds and flocks so much as before. I must tell sister Luka this thought so she can offer a prayer to Selene for making the deer return like they have. I have made suggestions before and she does use most of them. Everybody thinks the idea behind the prayer came from her, not from me, but that is nothing I care about. I turned to look behind me to see if Franklin Lee was bringing his cart, but he was not. Most likely he will take an age to come out and do what sister Luka wants, which will earn him a tonguewhipping if he does that, but he deserves it for disrespect.

There has been more and more of this disrespect lately. I have heard the big sisters talking about it when they think I am not listening, but I always am. For example when the spring offerings were made hardly anyone brought in crops from their fields to add to what the sisters contributed. We set out some of our best things, cheeses and honey and baked goods for Selene, but the sheaves of wheat and baskets of apples and so forth from the outlying farms were of very poor quality and the offerings were small. You could tell just by looking that the farmers had kept back the best for themselves, which is an insult to Selene. There was not so much of a crowd as usual either, and sister Luka's speech that she gave was not the one I heard her preparing through her window the day before, no, this speech was about not being properly grateful to our lady Selene who protects us all from calamity, and how there would likely be something bad happen because of that. We few humans that were left behind after the great stone came to destroy us had better start being grateful again or who knows, another stone might be flung at us from the stars and this time Selene would not place herself between the stone and the earth and we would all be destroyed for having forgotten how to be grateful. She was very upset all the rest of that day on account of so few people showed up to listen to her spring offering prayer. And then someone stole all the jars of honey and the loaves set out for Selene! It was sister Alicia who found that out at the end of the day and she wanted to not tell sister Luka who was already so disappointed, but in the end she did.

When I am High Sister I will make everyone in the valley come to the offering and they had just better bring the best of their crops or I will want to know the reason why. Not to offer Selene gifts out of gratitude is foolishness of the worst kind. Grover Styles should have offered something better than an old bag of weevilly flour to praise Selene. That was an insult and sister Luka should have sent him to the stocks for punishment and shaming. I would have thrown a clod at him myself. But he was not punished, which I think was a mistake. Sister Mattie says the people are worried about the sun shifting his path and the moonquakes that are getting worse on seventh night, but the last time Selene passed overhead there was not a rumble from anywhere, so that is not always true. I could see Selene as I walked back to the church, already on her way back out to the furthest reach of her looping path around the earth. In the daysky Selene is not so frightening, not just because she is smaller as she heads away from us, but because with Sol behind her it is her far side bathed in sunlight now, which we cannot see, and Selene is a soft blue, almost misty, with a thin golden curve showing the edge of her hidden face all ablaze with light.

8

Sister Ursula has asked if I am feeling poorly, because my daily name count has fallen lately. Of course this is because of my secret writing taking up time, but I could not say this or would risk punishment for neglecting my sacred duty. I have thought about this, about how I should be feeling guilty but do not, and it is because I do what I do for Selene. In the old world everything that happened was made a note of, sister Briony says, so everyone everywhere would know all about it, but we do not do that any more, so I will do it myself, just for me and of course for Selene who knows all our secrets. If I was truly doing wrong she would stop me, maybe with a handwriting cramp or a terrible headache like sister Marion gets sometimes and has to take to her bed so her duties are not attended to.

And I have a new secret to keep. The mess sister Kath made with the deer left a bowl of blood in the kitchen that was not thrown out directly, and when nobody was watching I snuck in there and took some blood from the bowl and put it in a jar with a wooden stopper. I hid it in my room, under the bed where Willa would not see it. The blood was already turning thick and I wanted it thin and running like fresh blood for my purpose, so I must not hesitate or delay on account of being scared to do this. It is another thing that I have to share with Selene, just between ourselves so she understands the reason why, which is to see our lady through the instrument like Willa was allowed to do just because she is older and has begun her bleeding. I will make a fake bleeding and be allowed also, which Selene will not be disapproving of because she will know I am her faithful servant anyhow, just impatient.

I told sister Ursula I had been feeling poorly just lately with stomach cramps, and she was so sorry for me she made me a potion from her herb garden that I had to drink down right there in front of her. It was horrible but worthwhile because now when I say I am bleeding at last there will be the story of my cramps and sister Ursula's potion to make it real. I asked her if sister Belinda was better today and she said no she was not and was wasting away very fast now from old age and sickness inside her, and why didn't I go cheer her up with a visit. So I went to the infirmary to see and sister Belinda was looking more awful than just a day ago even, so she is very sick, lying down not sitting up like yesterday. I waited by her bed to talk with her but she was not able to say anything, her eyes closed and her breathing very shallow. I stared at her, wondering why a blind person would close her eyelids when she can't see anything anyway. It must be because she had forgotten she was blind, she is so sick. Her mouth was open, making a funny little sound like something is stuck in her throat while she breathes. I waited a long time but she did not wake up, so I will not be told the secret yet.

Willa always sits next to me while we eat, and for prayers. She tells me everything about her lessons and how soon she will be able to read, but I know it will take longer than she thinks, she is just the kind that believes she is special and things will happen faster for her than for the rest. It is not so bad having her close to me now that she is clean and dressed like a girl, but I will not be sharing things with her the way she wants to share with me. Willa thinks she is my friend and there is nothing wrong with that so long as I know she is not. I have had some friends but only for a little while, then they annoy me with their childishness. For example Cicely and Janet were my friends for a short time but soon got to be more friendly with each other than with me, which I was expecting because it happened before with some of the others. I just do not want to bother with them after they show how they are not serious about Selene, not really thinking about our lady and what will happen to the world in time to come, just reciting their prayers and learning what they need to learn so when they are finally women they can pick and choose among the men on offer here, not that there is very much difference between these. I will not be choosing anyone because the High Sister must be alone to make her special, although it is permitted that the big sisters can be bedfriends if they want. I know from overhearing something sister Frieda said that a long time ago sister Luka and sister Belinda were bedfriends before I was even born, but later on they separated after sister Luka got to be High Sister, taking over after sister Rennie got sick from old age and went to walk with Selene in the gardens of the moon. They say that in sister Rennie's time everyone in the valley made sure to make offerings worthy of Selene and nobody showed disrespect for our church like now. When my turn comes I will put things back the way they were in sister Rennie's day. Someone has to do the things that will make life here better for all.

I will stop writing early today to make up for not naming Selene as many times as I am supposed to, though it is hard to go from setting down my own thoughts and back to *Selene Selene Selene* for more hours, but sister Ursula must not get suspicious about how many names I write each day.

9

I have done the thing I planned, used the deer's blood to make everyone think I have begun my bleeding at last. I woke up very early and made sure Willa was still asleep, then took the jar from under my bed and tipped it onto my little hairy patch, then hid the jar again. My smock was bloodied too but that cannot be helped and just makes it more real. When I heard Willa wake up I started making moaning sounds until she noticed, then I said I felt sick and lifted my blanket to see the blood down there. I pretended to be very shocked at the mess and even made a little scream that got her jumping out of bed to come see, and she said, 'Oh, is that all? Better wash your things out or it'll stain forever.'

Willa came with me to the well and even pulled up the bucket herself because I am still pretending to feel sick, then she helped me off with my smock and washed it out for me while I stood shivering in the early morning air and splashed water between my legs. Sister Ursula found us there because she is always one of the first to get up even though she is old, and she was not surprised about this because of my stomach pain yesterday. She gave me a hug and said, 'Now you can call yourself a woman.' Willa was twisting water out of my smock, just the bottom half, and gave it back to me. Pulling it over my head I almost felt like giggling because of the way I fooled them.

After morning prayers and breakfast sister Luka came to me and said the same as sister Ursula, and made an announcement to all the little and big sisters that now I am a woman. I had the strangest feeling when she said that in front of everyone and cannot decide if it was because I am so proud to be a woman now or guiltiness about the lie. I asked sister Briony if I could see through the instrument now and she said, 'Wait until seventh night comes again, that's the best time. You wouldn't want to be disappointed the first time you see our lady through the instrument, now would you.' So that was annoying, but a little later sister Ursula told me I could take the morning off and go into the forest to pick berries. My ink supply was running out and berry juice is mainly what is used to make ink with a little ash mixed in to thicken it. But I could not go into the forest alone, I had to take Willa with me so twice as many berries would be picked to make it worthwhile. This did not suit me at all. I wanted to spend the time by myself, not with her of all people, but of course I put on a smile and we went to fetch buckets from the kitchen, then set off.

Willa told me, 'It's better to have someone with you when there's danger.'

'What danger?'

'In the woods. There's wildcats and wolves and ghosts.'

'No there isn't, not ghosts.'

'Not in the daytime maybe, but at night.'

'Well, it's not even midday yet.'

'But there's animals there that'll rip you up and eat you.'

She wanted to make it an adventure, but that is just Willa. Someone like her just has to make more of something than it really is. That would be the reason she came to the valley with her trader friends, to be adventuring away from the sea and her stupid fish god.

I asked her as we walked along, 'Do you still believe in Fluke?'

She was swinging her bucket in circles, very happy to be away from the classroom. I think maybe she is not finding her ABCs as easy as she thought learning would be and was grateful to be given time away from the little sisters younger than herself.

'How do you mean?'

'Is he still real?'

'Of course he's real, I've seen him myself a long ways offshore, but you can tell he's really big and there's this hole in his back that blows smoke.'

'That's just silly. How could a fish blow smoke?'

'Because he's Fluke. Well, the others do it too, but he blows more than the rest.'

'I don't believe you.'

That stopped her swinging the bucket. 'Why not?'

'It's just too silly to be real.'

She was not happy about that. 'Well, what about you and the moon? It's just a big ball in the sky but you pretend it's a woman!'

If a man, or even a woman, in the village said that, they would be punished in the stocks. All I had to do was tell sister Luka what Willa said and she would be sent away back to the sea people.

'That's blasphemy!'

She looked puzzled, so I knew she never heard the word before, she is so ignorant.

'Saying that about our lady, it's not allowed.'

'Who says?'

'Sister Luka says, and all the High Sisters before her, that's who. You just did a terrible thing. I'll have to tell sister Luka about it. We have to when we hear someone say anything bad about our lady. She'll send you away, back where you came from.'

'But... you're my friend.'

She was very panicked now, which made it more fun, but it was her own fault. I made my own face very stern, like sister Mattie when she teaches about Selene.

'If I don't tell, it's breaking the rules and I'd be punished just like you're going to be.' The look on her face was very interesting, a mixture of anger and fear. I could not tell if her anger was for me or for what she saw as stupid rules, but either way it felt good to see her like that. She dropped her bucket and just stood there. 'No…' she said in a very small voice.

'I have to,' I said, trying not to smile because she looked so helpless.

'But I didn't mean it about Selene. I know it's not just a ball, there's a woman there in the invisible gardens… I believe about all that…'

'No you don't. You couldn't believe in Selene if you still believe in Fluke, and you just said you still think he's real. You can't believe in both.'

'Why not?'

I opened my mouth to tell her why not, but no answer came to mind. That does not happen very often to me, and as we stood watching each other I could feel time slipping past, silent time with no answers in it, and that made me feel almost as panicked as Willa but I did not show this.

'You aren't allowed, that's why.'

'But why couldn't they both be real?'

'Because they aren't, only Selene.'

'Why?'

'Because she is, that's why!'

She turned her back on me, very upset because I had shown how stupid she is to believe in Fluke but too proud to admit it. Willa was struggling with herself, I could see it in the way she held her shoulders and arms very stiff, and her hands were clenching and unclenching. Then they stopped and she turned around. Her face was different now, almost hard. She came three steps closer and I almost backed away, thinking maybe she would hit me.

'If you tell,' she said, her voice very soft but firm somehow, 'then I'll tell too.'

'About what?'

'About what I know that you don't want anyone to know.'

I felt a tiny tickling at the back of my neck when she said that. Had she peeked through the window into the room of names while I wrote and seen me writing in another book that was not the book of names? Nobody must know about the secret book, nobody. But then I knew it could not be that because one book seen through a yellow window would look like any other book, so that was not it. And then of course I knew.

'I found it under your bed, that blood.'

'My blood is nothing to do with you!'

'Well, it isn't your blood, is it, it's that deer's. You took some, didn't you? I knew soon as I saw your bush it isn't real, not all through your hair like that because it comes from your crack, not your belly button, but you wouldn't know about that, would you, because you aren't even a woman yet!'

I wanted to claw her eyes out for what she had done, that spying on me.

'Liar!'

She was smirking in a way that made her ugly. How I hated her.

'Who said you could look under my bed?'

The smirk got more crooked and scornful. 'Selene did.'

I tried to think what to say to that but nothing came.

'Selene whispered in my ear that there's someone trying to be a fake woman so she can look through the instrument even if she hasn't got the right to, not being a woman yet. Selene told me that's blastemy too.'

'Blasphemy.'

'Yes, so now you're going to be in big trouble for faking things, faking them in the name of Selene, hah!'

If I hit her hard enough with my bucket she might die, I was thinking, especially if I hit her in the head. But then I would have to explain about how that happened and could think of nothing that would sound real. So we stood glaring at each other with our faces all twisted, then she did something I was not expecting – she laughed. She was mocking me, and suddenly I wanted to cry. Willa had turned the argument around somehow and ended up on top, which was not right but I could not think how to change everything back again. Then she did something else I was not expecting – she stepped in close and hugged me, put her arms around me, trapping my own arms by my sides and squeezing me tight. She even picked me up and whirled me around herself twice, which made me lose my bucket. Then she stopped and opened her arms to let me go and I almost fell over from surprise. All that whirling and laughter had thrown aside Willa's loud words and my own, so once again we were standing there looking at each other, only now it was me feeling panic and alarm.

'Look at you,' she said. 'I won't tell. I'm not a snitch. You can tell if you like, I don't care. We should just be friends again.'

'All right.'

I had not meant to say that, it just slipped out. But it was the right thing to say because straight away I felt better.

'That's it, smile, it won't break your face.'

She picked up her bucket. 'I'm going to pick berries now, are you coming?'

I picked up my bucket too. We fell into step and kept going past the last of the fields and over the creek into the forest. I was very relieved Willa was not going to tell, and she must have been feeling the same. The sun was warm and for the first time I thought about what it might be like to have Willa for a friend. All those other friends I had for a little while were too young, even the ones my own age, and they never really treated me like a friend is supposed to because they could tell I am not like them, not really. I am not like Willa either, but she is older than me so I might not be as irritated by her silly ways. Of course she is very ignorant, but her mind is quick I must admit, so maybe we could try to be friends. It would most likely not work, but then again it might. Thinking about this, I saw that one of the reasons I would like to have a friend is so I can share the secret of the other book that is not the book of names. It surprised me that I felt a need to talk to someone about this because it had not crossed my mind until we took our first few steps into the forest, silent and dark, when having a friend seemed like a good thing.

The pine trees were very tall, their tops leaning sideways in the breeze and making a soft sighing noise like they were sad, but only a little bit. The ground was thick with fallen needles that made quiet crunching sounds under our feet. I knew the way to the nearest berry patch. Willa was singing a song about fishing that made it sound like fun, which it must not be from what I have heard, all that throwing of nets and rowing boats across the water. At the end of her song she started whistling a tune and would not stop. Then I knew she was afraid and was whistling and singing to keep away the ghosts because everyone knows ghosts do not like merriment. Sister Nell told me once that ghosts are the spirits of the dead that did not go to join Selene and walk among the gardens of the moon, meaning they are mostly men. They are supposed to have their own place but nobody really knows, and anyway who cares, they are only men, so I was not scared. But Willa was, and that made it easier to think of her as a friend even if she is older and knows about the bad thing I did. One of the bad things.

'Do fishermen whistle a lot?'

'Mostly they do. It makes the work easier. My brother Lonnie whistles a lot.'

'Do you miss him?'

'Sometimes. He doesn't talk much.'

'What about your ma?'

'We had fights. If my pa didn't die things would've been better, but I'm here now.'

That sounded like she did not want to go back to the sea, so if I want her for a friend there is lots of time. It was dark under the trees and cooler than in sunlight but we were sweating anyway from going slightly uphill and carrying those buckets that were heavier now than when we picked them up, and they did not have berries in them yet. Willa had stopped whistling. 'Where's this berry patch?'

'Not far now.'

'What kind are they?'

'Blackberries. We can eat all we want to but the ones in the buckets have to be saved for making ink. I have to squish them myself, that's the rule. The Scribe makes her own ink. Sister Luka says it's a tradition.'

'What's that?'

'Something people have been doing since waybackwhen.'

'Before the great stone came?'

'I think so. I have to squish them and squish them and my hands go purple and stay that way for days. I have to mix in charcoal ash too, that's really dirty. Two buckets will make a lot of ink, though. I make plenty before winter comes and there's no more blackberries. We make a lot of preserves too, sister Kath does, so she can make pies. What kind of pie do you like?'

'I'll eat anything. I like a nice food pie.'

That made us both laugh a lot. I was liking her more now. Having a friend is a nice feeling. I knew if I asked her to help me make the ink she would, but I could not ask her because only the Scribe is allowed to do that. Which is a shame because we could have had fun squishing the berries together and making a big mess with the charcoal. But that is what it means to be the Scribe. I must do the important things alone. Sister Luka told me the more important things you do, like being High Sister, the more alone you are even if the church has got lots of other sisters there. When I take sister Luka's place I will make sure Willa is given important things to do, like sister Ursula and sister Briony who are the ones sister Luka talks to the most, probably because they are getting old like her. I wonder what it would be like to have Willa for a bedfriend. She would never tell about the bad thing if we were that, and I would never tell about her still thinking Fluke is a god. Most likely she will stop thinking that after she has been with us a while, like she has already stopped wearing smelly leather pants. I am not sure what bedfriends do exactly, but they put their arms around each other to fall asleep, so that would be nice.

We finally got to the berry patch, which is in a wide clearing where the sun gets through, but there was someone else there before us, a small black bear. He looked at us but did not charge or roar, then went back to eating berries. He did not pick them, he ate them directly from the bush, but how he can do this without cutting his mouth on the thorns I do not know. Anyway, we did not want to go near him just in case he got angry at us for taking his berries. I whispered to Willa, 'There's another patch further in,' and we hurried away.

I asked her, 'When my blood really comes, will it hurt?'

'It's different for every girl. It never hurt me. Some get awful cramps but you might be lucky.'

'What about dribbles? I don't want to walk around with sticky legs.'

'You make a moss pack that soaks it up, I'll show you how.'

'I think I'll start soon. I don't know why I didn't already.'

'Don't be in such a rush. It's not so wonderful as you think.'

'But you're a woman then.'

'So?'

'To be a woman is best.'

'Who started that? Back where I'm from the men run things.'

'That's because you don't have the church. Having the church makes the difference.'

'But why?'

'Only through the church can we truly love our lady, and through loving her we learn to love each other.'

'But people love each other anyway.'

'No they don't, not the way they're supposed to, which is through our lady Selene.'

'Can you do it without learning how to read?'

'Not really.'

'Then how can the men learn if they don't get taught to read and write?'

'They can learn if they want to. Sister Luka says that not letting them learn is not right if they want to, that's called prejudice. But they never want to, or their fathers tell them it's nothing men need to know, so in the end we don't get any boys in class. There was one a little while ago but he only lasted for two seventh nights, so he wasn't suited for learning. None of them are, so that makes it nicer for us.'

'And the men like it that way?'

'If they didn't they'd say so.'

'The men from my village would say plenty.'

'But you don't live there now. The men here are different. We made them different because we don't let them run things like in the old world. They ran things into the ground, sister Briony says, so they don't deserve a second chance to do that. Our way is better.'

'Is that what your father says?'

'I don't have a father.'

'Did he die?'

'He was banished.'

'What's that?'

'Sister Luka made him go away for murdering my mother.'

'He *murdered* her?'

'If he'd just hit her he would have got put in the stocks and pelted with garbage to shame him, but he killed her with an axe and ran away. Some men hid him but their wives knew and told sister Luka, so then he was arrested and put on trial, and the punishment was to be banished. In the old world he would have been killed to teach other bad men a lesson, but we don't do the things that men used to do. He was sent away over the mountains without any food or a bow and arrows, nothing but the clothes he stood up in. I hope he got eaten by wolves.'

'Well, I guess he deserved it.'

'Murder is the worst thing in the world, then comes blasphemy.'

'We had a murder, but it was a woman that did it.'

'A woman?'

'They didn't banish her, just let her pick another husband. The first one was a bully and nobody liked him. The joke was, her new husband would likely be nicer to her – *or else*.'

'Well, if he was a bully...'

'So you folks here, you would've sent her away?'

'I think so. No woman has ever murdered anyone in the valley. That's the influence of Selene making things better than they were in the old world.'

'Well, she didn't kill the second one, so that worked out all right.'

Soon we came to the other berry patch where there were no bears, but someone had been there because the ground was all trampled, and in the centre of the clearing was the remains of a fire. It had been a big one with thick logs to burn, so it would have lasted all night but was cold now, so it burned some time ago. But who would go out into the woods to build a big fire like that and risk starting a forest fire? Willa did not give it a second look, just started gathering blackberries. She put the first few handfuls in her mouth and so did I. We had to be careful picking them or the thorns would have pricked us. One of our little sisters got scratched by a thorn last year and the scratch turned bad. Her whole arm swelled up until it looked like it would burst and turned very dark, almost black, then she died, so I was very careful with the picking. And all the time, as we ate berries and started filling our buckets, I wondered who made that big fire, and why.

10

For supper we had deer meat. Before that I spent the afternoon making ink, so now I have quite a lot to be going on with. Afterwards I used some of the new ink to write in my secret book as well as put about two hundred Selenes in the book of names. I must write the name of our lady with great care or the prayer in each word will not work, but with my own book I write very fast, almost as fast as I can think, even if it means my quill sometimes spatters ink around. That does not matter because this is my book, not Selene's. At supper Willa told everyone about the bear, only she made it twice as big and very threatening, roaring at us and chasing us away. She made it so real the littlest sisters stared at her with open mouths, very frightened, and all the big sisters laughed, even sister Luka, who has been looking very worried lately. Probably this is because sister Belinda is dying.

Watching Willa tell about the bear, I knew that yesterday I would have hated her for making people laugh, which is not something I can do. No, I cannot think of a single time I made someone laugh by saying something funny. Once I made up a joke to see if I could. Here is the joke. A big sister goes into the kitchen to see why there is smoke coming out the door, and she sees a skillet all on fire and rushes to get a bucket of water, but the kitchen sister says not to do that because she is making smoked beef! The joke is that you don't smoke meat right there in the pan, you get it from the smokehouse. I told it to two people but no one laughed, so I have no gift for this. But Willa does, and instead of hating her for that I was proud to see everyone enjoying the story because I have got a clever and funny friend now, and will make sure nobody else gets to be her best friend, only me.

After supper sister Luka told us sister Belinda was very sick and in need of our prayers, which would go to Selene and come back to sister Belinda, making her feel better. So for a longer time than usual we prayed over and over. Afterwards we were sent off to bed, but I went to the hospice instead to see if the prayers had worked yet. Sister Belinda was awake and not bending over with pain, so there you see the power of Selene to bring comfort and happiness. I sat on the stool beside her bed and coughed to let her know I was there. A small candle was burning because the sun had gone down even if sister Belinda could not see anything.

'Good evening, Rory,' she said, sounding stronger than the last time. She knew it was me even though she is blind, so the prayers had made her ears sharper somehow. Even so, it was strange to hear her say my name before I even said a word.

'Good evening, sister Belinda. We all said a prayer for you after supper.'

'Aah, that must be the reason I still live.'

'Did you feel the presence of Selene? It wasn't long ago.'

'I always feel the presence of our lady, but yes, a little while ago I felt something... extra, so that would be the prayers. Please thank everyone for me.'

'I will tomorrow. It's bedtime now.'

'And you came to see me.'

'I was wondering about the secret.'

'Secret?'

'You said you'd tell me a secret.'

'I did?'

'Just the other day. You said you'd tell me a secret before…'

'Before what? Before bedtime?'

'No.'

'Before what, then?'

'Before… I can't remember.'

'Would you remember a secret if I told you one?'

'Oh, yes!'

'Before I die, that was the part you forgot.'

She smiled at the room. Her hair was very grey and hung down over her breasts, which were very flat. Those pale eyes staring at nothing did not blink. 'Give me your hand, child.' I reached out and her fingers closed over mine, cold fingers with rough skin. She squeezed my hand tightly. 'Why do you like secrets?'

'I don't, but you wanted to tell me one.'

'You don't like secrets? I thought everyone liked secrets.'

'Well, sometimes I do.'

'And you wish to hear one from me before I die.'

'Only because you said.'

She stroked my hands, feeling how small and soft they are, I think, and not like hers. Maybe she was remembering when her own were small and soft.

'I wonder which secret I should tell you,' she said. 'There are two, you know.'

'Two?'

'One is the secret in Luka's desk.' It surprised me very much that she called sister Luka by her name alone, as if she was not the High Sister or even part of the church, more like they were natural sisters like our weavers sister Loren and sister Amanda. 'And the second is in sister Briony's thoughts.'

'I think I could keep both of them secret.'

'That may be, but I only promised one.'

I waited but she said nothing more. The candle sputtered a little but kept burning. Sister Alicia is our candle maker and she makes them from beef tallow with pine resin and a little honeycomb from sister Frieda's beehives so they do not smell like dinner, and the wicks are spun from goat hair by sister Loren and sister Amanda. We trade a lot of candles for meat and grain flour because candles from the church smell sweeter than anyone else's. We say our lady has made them that way, but really it is sister Alicia. I wanted to hear both secrets but it was like sister Belinda had fallen asleep with her eyes open and would not tell me even one, and I was supposed to be in bed by then.

'Which one will you tell me?' I asked her at last, to wake her up if she was sleeping.

'Which one? A good question. Both are dangerous. Maybe I shouldn't burden a young heart with awful truths. Is your heart strong, Rory?'

'Yes, very strong for my age thank you.'

'But the secrets are sister Luka's and sister Briony's to tell.'

'I don't think they'd mind, not if I kept them secret.'

'The thing about secrets is, they demand to be passed on, and some secrets are not for the ears of the very young. They might not understand.'

'I think I would.'

She began shaking her head slowly from side to side. Her neck was long and wrinkled so she looked like an old tortoise. I wanted to give her a shake to make her tell, or a slap, just a little one on the arm, not the face, which would have been disrespectful, just so she would finally tell me what she promised. Then she smiled and turned to me and said, 'But I may live a long time yet, if your prayers were sincere, so there's no reason to tell you any secrets just yet.'

'You could tell me one now and one later.'

'Or none at all, which would be wisest. Let me think about this.

I believe I may have made a rash promise I had no right to make.'

'That's all right, I won't tell.'

'I must think. Find sister Rose and tell her I need the pot.'

I made myself get off the stool and fetch sister Rose, who then made me go away to bed, saying I was 'out running around and setting a bad example to the others'. So I did not get a secret told to me at all, which was very annoying after going to the trouble of visiting the hospice, and sister Belinda did say she would tell me, so that was a promise not kept.

Willa was in her bed but still awake. I took off my moccasins and got into my bed and blew out our candle. 'Where were you?' she asked.

'Visiting sister Belinda.'

'Is she better now?'

'No, she's saying things and then not doing them.'

'Are you going to say extra prayers for her?'

'Everyone already did that.'

I hit my pillow to get rid of some lumps, then lay down with my hands behind my head, staring at the ceiling and wondering what those secrets were. What kind of secret could be kept in a desk, and what was the secret in sister Briony's thoughts? I could not just sneak into sister Luka's room and open up the drawers until I found it, and if I ask sister Briony she would want to know how I know she is thinking about a secret. It is all a very big annoyance and none of it my fault. I was being very patient with sister Belinda, and she had made me a promise after all.

'But Selene will help her if we ask,' said Willa. 'Prayers to our lady fly through the air to the ears of Selene.' She learned that from sister Mattie's lessons. I think she wanted me to think she believed the things being taught, but I could not have cared less right then what she believed. Sister Luka's room was never locked because we have no locks, none that work anyway, and the keys were all gathered up a long time ago, before sister Luka's time even, to show that in the church we share everything and do not have secrets. Hah!

'I wish we could go into the woods every day to pick berries,' said Willa, meaning she does not like the lessons and having to sit there listening with girls half her age. I like her more now than before, but she does not speak the truth a lot of the time, trying to fit in with us. But we are friends now so I must forgive her. I would never tell her a secret, though.

'Then all the berries would be gone and we wouldn't be able to.'

'Then we'd pick something else.'

'There isn't anything else, just some things sister Ursula picks to make remedies. She's getting very old now, so she might want to teach you all about that so someone can make the remedies after she dies.'

'I don't care about remedies.'

'That's because you're not sick.'

'I never get sick.'

'But one day you will, and if sister Ursula isn't here to fix you, you'll die.'

'So will you.'

'No I won't. Selene protects the Scribe.'

'Like sister Belinda,' she snorted, 'blind and sick.'

'She didn't get sick until after she stopped being the Scribe.'

Willa made that noise with her nose again to let me know she does not believe about Selene's protection. Her own people when they get sick most likely ask Fluke to blow smoke over them or something. She is never going to believe the things she needs to believe, but she will pretend to.

'Can I come over there?' she asked.

'Over where?'

'Your bed.'

'No.'

'Why not?'

'Because we aren't bedfriends.'

'We could be.'

'You have to ask permission first and the big sisters talk about it to see if you're suitable.'

'Well, we are, aren't we?'

'And you're not allowed until your blood comes.'

'I won't tell about the deer's blood. They'll all think you're ready.'

I wanted her to put her arms around me again like she did when we were going to pick berries. I would not have let her but she did it so suddenly I was not prepared. Now she wanted to do it again and I wanted her to, but at the same time I did not want her in my bed, because then if I wanted her to go away she might not. She might pretend to be asleep so she would not have to go away and then what would I do? Willa is bigger and stronger than me so I would not be able to push her out if I wanted. So I said to her, 'I'll come over there.' That way if she squeezed me too hard or would not quit talking I could just go back to my own bed. She flung back her cover. I went over and got in beside her. Straight away she put her arms around me and breathed a big sigh right into my ear.

'Don't do that.'

'Don't you like to cuddle?'

'Don't breathe in my ear like that, it tickles.'

'You think that tickles? Try this.'

And she started tickling my armpits, which I was not expecting and it made me yell, but then I was laughing, which I was also not expecting and she had to stop doing that.

'Quit it!'

'You're real ticklish, aren't you?'

'No, I just want to go to sleep.'

'No one's stopping you.'

'Just don't do that again.'

'I might and I might not.'

'You better not or I'm not staying.'

That made her behave herself. She gave me a peck on the cheek and laid her head on my shoulder, which was not very comfortable for me but I let her because she is my new friend and you must make allowances. I listened to her breathing. I had not been so close to someone else's mouth before, and breathing is louder than you might think if it is happening right next to you. At first she breathed through her nose, with just a tiny whistling sound that means she needs to blow some snot out, then she breathed through her mouth, which Sarah the mouse does a lot and it makes her look like an idiot. Someone is always telling Sarah to close her mouth and it makes her cry if more than one person tells her that. I would hate to be Sarah, she is so weak and silly. Soon I knew Willa was asleep, but I was wide awake still, not sure if I liked having someone lying so close beside me I could feel her ribs going in and out. Her arms were around me with one across my chest and the other one behind my back, making me uncomfortable, but I did not want to wake her up by leaving. In the end I fell asleep too, and woke up this morning still in her bed, which was a big surprise.

11

There has been a big argument between sister Luka and Grover Styles who mills everyone's grain to make flour. He has got two horses that go around and around in a circle to roll a big stone grinding wheel that took him almost a year to make. Before then everyone made their own flour with little grinding stones, but now everyone is happy for him to do it for some kind of trade. At the church we trade honey and goat yarn and apples from our orchard, which are popular for making cider, which we do not drink here. Cider is for men so they can talk loud and wrestle and later on fight each other, which is the reason we do not want it here.

Grover Styles has said to sister Luka we have to give him more to get our flour, and sister Luka told him we would not and he was greedy. This happened right beside our well so everyone could hear them, especially when he started shouting at her about thinking she is a queen and not just an old woman. Queens are something they had in the old world and were very hard to please. If you shouted at a queen back then you had your head cut off, so we do not need these, but I wanted to be a queen when he did that so I could cut off his head right there for shouting at sister Luka. I was on my way to the room of names when it happened and I stopped to listen because shouting is not heard very often. He shouted a lot with his long ginger whiskers going up and down and words flying out of his mouth all covered in spit, bad words that made sister Luka angry too and who can blame her, getting shouted at like that.

'You cunts think you own the world!' he yelled, and my mouth opened when he said that because that is the baddest word of all, being insulting to women. That is a word from the old world and good riddance, but there he was shouting it for us all to hear. He did it deliberately to make us feel bad. Grover Styles is a big man with a big belly and voice that he uses to get his way, only he cannot get his way with sister Luka because the church is how we are all made safe here in the valley, all thanks to our lady Selene, so really he is shouting blasphemy right in sister Luka's face, he is such a bully. Then along came sister Nell, about as big as Grover Styles, and she came stumping on her big heavy legs right up to him and shoved him over, shoved him right off his feet and told him, 'Mind your manners, mister!' He was so surprised about that he could not even talk, then he picked himself up and pulled his hat back on and pointed a finger at sister Luka. 'Don't think things can't change around here,' he said, then got on his horse and rode away without looking back.

'Thank you, sister.'

'That one needs a good whuppin'.' Sister Nell was very red in the face.

'He isn't speaking just for himself,' said sister Luka, looking all worried and upset.

'They all need to mind their manners and think again about all this nonsense they're spouting. I don't need to hear any more of it. None of us do.'

She was talking about the men, who have not been contributing as much as they should to the church. We educate their daughters and offer them the chance to serve our lady, but men are not grateful. The ones that only have sons say they should not have to give as much, or even nothing at all.

Then sister Nell saw me watching and yelled at me, 'Don't you need to be somewhere doing something, missy?' That made me hurry away before I got yelled at again. Sister Nell should not have done that. I am the Scribe after all and it was not my fault Grover Styles shouted at sister Luka that way. He picked a bad time to do that because Selene was in the daysky when he did, misty and blue and coming back again for seventh night two nights from now, so our lady saw what he did and now he will be punished for blasphemy. His horses that pull the grinding wheel around and around might die, but that would not be fair because the horses did not shout at sister Luka, so really the punishment should happen just to Grover Styles. He had a wife that before she died never said a word because he scared all the words out of her with his bullying.

And it is not just him. The other men are looking at us without respect. I have seen it in their faces when I go to the village. Just before the traders came I was walking past the blacksmith's place and his son who is around twenty saw me passing and called out, 'Hey, Spooky!' His name is Buford and I think he might have been drunk even if it was only the middle of the afternoon because he is known to be a maker and drinker of cider and something else called shine, made from potatoes I think. 'Hey, Spooky, where you going?' His hair stood out from his skull like porcupine quills and his mouth was wet and red. It was very disrespectful of him to talk to me like that because everyone knows I am the Scribe and my writing keeps all of us safe from calamity, but he did not care about any of that and was deliberately insulting to me. So I stopped and turned to face him. It pleased him that I did that because now he would have the chance to say more stupid things to me, which he could not have done if I kept on walking. I pointed directly between his eyes and held my finger very still as I told him, 'Now you are cursed.' His mouth dropped open and there was fear in his eyes that he tried to hide, but he could not say or do anything, as if my pointing finger had made him freeze. He stayed like that until I lowered my arm and turned away, very pleased by what I did. Walking on, I was waiting for him to call out something stupid to make himself feel better, but that did not happen, so he was truly scared by me, and that is how it should be. He is only a man and a fool besides.

So now it is clear something is happening in the valley with these men. After the great stone everything was changed to punish men for what they did to the old world, the way they destroyed it with acts of cruelty and foolishness that could not go unpunished, so that is what happened. There has always been a story that is only whispered by men, that if Selene had not been in the exact spot she placed herself, the great stone would have skimmed our sky and gone past the earth leaving just a line of fire in the air above, but because it struck Selene its path was turned towards the earth instead, all shattered into pieces that rained down upon all those places that had many people living there. So in that story Selene did a bad thing and made the world built by men go away forever, and now it is a world made for women, the creatures of Selene. We are in charge and stopping things from going back the way they were before. To the men this is bad, but they only see things that way because they have been pulled down from the high place where they ruled everyone so badly. But still some of them think they should rule just because they are bigger and stronger than us. Bigness and strength were what made them do what they did, all the killing and cruel things they did for generations until the stone came to change everything and make it better, make things the way they should have been all along. It is our sacred duty as sisters of Selene to make sure it stays that way. I have made a vow to Selene. I will never let the men take back what they used to have. I will kill them first.

And now I must use my quill to write down the holy name that keeps the world in balance, or sister Ursula will lecture me again on how many and I must not displease her.

12

Now that we are bedfriends Willa and I share a secret. She knows my blood was not real but she has said nothing. Really, Willa and I should go to sister Luka and tell her we want to be bedfriends, but we have not done this and I have been asking myself why. Of course it is because of my lie about the blood. If I went to sister Luka to ask permission for Willa and me to be bedfriends she would know somehow that I am not truly ready to be anyone's bedfriend. And sometimes I think so too. It was Willa who wanted this, not me. I think I went to her bed because if I had not she would have pestered me. That would have made a big mess that sister Luka does not need right now with all her problems already with Sol moving across the sky different to before so the earth is tilting over although we do not know how or why. Maybe that is the secret that sister Briony has got in her mind that sister Belinda spoke to me about. But that is not a secret, it is a mystery that nobody understands, so that must not be it. I have not been back to the infirmary because I know sister Belinda will not tell me the two secrets, and it was not right for her to say she would. Maybe her mind is sick as well as her body, that would explain it. But the way she talked, those secrets are real, which if they are is making me angry. I am the Scribe and should be told.

Willa holds me in her arms and pours her breath over me all night.

If we are discovered like that there will be trouble. The big sisters are allowed into all the bedrooms whenever they want, even though this hardly ever happens. They do not think they need to snoop for bad things because the rules are hardly ever broken. But we are breaking them. And I am the Scribe. So this must stop. Or else we should make the lie complete and ask permission to sleep together. But that would make everything worse in my opinion, because telling one lie is bad enough, but asking permission would be like telling another lie on top of the first, so now I do not know what to do. Is it Willa's fault for wanting to sleep with me even though she knows I am not blooded, or is it my fault for letting her? I could stop getting into her bed, but that would make Willa sad. Or it might make her tell. *SeleneSeleneSeleneSeleneSeleneSeleneSeleneSeleneSeleneSelene*

13

Last night was seventh night and I was invited by sister Briony to go up into the tower and look through the instrument. I was so excited I forgot to feel guilty about the blood lie and could not wait to see our lady closer than ever before. The tower is open at the top with just a roof supported by pillars, and Selene was so close already her light filled the top of the tower and shone upon the long metal tube on its three legs that sister Briony set up for me. She showed me where to put my eye for looking, and when I looked our lady was so big it seemed like she was about to come right into the tower. The moon looked close enough to reach out and touch, as if my fingers could graze against that spinning ball and slow it down. Selene was so near she filled more than the circle that the instrument lets you look through, a greyish-yellow surface turning, always turning, but not so fast I could not feed my eyes on the strangeness there and store away in my head every crease and fold, every jagged mountaintop and dusty plain as it came into view. Best of all was the sacred wound, very long and deep, sunshine from behind the earth filling it with light so I could see every detail of the mighty gouge marks.

Some of the other little sisters were down below in the yard, gazing up at Selene hanging so huge and low in the sky. It was too soon to see the shadow of the earth pass across the face of our lady, but I would be allowed to stay up as late as I pleased, or as late as sister Briony pleased. 'Can you spot the gardens?' she asked, but I think she was teasing. She probably asks that every time a newly blooded sister looks through the instrument for the first time. I told her no, and then, feeling that sister Briony was in a good mood, I asked, 'Are there secrets?'

'Secrets? Where, on Selene?'

'No, not there.'

'Where then?'

'Sister Belinda was going to tell me a secret.'

'Well, she'd know about that, not me.'

'But the secret is in your mind, she said.'

'In your mind?'

'In *your* mind. That's what she said.'

'In *my* mind? Are you sure?'

I could have mentioned the other secret sister Belinda hinted at, the one in sister Luka's desk, but sister Briony could not be expected to know about that. She did not even seem to know anything about the secret in her own mind, or else she was faking.

'Yes.'

'Was she making sense when she said it?'

'Yes.'

'Wasn't in pain or anything?'

'No,' I said, and then I did a reckless thing. I made something up. 'She said I should ask you.'

'She did, did she?'

'So will you?'

I could hear her fidgeting behind me. My eye was still placed against the instrument, watching Selene turn in silence.

'Sister Belinda should mind her business, is what she should do.'

'I think she thought you might like to tell me.'

'Well, she thought wrong about that. I wouldn't know what she's talking about, and neither does she, most likely. You know she's close to joining our lady.'

'I know, but she was talking about secrets, and she says you've got one that you should share.'

'Well, I won't, and you can tell her that. No, I'll tell her myself.'

She sounded peevish now, and I did not want her to be talking with sister Belinda about secrets or she will find out I am fibbing a little bit, and then sister Luka would be brought in to sort everything out, meaning I would be asked a lot of questions and found out to be a liar, not just about what sister Belinda really said to me, but about the blooding too. And I do not want this to be revealed.

'She might have been a bit sleepy,' said the coward inside me.

Sister Briony sniffed but said nothing. I continued staring at Selene, and something inside me opened my mouth to say, 'And sister Luka has a secret too.'

'Is that what sister Belinda says?'

'She might have been a bit sleepy then, too.'

'You shouldn't take everything so serious. Sister Belinda has got potions inside her from sister Ursula's treatment herbs. Some of that stuff makes you see things and say things that aren't real. You should just ignore what she says.'

'Yes, sister.'

'Someone that's dying, they need to concentrate on what's to come, not leftover business from their life that's ending. She won't even remember telling you things like that by the time she wakes up in the gardens with Selene.'

'Yes, sister.'

'All right now, here comes the shadow.'

Our earth was beginning to throw its black circle onto the land of Selene, like a bite taken out of the moon's side. I could not take my eyes from the shadow's edge as it rippled and flattened and rippled again, passing over those ridges and valleys. This time it did not go into the sacred wound, just ran alongside it.

'Why is it different every time?' I asked.

'Why is one tree different to the next, even if they're both the same kind? All things that grow or happen over and over are different each time.'

'But why?'

'So we don't get bored watching it all. Would you want to eat the same thing for breakfast, lunch and supper?'

'If it was pie.'

She laughed, which made me think she would forget about those secrets and not talk to sister Belinda or sister Luka, so I would not be discovered for a liar.

When I went to bed Willa was waiting to ask what I thought about the instrument. I was still annoyed that she had looked through it before me even if she is just a newcomer, so I told her it was all right, nothing more, and she seemed satisfied with that. I would not have been if *I* was asking, but with Willa you cannot be sure her questions are sincere, so a poor answer is enough. The room was not at all dark because of Selene's light coming through the window. I got into my own bed and she came over to join me, even though I did not invite her. Willa thinks she can do whatever she pleases without asking, just because we are friends. I asked her, 'In your village, why do they think the earthshadow passes across the moon a little bit differently each time?'

'I don't know.'

She wasn't curious at all about this.

'But someone must have asked.'

'Who?'

'Someone who wanted to know. Don't your people want to know things?'

'We know enough. We look at the sea, not the sky.'

'Well, if you asked more questions you wouldn't believe in a fish god.'

'Why wouldn't we?'

'Because the answers would make you see it's silly.'

'You're silly.'

'No, you are.'

'No, *you* are!'

She started to tickle me, which has become a habit with her. Her fingertips dug into my ribs too hard and I smacked her to make her stop, smacked her in the face. She gasped, very surprised, then smacked me back. Her hand hitting my face made me so angry I smacked her again, really hard, and this time instead of smacking me back she punched me in my side. She punched the Scribe! I could not believe she did that, not because it hurt a lot, which it did not, but because you do not do that, not to a friend, never mind the Scribe. So I was very angry and hit out to punish her for doing that, only we did not have enough room to be swinging punches under the bedcover and ended up wrestling instead, but even this was not taken seriously by Willa. She snorted and giggled through all our grabbing and squeezing, making a big joke out of it. It is always hard not to laugh if someone right next to you is laughing, so I started laughing too, even when we tried much harder to get the better of each other, so we were both cackling like chickens when we fell out of bed and hit the floor together, which did not stop anything because my pillow came off the bed alongside us and Willa grabbed it to use for a weapon. She whomped me right in the face but of course it did not hurt and I scrambled over to her bed to get her pillow to use the same way. Still sitting on the floor, we hit each other with our pillows, giggling and grunting with every swing, hitting as hard as we possibly could. Then her pillow came apart and corn shucks and goat hair went everywhere, so we both had to hold our mouths so nobody would hear, it was so funny to see the pillow wrecked that way. Finally we got back into bed with our heads close together on the one pillow.

'You'll have to clean that mess up in the morning,' she said.

'No, *you* will.'

'No, because you're the one that did it.'

'With *your* pillow.'

'That you didn't ask permission to use.'

'Neither did you, so you can clean it all up.'

'No, *you* can.'

All of a sudden she was kissing me on the mouth. I have never been kissed on the mouth before, not by anyone, only on the cheek, so this was different to that. I could feel her tongue all wet and squirming against my lips, even feel her teeth hard and slippery, then our tongues were wrapped around each other like those mating snakes I saw last summer, and the blood rushing through my face and ears made me faint almost it was so strong. The smell of her skin filled my nose and her arms squashed my ribs they were around me so tight. Then her front teeth banged against mine and we both pulled back, sucking at our teeth to see if they were chipped.

Willa said, 'Ow.'

'That was your fault.'

'No, yours.'

But I did not want to play that game any more. She let me wriggle out of her arms so I could sit up. I touched my teeth again with my fingers, checking, not wanting to lose teeth like sister Belinda. 'Sorry,' said Willa, so I forgave her because we are friends after all and my teeth were not chipped or even loose. I lay down again but she kept her arms to herself. My heart was still pumping very fast from all that fighting. Then we went to sleep.

14

A new thing has happened. A farmer and his wife came to the church and said they wanted their daughter back. Their daughter is Irma who said she could see the invisible gardens of Selene. Her parents said they want her back at their farm so she can help out with the chores. Now this has never happened before, someone demanding their daughter back. I heard it all from Willa, who saw and heard everything. They came into the classroom looking for Irma and told sister Mattie they are going to take her away right now, and sister Mattie asked them to wait and talk to sister Luka, which they did not want to do, saying that was a waste of time because their mind is made up. Sister Mattie sent a girl to fetch sister Luka, all the while trying to make the farmer understand that Irma had to stay with the church until she is sixteen, but that only made him angry, shouting that he wanted his daughter right now and where was she! Irma was in the weaving room, which is at the far end of the church, but sister Mattie did not tell him that, keeping him in the classroom until sister Luka got there. And then there was a big argument when she did, because by then Irma's father was in a fury about having to wait and talking very loud. His wife just stood there looking upset. Sister Luka would not say where Irma was and that made the farmer even angrier and he pushed her out of the way even if sister Luka is old and not so steady on her feet, and went looking for his daughter. He went to every door that was shut and opened it, and that is how I learned something was happening because he opened the door to the room of names and stuck his head inside. I was frightened by him but he only glared at me then slammed the door shut again. Of course I went outside to see what had made him do that, and saw a bunch of people all clustered around him and his wife, with sister Luka telling him to stop, stop!

Everyone from the class had followed them outside, and Willa told me everything as we joined in. His wife must have known that Irma was learning to be a weaver, and she must have known where the weaving room was because she lived here herself until she turned sixteen, but she kept her mouth shut and hurried along after her husband. They were just two doors away from the weaving room when sister Luka grabbed hold of the man's arm. He shook her off and sister Luka fell down, which made everyone gasp. There was silence for just a moment, then he went to the door of the storeroom and yanked it open. Irma was not there so he slammed it shut just like he did to my door. There was so much noise and confusion by then that the weavers all came outside to see what was making such a fuss, and as soon as her father saw Irma she was grabbed. He started hauling her away to his wagon over by the main gate. Sister Luka was trying to get up, so Willa and I helped her to her feet again, but it was too late to keep Irma from being taken away. She looked confused about everything, maybe not wanting to go back home, but too afraid of her shouting father to say no. The wagon was gone and so was Irma, and nobody knew what to do because this has never happened before. It is just a shame sister Nell was not there to knock the farmer down when he did that to sister Luka. Willa and I were still holding onto her arms to support her and she was shaking, that is how upset sister Luka was. She pointed to the old bench under the elm tree and we helped her get there. Sister

Luka sank down onto it and sat looking at the ground, her whole body trembling.

'Fetch sister Ursula…' she said to Willa, and off Willa went in the direction of the herb garden. To the rest all crowded around she said, 'Go back to your classroom, nothing has happened here,' which was not true, only what she wanted to believe. Sister Mattie led the little sisters away, then the weavers were shooed off with a wave of sister Luka's arm and there was only her and me still there under the elm. She took a deep breath, then another, trying to calm herself, then she said in a small voice, 'It has happened. I was waiting, and now it has happened…' So Irma getting taken away was something she expected, which was surprising to me, because how can you expect something to happen that never happened before? 'This is the beginning,' she said, not looking at me, not looking at anything really. Then she put her head in her hands and did not look up until Willa came back with sister Ursula, who told Willa and me to go do what we were supposed to be doing, so we did not get to hear what they talked about, but Willa said to me before we separated, 'I bet there's more that'll come and do the same.'

I went back to the room of names and have written down what happened. I think Willa is right, more people will come and take away their daughters now that it has been done once with nobody to stop it. I am not able to write the name of Selene. I am sitting here wondering what will happen now. Sister Luka has been the leader for such a long time, like the High Sisters before her, telling people in the valley how to live their lives and the rules they have to follow, and if they don't then Selene will come crashing down upon us all even if I have been writing down her name all this time like the Scribes before me to keep this from happening. But now sister Luka has been knocked down, and the other day she was shouted at by Grover Styles, who most likely told everyone about that. Maybe that is why Irma's parents came to take her away, because Grover

Styles insulted the High Sister and nothing bad happened to him, so now they all think they can do whatever they want and will not be punished. When Irma's father banged open my door and put his head inside all red-faced and angry, the first thing that came into my mind, now that I think about it, was that he was here to kill me. His face told me that. No, it did not happen, but why is it that I thought what I did when he looked at me? It is like I have had this happen before, but then forgot it.

But now I remember my father, how he came to my room when I was small and stared down at me in my crib with an awful look on his face, a look so unlike his usual self I began to cry, and that made him go away. That was the day he murdered my mother whose name was Angela. I will not say what his name was, he is dead and gone and did such a bad thing he should not be remembered, but now I have remembered, and Irma's father gave me that same look that says he wants to kill me. And it is because I am female. I know this even though I do not know how I know. I just know. So now I am very uneasy about Grover Styles and Irma's father and Buford the blacksmith's son. They are all bad men like my father was. So they must all be sent away out of the valley for being bad men, before something else happens to sister Luka. If more men come to take away their daughters, who will stop them? After today the men will not respect sister Luka any more and will take away their daughters and do whatever else they want, like making us pay more for our flour or blacksmith work or anything else to do with bartering for what we need. Now they will say we are not offering enough and will refuse to give us those things. And nobody will stop them. I am shaking now like sister Luka, just thinking about all this. She was right. This is the beginning of some new thing, and it may be a bad thing.

15

Last night we all gathered in the prayer hall and asked for guidance from Selene. Everyone knows what happened yesterday and is worried, especially Sarah the mouse who does not want to go back to her parents because they do not like her, she says. Some of the other little sisters do not seem so upset, the ones that most likely would have left at sixteen anyway, girls like Eunice and Cicely who are not very bright and want husbands instead of being big sisters for life, so now they must be thinking they will have husbands a lot sooner. Nobody is supposed to marry before sixteen, but that rule might be tossed aside now that sister Luka has been shouted at and knocked down. Anything can happen after something like that. I have done my Selenes for the day and gone to the secret book for setting down the important things that happened. No, I am fibbing. I have not done all my Selenes, only half of what I usually do, but that can wait. I know sister Ursula will not give me a talking-to when I deliver the book of names to the room of numbers. I think maybe she will not even count them, or if she does she will not care that I have only done half the number.

All the big sisters are looking very worried today because of what happened with Irma. I know everyone has got one eye watching the gates to see if other people come to take away more of our little sisters. I have gone to my window three times to look but so far there is nobody. While I was looking a fourth time I saw sister Luka and sister Ursula walking across the yard in the direction of the herb garden. They often stroll there together when they have important matters to talk about because the garden is very nicely laid out and restful to the eye, as sister Ursula puts it, and there is a high stone wall around it for privacy, so they have gone there to talk about Irma and what it means. So sister Luka would not be in her room for at least a little while.

I thought about that and made up my mind. It was easy because I really wanted to know what kind of a secret was in her desk. Sister Briony is never going to tell me the secret in her mind, but sister Luka could let me know the secret in her desk just by not being there, so she would not have to think about it, which would be a good thing because she has so much else to be thinking about. It only took a moment to slip out of the room of names and hurry along to the staircase and up to sister Luka's room. It was not locked of course, and I went directly to her desk after closing the door behind me. It was a very old desk with lots of drawers. I opened them one by one, and was surprised to find most of them empty. Some had pieces of old yellow paper with words that were not written by hand, they were very exact and perfect like 'Accounts' on the front of my secret book, and I could not understand what the words were talking about, so they could not be the secret. I opened one of the bottom drawers and saw something mysterious, some kind of tool from the old world I think. It had a curved wooden piece at one end and a metal tube at the other, with a thick part in the middle, all of it very rusty. I picked it up and it was heavy. I thought it might be a hammer, but the part you would hit the nail with was wood, so that did not make sense. Anyway it was not the secret, so I put it back and opened the last few drawers, which had nothing in them. Sister Belinda was a fibber, or else so sick she was imagining things. It was very disappointing not to find anything.

I stood there thinking about things instead of leaving, which was foolish of me because the door opened and sister Briony came in. At first she was surprised to see me there, then suspicious, I could tell. 'What are you doing here, Rory?'

'Looking for sister Luka.'

'What for?'

'I want to talk to her about something.'

'What kind of something?'

'It's… private.'

'Sister Luka is very busy today.'

'I'll ask her tomorrow then.'

When I came out from behind the desk she looked at my hands. She was looking to see if I stole anything, and I was ashamed that she would think that about the Scribe, but then sister Briony is a very down to earth type of person that would think the worst of anyone if she had reason to, but that did not make me feel any better. She was looking around the room as if trying to see what was different, what had been changed by my being there, but of course she saw nothing. That did not change her face, though. She did not believe me, it was just so obvious, and that made me angry, which I could not show. I had to make her believe I had truly come to sister Luka's room for a reason, something personal and private.

'Can I ask you instead, sister Briony?'

'Ask me what?'

'It's about Willa and me.'

Her face softened a little. 'Bedfriends?'

'Yes.'

I was blushing, but only from guilt.

'I'll tell sister Luka you want permission. You're both sure?'

'Yes, sister.'

'You love each other truly?'

I nodded my head. Sister Briony had a sad look on her face now, very different from when she came through the door and saw me standing there. 'First the instrument,' she said, smiling, 'and now true love. Things change fast once you're blooded, don't they, Rory.'

'Yes they do. Sister, will there be others that get taken away?'

'Sister Luka has that matter in hand. What happened with Irma doesn't mean there'll be others. Willa won't be taken away, you can both be sure of that.'

'Thank you, sister.'

'Don't thank me, thank her parents for being dead or a long way away.'

'Yes, sister.'

'And don't enter the High Sister's room when she isn't here, that's not right.'

'I knocked. I thought I heard her tell me to come in.'

'Clean your ears out,' she said, but not unkindly. 'Now scoot.'

I went away. She had been fooled completely, but I had gone and said out loud that Willa and I wanted to be bedfriends, and I was not sure I wanted that. Once we were bedfriends in sister Luka's eyes, Willa might not get out of my bed when I told her to, and she did not put my pillow back together like she should have, I had to do that myself. I had spoken too soon, but it did get me clear of sister Briony's suspicion, so that is good.

Before going back to the room of names I visited the hospice to see what sister Belinda had to say for herself. I could not tell her there was no secret in sister Luka's desk, not without owning up to being a snoop, and it was plain there were also no secrets in sister Briony's mind the way she said. Sister Belinda has told me things that are not real, only imaginary things in her own mind, so I must forgive her for that and not be resentful that the secrets are not there, but it is a shame because secrets are interesting to know. She was awake and did not seem to be in pain but was lying down anyway.

'Is that Rory?'

'Yes, sister.'

'Come sit with me. Is it afternoon yet?'

'Yes.'

I sat on the stool beside her bed. She did not bother turning her head since she could not see, and it was strange to talk to the side of someone's head.

'That salt trader girl,' she said, 'I hear you and her are sharing a room.'

'Yes we are.'

'Sharing a bed too?'

'Well… yes.'

'Bedfriends, or just to cuddle?'

It was rude of her to ask that, and I did not want to tell her anything because she told me about secrets that are not there, so I did not have to be truthful with her in return. And anyway she was dying, so it made no difference if I fibbed.

'Just cuddling.'

Hearing myself say that, I wondered if it was true or not. Real bedfriends do sexual things, everyone knows that, but all Willa and I had done was kiss, which is not sex, more like affection. I do not want to do sexual things with Willa, just be friends but not bedfriends, but that will not be possible now that I told sister Briony, so I have traded the truth for something I am not sure about. I think Willa wants to do sexual things, and when sister Luka blesses us as bedfriends Willa will be expecting more sex and not so much of the ordinary cuddling. The kissing was very nice but sexual things are all about your crack, and I do not want someone touching me there. Maybe if I was truly blooded I would not feel this way. Maybe if I had not lied I would be ready to do sexual things. I had wanted to tell sister Belinda a lie to punish her for the fake secrets, but now I am not so sure what is a lie and what is not, or if something can be almost true.

'That's how it starts,' she said, her blind eyes not seeing the ceiling they looked at.

She sounded sad, just like sister Briony when I told her Willa and I wanted to be bedfriends. What is it that makes old women feel sad because someone young wants to have a bedfriend? They should be happy, not sad, because having a bedfriend is true love like sister Briony said, so why is there sadness?

'At least her parents won't take her away.'

'No.'

'That shouldn't have happened. That's bad. There'll be more.'

'How do you know, sister?'

'Bad things come in bunches. No salt traders last year, then bad crops on account of crazy weather, and now they say the sun has got himself a new path across the sky, comes up in a different place and sets in a different place than before, is that right?'

'I'm not sure. I think it's different, but only a little bit. Our lady isn't different.'

'When our lady does something different, that's the end of everything.'

'Why?'

'Because ever since the great stone nothing has been like it was. Before, there was a regular way of things happening, but now there isn't. In the old world they knew when and where the sun would be, anytime, day or night. They could point to the horizon any day of the year and say, That's where the sun'll be coming up today, and point somewhere else and say, That's where he'll be setting tonight, and they were always right. But we can't be sure any more, not now. Our lady used to roll in a circle, now she's in a long loop, but at least she's regular in the loop. She stops doing that, it'll mean bad things heading our way. Think I'm crazy?'

'No, sister.'

'Well, I am. I'm crazy and getting crazier. All the things I know, they'd drive anyone crazy if they knew.'

'What things?'

'I told you already, the secret things.'

'But what are they?'

'You didn't ask yet?'

'Not really.'

'Not really. Well then, I guess you shouldn't bother. You'll know anyway when the time comes. It's coming, and then there'll be trouble.'

'What kind of trouble, sister?'

'Every kind available. All the trouble that almost happened when the great stone hit, and maybe some more we can't even guess at.'

'There haven't been any moonquakes for a long time, not even a little rumble underground the last few seventh nights.'

'Oh, what a relief.'

She was only pretending to be relieved, was behaving very strange.

'Nothing bad can happen to our lady,' I reminded her, 'because the Scribe has never stopped writing down the name of Selene. All those scribes, going back to the great stone, writing and writing in all those books.'

'The Scribe,' she said, then again, 'the Scribe.' She sounded like I did when talking about Fluke, but how could sister Belinda do that, make the Scribe sound like something silly, something for ignorant people like the sea traders?

'And aren't you supposed to be writing the name of Selene right now?'

'I had to see sister Luka.'

'Poor Luka, it's all coming down on her head.'

'What is, sister?'

'You don't listen. We're an old blind woman and a young deaf girl, and sister Luka... she's a rock. You should be saying extra prayers for Luka because she'll need them soon, but don't say I told you so.'

She lay very still after saying that, while I waited for more of her opinions, but then she began to snore and I tiptoed away to the room of names.

16

After supper and evening prayers last night sister Luka came to our room to talk to Willa and me about being bedfriends. Usually the two girls have to go to sister Luka's room to discuss this, but like everything else around here that has changed. We had no chair or stool so sister Luka sat on Willa's bed and we sat on mine. It was past time to blow the candle out but we kept it burning, filling the room faintly with the smell of pine resin and honeycomb. She took a long while to begin talking, and I could see that everything is piling up inside her, all her worries about this and that. She seemed much older, and was even walking with a slight limp when she came in, something I never saw before, most likely a bruise from Irma's father pushing her over. Looking at her, waiting for her to start speaking, I made up my mind to do everything she asked and not to question anything, because sister Luka is under a lot of strain about things and we must all do our bit to make her happier.

'Rory, Willa, as you know, we are a society of women. Can you tell me why?'

I put up my hand, then felt silly because we were not in the classroom. Sister Luka smiled a crooked smile and invited me to speak just by lifting an eyebrow. 'So we can follow our own interests without interference from men, who have no idea.'

'And why is this our tradition?'

'Because it works?'

The crooked smile again. 'Because that is the legacy of sister Winona, blessed be her name and without whom we would have nothing.'

'Blessed be her name,' Willa said, too loudly, trying too hard to do the right thing.

'Sister Winona was a woman ahead of her time, girls. She knew change was coming to make everything different, and she gathered around herself a band of women, some of them friends and some of them lovers, and came here to the valley to establish a community dedicated to the happiness of women. Such a simple thing, happiness, and different for everyone, but the one thing happiness must have to thrive and expand into the lives of others is… what?'

'No men,' said Willa, grinning, expecting to be right. I wanted her to shut up and just listen.

'Not quite. Men have their place in the world, Willa. Without men we could not have children. Men must be accommodated as part of the natural order of things. But we cannot allow them to tell us what to do, the way they did in the old world, they are simply too narrow in their understanding, as nature made them. It's up to us, the women, to direct everyone in the ways best suited to happiness for all. And to do that we must have…?'

'Freedom from interference,' I said.

I was right but sister Luka did not say it out loud so Willa would not be hurt. She knew Willa was trying hard. Sister Luka is so understanding like that, and this is why she has been High Sister for so long. I will be the same way when my time comes.

'In all our time here, following the rules laid out by sister Winona, the valley has been peaceful and secure. We have enough land for all and our farms are prosperous. Disputes arise because we're human, therefore flawed by nature, and are taken care of by talking, not by violence, which was the way of life when men were in charge of everything. Our way is better, as anyone can see. And what is the secret of our way?'

Willa couldn't help herself. 'No men running things!'

'That is our rule, Willa, not our secret. What is the secret, Rory?'

'Love between women.' It was easy, really. If Willa had been studying longer under sister Mattie she would have known that answer.

'Love between women,' said sister Luka. 'Everything else comes from that. Love practised among ourselves is the foundation, the bedrock and cornerstone. Without love there can be no peace, no happiness. Therefore love must become part of ourselves from an early age. We must wake up in the morning with our hearts filled to overflowing. Love is the main ingredient in everything we do, all our thoughts and all our actions performed in the name of Selene. In the old world men bowed down before a god who was made in their image, harsh in his judgements, vengeful and intolerant. This was the god men used to justify their bloodlust and greed to possess everything in the world for their own use, and to make sure no woman ever was able to raise her voice in protest at their selfishness. Sister Winona would not allow herself to live among that kind, and made her way here in the last days before the great stone came to destroy the world of men. She established as perfect a society as humans are able to make for themselves, and it has succeeded, all thanks to the power of our lady.'

She stopped, staring for a long time at the candle flame, then went on. 'So now, in her name, we love one another. Love always knows itself when it sees love reflected in the face of another. The love we feel inside ourselves is never so strong as when held in the arms of our lover. Love is a circle, and a circle is the strongest thing in this, our world, and even among the stars. The earth is a circle, and the moon, because these things were made with the power of love by our lady Selene, whose outpost and refuge hangs above us for inspiration and as the object of our prayers. We are nothing if we do not love, and a part of love is physical love, its demonstration through our bodies of the loving power within our hearts and minds. Among ourselves we feel love in its most perfect form, since there are no children to be made. Our love here in the church exists for its own sake, to strengthen us and make our time on earth bearable. For some, this will be their only means of knowing love. Others will want to leave us and know the bodies of men in order to create new life. Few of us know at the time we first feel the power of love if we will remain true to that first kind of love, or if we'll go out among men to find the second kind. That doesn't matter, because only the fullness of time can reveal our true nature, our essential self. Rory, Willa, do you truly love each other?'

We nodded, too moved by her words to speak. Sister Luka had never seemed so wise and strong, our lady's voice on earth. 'Come here,' she said, and we joined her on Willa's bed. Sister Luka's arms went around us both, holding us tightly to her sides. I could feel a tiny trembling in her arms from the effort, and she said, very soft and low with her head bowed, 'Lady Selene, under whose protection we live, shield these lovers for the full term of their love, one for the other and each for all, to serve your children of the sacred gender and the lesser, for the furtherance of your design and the fulfilment of your dominion over our world. We beseech you in the name of love and wisdom and our obedience to the wishes of your daughter on earth, sister Winona, blessed be her name.'

'Blessed be her name,' I said, with Willa hurrying along a heartbeat behind, snuffling a little because she was trying hard not to cry, which surprised me because I had not thought her able to feel so deeply as this. She seemed almost to be taking sister Luka's words with more seriousness than me, but that could not have been right. We sat for a long moment, held together by sister Luka's trembling arms, and then she released us, giving us both a little kiss on the forehead with her thin dry lips. She kissed Willa before me, I think because she wanted to reassure Willa that her silly answers had been forgiven. Then she stood up and moved slowly to the door, with that same limp I noticed, and after turning to give us a long look – there is that sadness again – sister Luka left our room. Willa and I had both been holding our breaths, and we let them out together and smiled. Willa picked up my hand that was closest to her and took it to her mouth. My fingers had never been kissed before. That is a strange thing to do but it felt nice. 'Now we're real bedfriends,' she said.

'Yes.'

She had completely forgotten that only the blooded are allowed to be real bedfriends, but her face was bright with happiness, eyes shining in the candlelight, so I could not say anything. Sister Luka had left us a room filled with love. Willa moved along the bed and put her arms around me, which felt a lot stronger than sister Luka's arms had. She said straight into my ear, 'I love you.' Nobody ever said those exact words to me in my whole life, and for a moment I did not know what to do or say, or even know if I should do or say anything. Maybe when you are told this, the right thing to do is say nothing, just accept what you have been told, or maybe smile with love back at the one who said it, I do not know. But she did not seem to notice my silence, just sat there with her arms wrapped tight around my shoulders and the side of her head touching mine.

Knowing Willa loved me was the strangest feeling, a good feeling, but love is supposed to be given as strong as it is received, and somehow I was able to compare the two while listening to her breathe, and my own love for her was not as strong, so that is a betrayal of love's promise but I could not help it. I knew I should feel different to this, and wanted to. The thing not allowing me is knowing I have not begun to bleed and have faked that to get my chance at looking through the instrument ahead of my rightful time. So now I can only give half the love to Willa that she wants or even deserves. If I tried explaining this to her she would be hurt, which I did not want, so the best thing was to say nothing and be held silently and feel her love pouring into me like warm water into a bowl.

She stood up, lifted her smock over her head and let it fall to the floor, then grabbed mine by the shoulders and lifted. My arms rose without meaning to and my smock came off like skinning a rabbit but I stayed sitting on the bed until Willa took both my hands in hers and made me stand up just by lifting ever so lightly. I was very nervous now, not really wanting to do sexual things yet, but sister Luka had made us bedfriends and so this was to be expected.

Then Willa showed me how to row the boat.

17

Two more girls have been taken away by their parents. Nobody tried to stop them because the girls did not mind. They were never going to be big sisters anyway. Sister Mattie tried keeping everyone in the classroom, but once the parents came in and demanded that Cicely and Janet leave right now it was not possible. All their friends trailed after them to their room and helped them pack, which did not take long, and then they were gone. Class was over for the day even if it was not even noon, and that is when Willa came to tell me about it. I set down my quill, went to the door and looked out. Little sisters were gathered here and there in bunches, talking and seeming a little lost, waiting for someone to tell them what to do. There were no big sisters in sight, and Willa told me they had all gathered in the prayer hall to talk about what happened. 'Come on,' she urged, 'you don't have to stay here working, nobody else is.'

'I have to complete at least another five pages.'

'No you don't.'

'Writing down the name of our lady is what keeps her above us and not among us.'

That was something sister Luka told me when I was first made Scribe, to let me know the importance of my work, but all of that was lost on Willa. She just wanted to go out and play in the sunshine. With me. And I wanted to do that too, which made me feel an awful sense of guilt on top of the blood lie. But it was hard to keep reminding myself of my duty because having Willa there with me in the room of names was a big distraction. Because of what happened the night before when we were naked and together. Rowing the boat. I did not know such feelings were there inside my body before, and now, with the day disrupted by those parents and the loss of two little sisters, and Willa breathing her excitement into my face and the sun shining down warm and inviting, keeping Selene in the sky by way of writing down her name in an old yellow-paged book did not seem to make sense. And when I felt that feeling I knew something terrible had happened inside me to make me think such a blasphemous thought. I knew I was being weak by not telling Willa never to say such things again. I made myself weak by simply looking at her face all excited about the changes and seeing there a chance to take advantage of all the big sisters being together somewhere talking about this bad thing happening and nobody in charge.

'Let's get some berries,' she said, 'and not bring any back.'

That first part of her plan was not so bad, just human appetite for something sweet, but the second part was a small blasphemy because she knows that berries are mostly for making the ink for writing down the name of Selene, which is holy work and not to be ignored just because something unexpected has happened to break our routine. So I did not know what to do now. Willa saw it in my face and put her hand on my shoulder. 'Come away,' she said, 'and we can be together, just us two with no one else around. We can do anything we want. Don't stay here and be miserable, please, Rory.'

I had set my quill down on my desk beside the book when I went to the door. I was closer to the door than to the book, so it seemed like the most natural thing in the world to ease myself out through the doorway and watch Willa close it behind me. I knew I was being bad, allowing this to happen. Willa understood I had to be forced to do it. She took my hand to drag me away past the storeroom and kitchen, away from where the other girls were gathered in the yard, and we went behind the firewood stacks so nobody could see us. From there it was easy to just walk away from the church and go through a gap in the wall where the bricks have crumbled. Beyond the wall were empty fields, and beyond the fields a line of trees, dark and inviting. The further we ran from the church and my duties, the lighter my heart.

We wandered in the direction of the blackberry patch, our faces kissed by sunlight, too happy even to talk about ourselves and our new situation, and in no mood at all to be discussing things that were happening far behind us at the church, because none of that was real. Nothing could have been more important than to kick our way through thick carpets of pine needles and run together beneath the trees with arms outstretched and merriment spilling from our lips. We arrived all puffed out and panting and threw ourselves down in the clearing to feel the sun on our eyelids and catch our breath. Willa's hand reached out for mine and we lay quietly, listening to the birds and cicadas and the sound of wind sighing through the pines. It was a perfect thing to be part of, the best hour of my life, and every shining moment of it was the work of just one person. Willa drew lazy circles in the sky with her free hand, linking clouds, and hummed another of her strange fisherfolk songs. I was in love with her.

I asked, 'Why do you call it rowing the boat?'

'It's just a name.'

'But what's it got to do with rowing a boat?'

'Nothing, but you wouldn't want to call it cuntrubbing, would you?'

'That's awful.'

'So it's rowing the boat.'

Here is how you row the boat. You take off your clothes and lie down beside each other, but head-to-toes, then you lift one leg and your partner lifts one leg and you kind of roll onto each other with the legs intertwined, so your private parts are jammed up close. Then you reach for each other's hands and take hold and grip tight, pulling each other closer still, so close your crack and the other's crack are like two mouths kissing, and you squirm and pull and grunt against each other until something wonderful happens that makes you cry out with happiness it is so good. It is nothing like what happens when you do things to yourself. This is different because there is another person doing the rubbing, and not with her hands, so that must be what makes the difference.

'Do you want to?'

Willa's eyes were more than smiling, they were dancing in her face.

'If you want to,' I said.

'But *do* you?'

'If you like.'

'Stop pretending you don't want to.'

'I'm not pretending.'

'You are.'

'No I'm not.'

'Take off your smock then.'

It was different to taking off your clothes in a dark room. Here there was bright sunlight and everything could be seen, right down to the last hair and freckle in places that are never touched by sunshine. I folded my smock into a pillow and Willa did the same, grinning at me. I wondered how she saw me. My breasts are hardly there at all and my patch is just a little dab of hair like the down on a baby bird's chest. To me I am nothing, but Willa's face told me she found me pleasing, and that is how I found Willa too. She has proper breasts and a real tangle of hair down there all curling

120

around her wet crack that she opened with her fingers so I could see inside where it is pink and shining, but I could not show her mine like that because I am shy. So we went there to pick berries but ended up rowing the boat instead. I am only writing this down because nobody will ever see it, not even Willa. Afterwards I was embarrassed because I made such a lot of noise. I just could not keep my lips clenched like in our room so no one would hear us. Out there in the woods was so different with nobody around, just us rowing the boat until we slid off each other all covered in sweat. We lay there panting and feeling the sun on our skin, then after a while sat up and cleaned each other off with little slaps to get rid of the grass stuck to us.

We had come to the first berry patch, the one we could not gather from because of the bear, so when we finally got up to begin picking we found there were hardly any berries to be had. Most likely mister bear had eaten himself silly and no more had grown to replace them. So we decided to move on to the second patch, the one we harvested last time. Willa said we had to sneak up in silence because the bear might have found this patch too, so we pretended he really was there and waiting to pounce on us and could not stop giggling, especially when Willa farted and said the stink would protect us. There was no bear in the second clearing, just a deer that looked up as we came near and darted away into the shadows. But something else was moving, just a wisp of smoke but it should not have been there.

The cold ashes we had found last time were now warm again, with a few barely smouldering embers that sent a trickle of smoke into the air. Whoever had made the fire, they were fools not to have smothered it completely before going away, and it did not take long to work out what kind of fools, because at the far edge of the clearing was a rock, and on the rock was the head of a goat, and in the goat's mouth was a bone, most likely one of his own because scattered around the ashes were other bones swarming with ants, also a broken cider jug, or maybe shine. So the story was an easy one if you had eyes to see – some men had come here and slaughtered a goat and eaten it and gotten drunk while they did that. The grass all around was trampled down and there was a stain of deepest red where the goat had its throat cut. The hide was not there so someone had taken that away, leaving just the head with that stupid bone held between its teeth. I do not like goats but this made fun of something that had given its life for humans to eat. Only men would have insulted a fellow creature this way. Its eyes were squirming with flies laying eggs there. I do not like to look at a goat because of that sideways slit in their eyes, but this was just awful to see. Animals that surrender their lives so we might eat and live should be treated with respect, not made a joke of with a bone between the teeth like it had been snacking on itself. Only men would have done this terrible thing because that is the way they are.

We did not want to pick berries in a place like that. The clearing had been spoiled somehow by the spilled blood and buzzing flies and broken jug. Men should not have been out there in the woods building fires that might make a spark that sets fire to the whole forest. Men should stay in the fields where they belong, working and being useful, not wasting time drinking. And all this must have happened at night or else someone would have seen the smoke and rung the fire alarm bell in the village. So why are men doing this? Or maybe it is Chad, the only man who has the natural right to be away from the fields because he is a hunter that we all benefit from when he kills wolves and cougars that threaten us. I pictured Chad on his own beside this big fire, killing a goat and eating it, but one man could not have eaten a whole goat. And would Chad have set the goat's head up that way to be laughed at? That did not seem right, even if it is very hard to understand someone like Chad, who most of the villagers say is simpleminded. Maybe I have a soft spot for him because he brought the deer to my door. I still do not know why he did that, but nobody else has been wondering. What I really think is this – Chad brought me the deer because he knows somehow that I am going to play an important part in something that will happen soon. They say that animals are able to sense things before they happen, like the way dogs in the village start baying a long time before there is a moonquake because they know it will happen, even if the quake is a long way away when it comes. So I think Chad is like that, and can see something in me that nobody else can, and because he does not talk or maybe does not understand what he feels about me, he brought me an offering instead, like the harvest offerings we make to Selene. But I could not speak about any of this without sounding very vain and foolish, not even to Willa.

'I don't like this place.'

'I don't like that goat.'

'Let's go somewhere else.'

We wandered away, wanting to put the clearing behind us, and found another sunny spot to lie down in and listen to the wind and talk.

'What's going to happen now with sister Luka and the rest?'

'What do you mean?'

'Soon there'll be no little sisters left except you and me.'

'That's silly. There have always been little sisters that grow up to be big sisters.'

'But that was because the people here wanted to give their daughters to sister Luka. Now they don't.'

'That's just a few of them. The others won't do that.'

'You don't know.'

'Yes I do.'

'If it happened you could come back to my people. I'd teach you how to fish.'

'I don't want to.'

'But you might have to if there's no more sisters of Selene to belong with.'

Even though I love her I wanted to smack Willa's face for saying such a thing. Without the church there is nothing but growing food and making babies to do. That is not enough for me. I could never be a farmer's wife, and I do not think Willa could be either. She would talk back and be hit by her husband and would not like that and maybe would kill him like that woman in the fisher village she told me about, but here she would be an outcast, not given another husband. Without the sisters of Selene the valley would be no different to Willa's home, and that can never happen. The church is not here because the people are. The people are here because the church is. Without the sisters our earth will be crushed by the moon, so the risk they are taking by showing disrespect to sister Luka is just awful, but they are too stupid to see this. Sometimes I think Willa is too stupid to see it too, the way she talks, like becoming a little sister herself was just something she did as part of her adventure away from the sea. Which means that to her I am just a girl. She does not respect the Scribe, only loves the girl wrapped around the Scribe. But the part of me that matters most is the part that belongs to Selene. Willa only has the leftover girl part, and yet she seems happy to have this. Willa does not know me, only loves me. Do I love her more than I love Selene? I do not respect her because she has nothing to set out and be respected for, only herself. But I do love her. But would I love her the same if there was no rowing the boat? If there was only friendship and being sisters of Selene together I might be irritated by Willa's easygoing ways. I just cannot see her as a big sister even if she would be good at looking after the beehives or baking bread. The believing part of our sisterhood is beyond her understanding, I think. We should not be together, not even as bedfriends, because we are not suited. But not to have

Willa beside me in the night would be an awful thing now that I have done what I have done with her. It is rowing the boat that has made all this trouble, because now I want Willa almost as much as I want to be High Sister. Did sister Luka have this problem when she was bedfriends with sister Belinda? No, because sister Belinda believes in Selene, which made them suitable bedfriends. Willa and I are unsuitable, but I will not give her up for anything. It is all the fault of rowing the boat.

'So you wouldn't come back there with me?'

'No, I belong here.'

'Only because you were brung up that way. You can change your mind.'

'No!'

'No need to be shitty with me.'

'Just stop saying that.'

She made a huffing sound to let me know she was not happy, and turned away from me to look at a wasp, just an ordinary yellow and black wasp so it was not as interesting as she wanted me to think. And that simple turning away hurt me, which is the proof that love is the worst kind of distraction from the serious matters that everyone should be concerned with, even Willa. I wanted to scold her for her lack of understanding of what is important, wanted to tell her how unsuitable we are, but the words would not come. Watching her from the corner of my eye, knowing she would never betray my blood lie, knowing she loved me too, I felt like the lowest kind of creature. Just looking at the line of her nose and lips and chin made me want to cry out, she was so lovely. Without even wanting to I reached for her hand, but she pulled it away. That pushed a thorn so deep into my heart I could feel tears prickling my eyes. Such feelings as these are only suitable for Selene. They are too powerful to be used between people. When I am High Sister I might make the little sisters choose between having a bedfriend and dedicating themselves only to Selene. Maybe this is why the people in our valley are showing disrespect for sister Luka, because she has allowed the little sisters to become friends and more than friends, some of them, when everyone should be thinking about nothing but our lady. But the church has always been run like this, even farbackaway before sister Luka was born, so that cannot be the reason. Even sister Winona had a bedfriend, they say, so who am I to be thinking it all must change, and why do my thoughts keep on running in circles like this?

The wasp had landed on Willa's palm and she was staring at it with a look of concentration on her face. Maybe they do not have wasps by the sea and she did not know it could sting. I told her to watch out but she let the wasp sit there, then she said, 'Will it hurt if I let it bite me?'

'Yes.'

'This is how much I love you.'

She closed her hand over the wasp. My mouth opened at her foolishness, then Willa cried out suddenly in a way that tore at me. Her fingers opened and the wasp fell out, its wings crushed. There was no mark on her palm but she kept staring at it anyway while her mouth made little sounds of hurt.

'Why did you do that?'

'Shut up...'

Tears were starting to dribble from her eyes. She hugged the stung hand to her breast and began rocking back and forth, moaning, her good hand closed around the injured one. I could not bear to see Willa like that, so I put my arms around her for comfort and buried my face in her hair, and that made her stop, then she said, 'I feel sick...' and fell over. Her eyes were open but she was not there behind them. I shook her and shook her but she would not say anything or even sit up. I thought the wasp had killed her, but could see blood pumping in the veins of her neck. 'Willa... Willa!'

I smacked her on the cheek but that did not help, so now the only thing to do was run and fetch sister Rose from the infirmary. 'I'm going to get sister Rose!' I stood up and started to run, truly thinking that Willa might die. I was crying as I ran, blaming myself somehow for what happened even if I warned her about the wasp. She must be one of those people who can be killed by just a bee sting and it only has to happen once. I kept calling her name as I ran, as if she was ahead of me and I was trying to catch up, which did not make sense so I made myself stop that and save my breath for running.

At the edge of the woods I had to stop because of the pain in my side, and that is when I saw Chad. He was walking along the trail at the edge of the furthest field from the village, bow in hand and a quiver of arrows slung over his shoulder. He had not seen me come out from the trees so I called out to him, 'Chad! Chad!' and he turned. I waved my arms to make him come, and he began loping across the open ground between us. When he was close I shouted that Willa was hurt and turned around to go back into the woods. He caught up and ran beside me like a dog. I had to stop twice on the way back to the berry patch and hold my side again. Chad said not a single word all the way, and when we reached Willa, lying very still on the ground, he handed me his bow to carry and picked up Willa like I would pick up a bundle of clothing. He could not run with her but he could walk very fast, sometimes jogging for a little way, then walking again, which suited me best because my lungs were gasping by then. I told him about the wasp but he seemed not to listen, just kept on walking with Willa lying limp in his long skinny arms.

We passed through the gap in the wall and hurried around the woodpile to reach the infirmary. Sister Rose was right there looking after sister Belinda, who was lying down and very quiet. I gabbled the story of the wasp while Chad placed Willa on a bed. Sister Rose smacked her cheek but still Willa did not respond, and I began thinking again that she had died. Her stung hand was swollen to half again its normal size, and her arm was swelling too, and her face, especially around the eyes. She did not look like Willa any more. 'There's nothing I can do,' said sister Rose, 'but she'll likely be all right. We just have to wait for the poison to weaken inside her.'

'But she might die from it,' I said. 'There are people that do that.'

'If she was one of them she'd be dead already. It's just a bad reaction, nothing fatal.'

We watched Willa breathing slowly, eyes closed now, her lips parted and her face very pale, then sister Rose went back over to sister Belinda, who had not lifted her head at all despite all the excitement so she must have been asleep or very sick. I looked around to tell Chad thank you but he had already gone, which was a pity because I wanted to ask him why he left the deer outside my door. 'No use you waiting around,' sister Rose told me, 'she'll come to when she's ready.'

I went outside and saw sister Luka hurrying along towards the infirmary, so some of the little sisters who had seen Chad carrying Willa must have fetched her. I went back inside with her, telling about the wasp, only to get shooed out again by sister Rose, who seemed to be more worried about sister Belinda than Willa. Everyone who should have been in class was not, so I had to tell the story all over to satisfy them. Sarah the mouse started crying and had to be comforted by the others, and I could not bear to listen while she sobbed and sobbed like Willa was her closest friend, even though everyone knows Sarah does not have any close friends because she is peculiar and annoying. There were too many little sisters underfoot for my liking so I took myself away to the cool room in the cellar where all our preserves and such are kept. I wanted an apple for Willa to eat when she woke up. Our orchard is covered in pretty white apple blossom but would not bear fruit for a long time yet, so an apple from last year's crop would have to do. I went to the basket where they are kept and found three left. Two were very wrinkled and not fit to eat, but the third was all right, barely wrinkled at all and still firm. I would peel it for Willa before handing it to her so she would not notice how old it was, and enjoy eating it.

By the time I went back to the infirmary sister Luka had gone again and sister Rose was sitting with sister Belinda, who still was not aware of anything. 'She's not got too much longer,' I was told, which let me know I would not be getting any secrets revealed now. I was thinking sister Belinda had made it all up anyway, so it is not a real loss. Her breathing was harsh, her white eyes seen through half-closed eyelids.

'Why is she dying?' I asked.

'She's old. When you get to be old enough you die from it.'

'Do old people dying from it make things up and tell people?'

'Not unless they're born liars. Did she tell you some things?'

'No. She said she would but she didn't, not yet.'

'Maybe she was just remembering something and got it all tangled up with something imaginary. That happens. Who's the apple for?'

'Willa, when she wakes up.'

'It's old too. Are you sure you want to give that to her?'

'It's the last one in the cellar.'

She looked over at Willa. 'You can never tell who's going to be the kind that can't be stung. I'm surprised at Willa, though, she just doesn't seem the type somehow. But nothing should surprise me any more. The sun goes wandering, and there was a woman gave birth in the village two days ago to a monster.'

'A monster?'

I pictured something with huge fangs and claws, like a giant wolf, or maybe a wasp as big as a man.

'Like a normal baby,' said sister Rose, shaking her head sadly, 'only no top to its head and no arms. I've seen some disappointing births but the mother was beside herself looking at something like that. I was surprised it wouldn't quit breathing. The husband drowned it in a bucket to make his wife stop crying, which it didn't but she'll get over it after a while. Better that than trying to raise a child with only half its head.' She smoothed the cover over sister Belinda even though it made no difference. 'In the old world it didn't matter so much, the misbirths, because there were plenty of people all over before the stone came, not like now. You have to wonder sometimes what everything is supposed to be like. I don't think it's supposed to be like this, stone or no stone.'

'But we were spared by our lady.'

'Yes, we were, and for what?'

I have never heard a big sister talk this way and cannot decide if I should report her to sister Luka for blasphemy, saying that about Selene. If we were saved it had to be for a reason. I think we were saved so that we could begin our neverending duty to write down the name of Selene and keep the poor scarred moon in the sky to remind us how close we came to complete calamity that did not happen thanks to our lady and all those Scribes of which I am the newest and very proud. It was not right for sister Rose to be saying something different that might upset people if they heard. But maybe she is sad that sister Belinda is dying, and just saying out loud the things people say that they might not mean if nobody was dying and there were not half-headed babies to be thinking about. I wondered how many dead people sister Rose had seen since she was put in charge of sickness and birthing. She was one of the older sisters, like sister Ursula and sister Luka, so she would have seen a lot of things I have not seen yet. I wanted to tell her that soon a wonderful thing would be happening to make up for the baby in the bucket and sister Belinda, something that would make everything right again and take that worried look from the faces of the older sisters. I wanted to but did not, because it is too soon and she would not believe me, also I do not know yet what kind of wonderful thing will happen and could not describe it to her, so silence is best.

I stayed a little longer but Willa did not wake up. I left the apple there beside her, then went to the room of names and have set all this down in the secret book. Now it is late in the day and I have not written down the name of Selene even once! I will do some pages of names, as many as I can before the supper bell rings. Selene will understand because this has not been a normal day.

18

Sister Ursula did not say anything when I told her I had not done all my work, just told me to go and have my supper with the rest. There were empty chairs from those little sisters who were taken away, and sister Kath said her work preparing food would be easier now. It was supposed to be a joke, but nobody laughed. After eating I went back to the infirmary but Willa was still not awake. Her face was not so swollen, though, and the apple was in her hand so she must have woken up for just a moment at least. Sister Rose was not there, and sister Belinda suddenly sat up, startling me. There was just a small candle burning in the room, and sister Belinda's shadow filled a whole wall. She pointed into a corner, even though she is blind, and said, 'You are not welcome here! Go!' There was no one there, of course, so maybe she was dreaming, but then she fell back onto the bed and an awful sound came from her throat, a kind of gurgling that made the hairs on my neck stand up.

I went to her but the sound stopped even as I leaned over to see her face more clearly, then came a long long sigh from her lips. It seemed to go on forever, but faded away as I waited, and I knew sister Belinda was dead. It did not make me sad because she was an old woman, and now she can see again as she walks through the gardens of Selene and talks with all the sisters who went before her, so she is among friends still. It was strange to see her white eyes staying open, though. 'Goodbye, sister,' I said. 'Tell our lady I love her.' There was nothing else to do. Sister Rose and sister Nell always lay out the dead, because sister Nell is strong and can turn the body over easily and so forth, getting it ready for cremation. I looked into sister Belinda's eyes that were already looking about her at those wonderful trees on the moon that we do not have here, taller and with more shade from the sun, and I have heard they are a different colour too, not just green. I think trees on the moon are probably blue, like the face of Selene when she is in the daysky and far away on her loop around the earth. Blue trees would be so beautiful to see, and one day when I am old and dead I will see them, and see for myself if the dress of our lady is truly made from the shining webs of silver moon spiders.

I went to Willa's bed and told her sister Belinda had gone to Selene, but she just lay there with my apple in her hand. It had been a silly thing to give her, all wrinkled like it was, but maybe with the skin peeled off it would be all right. Anyway I did not have anything else to give except a kiss that I put on her cheek, then I went to find sister Rose. She was not downstairs so I went upstairs but nobody was there either. I went along the corridor to sister Luka's room to tell her about sister Belinda. Her door was open and I heard her voice talking, then sister Ursula's voice. I am not a snoop but I wanted to hear what they were saying. The big sisters talk about things among themselves that they do not talk about with us. Sometimes they will stop talking when a little sister comes near, and start again when she goes away, so they talk about things they do not want us to know. So I wanted to hear some of that talk, just to see what kind it is. I stood beside the doorway and listened, feeling guilty but also excited because the first word coming through the doorway that I could hear properly was my own name, then some more words I could not hear. I tiptoed closer to listen.

'But how likely is it?' sister Ursula was saying.

'About as likely as anything else that's happened recently. Do you doubt it?'

'I'm sceptical by nature. We need to think about this and not go rushing into anything, it's too important.'

'I agree, none of this should be discussed openly. What if we're wrong?'

'If we're wrong Selene will be harsh in her judgement.'

'Our lady knows her own moods best. Someone as young as this, though, did you ever expect it would be her?'

'My expectations are an empty basket and have been for a long time.'

Sister Luka laughed, but not a lot, then she said, 'She's obviously unaware. I think we should keep her in the dark until later, when it's clear.'

'We should be cautious, yes, but don't you think she's aware already?'

'I see nothing to indicate that. She's just a girl like any other.'

'Or not.'

'I'm fairly certain. In any case we can wait and see. Telling her who she is might throw her off balance, and the other girls are going to be jealous, don't think they won't be.'

'Just don't hang a sign around her neck and they'll be fine. The little sisters are not mature enough to understand fully anyway.'

'I just wonder if *she* does.'

'When we explain it to her she will. We can't have the Seer among us at last and not have her know who she is.'

The Seer. That word came floating through sister Luka's doorway and into my ears like a firefly, and set my brain alight. The Seer. We have been taught about her by sister Mattie and sister Luka. The Seer is the sister chosen by Selene to be given secret knowledge that is so important it can only be given to one person who can see things the rest can never see, and she will tell them what she sees

that was shown to her by Selene. There can only be one Seer alive
in the world at one time, and they do not come along very often.
There have only been two Seers since sister Winona, blessed be her
name, made the church of our lady Selene so long ago. The Seer
only happens when things are very bad all over, and the message she
brings is one of hope and wisdom. Sister Winona herself was the first
Seer. She saw that our world was going to have bad things happen
to it, so she took her followers away into the wilderness and found
the valley, a protected place, protected by our lady who whispered
in the ear of sister Winona to let her know she must go find the
valley before the stone came from the stars to pass judgement on
the way men had ruined everything. The next Seer, who came along
a long time after sister Winona had gone to Selene, was a big sister
who went into a strange kind of sickness that made her say strange
things, like there should only be one Scribe. Before, there were
lots of Scribes writing down the name of Selene to make sure the
moon did not fall down among us, but the Seer was told by Selene
that there should just be one, and she would be Scribe for life. The
next Seer, almost eighty years ago now, was a big sister who heard
the voice of Selene telling her not to allow any woman to have
more than one husband. Before then it was all right to have two
husbands after you left the church to marry, since choosing a mate
is done by women, and some women wanted to have more than
other women by having two husbands to provide for them. Those
women got richer than most and began wearing better clothes and
eating more food that their husbands grew, which was not a good
thing and made other women jealous. So that had to stop and the
Seer made that happen. Now there is only one husband for each
woman, if they even want one that is.

But now sister Luka and sister Ursula are talking about the new
Seer finally being among us after all these years, and this time the
Seer is a little sister, not a big one, which is unusual but not against

the rules. This will be the first time a little sister gets to be the Seer, which is so exciting because standing there, listening to them talk about this, I suddenly understood who the little sister is that they are talking about. It is me! I have been feeling for some time now that something important will happen soon that I am part of, the most important part of whatever happens. I knew this but could not speak to anyone about it because I could not explain why I knew it would be me who had the important part, so I set it down in the secret book instead, because if I did not set it down in writing I would puff up and burst from the secret inside me. And now I understand! It is me! I am the new Seer! Everything makes sense to me now, all the feelings I have had that I am different to the rest and special in the eyes of sister Luka and especially in the eyes of our lady, who has chosen me, young as I am, to bring a message of hope and wisdom. I do not have the exact message yet, but Selene will tell me when the time is right, I am absolutely sure about this. I have been chosen without any fuss just because I am the only one ready to be made Seer, because I am different to the rest and here is the reason for that.

I almost slid down the wall beside sister Luka's door as understanding came inside me to fill me with a white light that could only come from Selene, letting me know that yes, I have understood correctly and now I must prepare myself for this important work for our lady. I will receive my message from Selene and tell the world, and the world will be changed because of that, just like the world was changed by those other two Seers who came after sister Winona. I am the new Seer, and my message will be more important than theirs because things are worse now than when they were given their message from Selene to change things. Of course it is an honour to be chosen this way, but I will not allow myself to become vain about that. Our lady would not have chosen me if I was that kind. The Seer is chosen from among the sisters because of her special qualities that make her right for the task. I have been tasked by our lady and will not let her down. But it will be so hard not to tell the other little sisters I am the chosen one. They will walk past me and not even know this has happened, not until sister Luka decides to tell everyone about this wonderful thing after all these years. They will act different towards me when they know. There will be respect, even from the big sisters, even from sister Luka, because to be the Seer is better than to be High Sister even. And this means I will be the first little sister to be made the Seer, and then the first Seer to be made High Sister, which those other two Seers did not. Sister Winona was the only Seer who also got to be High Sister, and I will be the second one, but really I will be the first because sister Winona was a very special person who started everything, so what happened to her cannot be set alongside what happens to anyone else. So I will be the first Seer who gets to be High Sister afterwards, and that will make me almost as special as sister Winona, who has been looking down from the gardens of Selene and watching me grow up and choosing me to be the one, talking it over with Selene herself and they both decided it will be me and not someone else.

Sister Luka and sister Ursula had kept on talking but I did not hear a single word. My head was filled with light and my heart was filled with joy, and those things together made everything else fall away from me and be nothing more than mumbled words from a long way off. They were moving around in sister Luka's room now, and I did not want them to find me by the door if they came outside, so I sneaked away down the corridor and then turned around to run back, this time making as much noise as I could, slapping my feet down hard on the floor so they could hear me coming. I stopped in front of the door, panting as if I had run all the way from the infirmary, and looked inside. They were both looking at me, most likely being amazed that the one they were just now talking about is standing before them in the flesh. I told them, 'Sister Belinda died…'

'She has?'

They did not move quickly as I followed them back down to the infirmary, and they did not talk, not wanting me to know that I am the Seer because that would spoil the surprise. When they looked at sister Belinda they were not sad, not even sister Luka who was her bedfriend when they were young, but this is because their sadness about sister Belinda has been overcome by excitement about me being the Seer, so who can blame them for just pulling the cover up over sister Belinda's dead white eyes and talking about having enough firewood for her funeral pyre tomorrow. I wanted Willa to wake up so I could tell her about everything, but she just kept on sleeping. My gift apple had rolled off the bed onto the floor, so now it would be too bruised to eat even if I peeled it. I put it in my pocket to take away, then put Willa's arm back under the cover so she would not catch cold. How proud she will be of me when all is revealed!

When someone dies they have to be sat with through the hours of darkness until the next day, so their spirit will not be sad as it flies away to Selene. Most of the sisters were asleep so sister Luka and sister Ursula agreed they would be the ones. I offered to stay with them and keep watch over Willa, but they said I am too young to be staying up all night and must go to bed and leave my new bedfriend in their care until dawn along with sister Belinda. I think as the new Seer I should have been allowed to do what I want, but they have not said anything to me yet so I went away to bed, but of course I could not sleep, just kept thinking how all of my certainty that I am special somehow has been proved true.

Today I rose early and went to the room of names even before breakfast and set down everything that happened last night, which did not take long because Selene has given wings to my quill. I am so happy now! At breakfast I ate a huge amount, not like me at all, and when sister Kath asked why, I told her I was eating for Willa too so she will get better sooner. Sister Luka came in to make an announcement about sister Belinda, and Sarah started to cry even if she had not been especially fond of the dead sister, but that is Sarah for you, just a nervous mess about anything at all these days.

Then everyone had to lend a hand building sister Belinda's fire, and it was during this that Willa came out of the infirmary and sat down to watch, still looking a bit pale but her arm and face were not swollen any more. Sister Rose told her just to watch and not carry any firewood. I was very busy and could only give her a quick wave but she did not seem to notice, so maybe she still did not feel well. The pyre was built where they always have been, in the stony field beside the church where no crops have ever grown properly. I have heard villagers say this is because there have been too many sour old ladies burned there and it has poisoned the ground. When I am High Sister that kind of silliness will not be allowed. It is insulting to the older sisters, and there have been one or two young ones who died also and were burned there, so it is sacred ground, not poisoned. The villagers bury their dead instead of burning them because they say this saves firewood, and it is better that they do things differently to us because they are not like us at all, most of them, even some of the wives that come back to the church once in a while to make a complaint about their husband beating them or similar behaviour that is not right. We do things our way and they do things their way.

Sister Belinda was brought out to the field in the funeral wheelbarrow that is kept in sister Ursula's garden shed and laid to rest on the pile we had built, then sister Luka said a long prayer and used her flint striker to set fire to the small brush underneath. It caught quickly and soon sister Belinda's body could not be seen behind all that flame leaping up into the sky. We prayed and sang for her soul and I could not help looking up at Selene, all blue and very large again overhead as she heads back towards the earth for seventh night.

The fire burned for a long time. Nobody does any work or learning while a funeral pyre burns, so only after it was obvious sister Belinda's body had been completely destroyed did the mourners begin drifting away. I was not excused from my work once the fire collapsed into uneven piles of embers, and took myself away to add to the names of Selene. Willa was nowhere to be seen, and I did so want to tell her about my new secret, but that will have to wait until this evening.

19

After supper and evening prayers I still had not said anything to Willa, who had been looking strange all day but that is understandable since she is a person very easily made sick by wasp stings. I was expecting an announcement at supper about me being the Seer, but that did not happen. I think it must be because of the funeral, but in my opinion the announcement should have been made to balance the sadness about sister Belinda. Sister Luka has not been thinking about things clearly because her old bedfriend has died, so this is understandable and I forgive her, but surely she will say something before seventh night, which would be the perfect time to be announcing the new Seer chosen by Selene. I must be patient. Keeping the secret to myself is good training for being Seer because it makes me feel strong, knowing something like this, and the Seer should not be an excited little girl, more like a grown-up woman, very calm about things that are important.

I have penned a lot of Selenes so far today to catch up and am working on the secret book again. I was thinking that in years to come people will be able to read this book and know about how I became Seer. All the big sisters will read it for inspiration and the High Sisters that come after me will read aloud from it to instruct the newest little sisters, and these will not be allowed to be taken away by their parents until they are sixteen. It is a disgrace that this has happened, and it has just happened again, with two more families driving their wagons up to the church and taking their girls away. I heard the fuss and shouting and went outside to see, and this time it was two of the youngest being dragged away even if sister Luka was arguing with the father of one of them and sister Briony was talking with the mother of another. It made no difference and the girls were taken away, which means another day of learning has been disrupted for all by selfish stupid people that do not know what is best for their daughters. It is the men doing this, making their wives do something they have been trained not to do, which is turn against the church that all these women were educated by and given the power of choice when it came time to pick a husband. Without sister Winona, blessed be her name, none of these wives and mothers would have been given a chance to be happy. And now they are letting their stupid husbands tell them what to do and taking away all our little sisters, and when they have all gone what will be left? Of course stupid people cannot see this. What I would do is banish some of these men, the worst of them, make them go away out of our valley and be stupid somewhere else where they can do no harm to their own children like this.

After the wagons rolled away sister Luka and sister Briony sat down on the bench under the elm tree and began talking together. Now that I am the Seer I should be told things that are important, which having the little sisters taken away is, so I went around the edge of the yard and walked over to the elm from behind, so they did not see me there listening. Sister Briony was saying there will soon be less than half the usual number of little sisters for teaching the ways of Selene to, and if bringing their daughters to the church gets to be something parents have a choice about, it will mean ruination for us because the men will not allow it even if they are supposed to do as they are told and not start running things again like before. It is always the men doing bad things like that and the women and children have to suffer. So now this is a very bad thing sister Briony is saying, about how everything will change for the worse if the men are not stopped. And things are even worse than you might think, because one of the mothers that came in the wagons told sister Briony that her husband and some other men have been gathering in secret at night to talk among themselves and make a plan for taking away sister Luka's natural right to be the one in charge and replace her with some man who will be elected by all the other men, so no women can say anything about it. This will be the new way of things in the valley if something is not done.

I know where those men go to hatch their idiot plans. It is the clearing where the blackberry patch is, where the fire has been and the goat was eaten. I know this because then sister Briony said the woman told her the men did not believe our harvest offerings mean anything at all and Selene should not be the one to worship. Grover Styles is the man spouting this nonsense and the other men are listening. We should be worshipping Sol instead of Selene, these men think, because Sol makes the crops grow and all Selene does is make the ground quake sometimes on seventh night when she passes so close to the earth. And the harvest offerings of grain and other crops should be replaced by what they did in the old world, which is animal sacrifice, because only blood can win the favour of the gods. So that poor goat was not just slaughtered for eating, he was meant as an offering to Sol. That is what Grover Styles has been up to. And how stupid to make a sacrifice to the sun in the middle of the night! That shows what kind of brains men have.

I could hardly believe what sister Briony was saying this woman told her, and sister Luka was silent too, then she said, 'The Seer comes when times are bad, we've always known that, and this time may be the worst. Now the question is, do we reveal her and hope they take her seriously, or keep her as our secret? If she was a fully grown woman they might listen, but to a young girl? I'm not hopeful.'

'What choice do we have? What they're doing is nothing less than stripping power away from the church, interfering with the natural order and trying to set themselves up as lawmakers. Sister Winona would not have allowed it.'

'Sister Winona was still a young woman when she did what she did. I'm exhausted.'

'Sister, you have to be strong, for all of us.'

Then I heard a terrible thing. I heard sister Luka sobbing. My heart felt like a lump of wood when I heard that. Sister Luka is a good woman who has done her best to make everyone in our valley happy by following the rules laid down by sister Winona. Those rules have kept us all from harm for generations, and now these men want to change everything and run the risk of bringing calamity down upon us all like they did so long ago. How I hate them! I hate them for their ungrateful complaints and their lack of respect for all the sisters, big and little, and I hate them for being so stupid they will not see that they are going to destroy everything all over again. I do not know all the men in the valley, but I think the only one among them with any worth is Chad, who is the lowliest man around here on account of his animal hide clothes and because he does not talk. How wise is the voice of the mute. I would banish all men but Chad, who does good work killing wolves and deer. The rest can wander among the mountains and die there for all I care, like my murderous father. Poor sister Luka, to be brought to tears by the acts of fools.

As the Seer it will be my duty to tell everyone what they must do to avoid calamity, but this is the part I do not understand – I do not know what must be done to set things right here. I am the Seer, sister Luka and sister Ursula said so, and yet I do not have a message like those other Seers before me. They gave orders and these were obeyed and things got better, but I do not have a message inside me that I know of, and if I do not know what the Seer's message is, how can it be told? I am thinking that things are not yet bad enough, and the message inside me will not mean anything until things are so bad even the men will be scared, and will listen and obey. The message will just pop out of my mind and into my mouth when the time comes. I might even be just as surprised as everyone else when that happens. It will be the voice of our lady, after all, and not really my own, so that would explain why I do not know the message yet. Most likely the other Seers had this happen to them the same way. It was a long time ago and everyone from then is dead now, so this is most likely the way it will happen again.

Sister Briony was making small sounds of comfort and I felt guilty for overhearing this, so guilty I was about to go away before they found out I was just the other side of the elm, but then sister Briony said something that made me stop. She said, 'We can't tell ourselves we didn't see some of this coming. Look at my observations, the way Selene has been moving closer for as long as I've been in charge of the instrument. Sister Joan said the same thing before me. That can't go on without Selene coming so close we collide, yet here we are writing down her name over and over like it's having an influence. Well, it isn't. It isn't having any influence and one of these days that moon is going to come down and crush us like ants.'

'Our lady will not allow it.'

'Our lady hasn't shown any sign of not allowing it. If my observations showed her getting further away I could sleep easy, but they don't show that, they show the opposite, and we keep on keeping it a secret. Maybe all this secret-keeping is to blame.'

I had to put my hand to my mouth when she said those things, because here is the secret that sister Belinda hinted at, the second secret, the one belonging to sister Briony. Selene is coming closer all the time, not staying the same distance when she passes the earth on seventh night. But I am the one keeping her in the sky with my writing down of her name. That has been my task all this time, and all the while sister Luka and sister Briony and sister Belinda and maybe some more of the older sisters have known that it is not working. But they did not tell me this and so I have been making ink and sharpening quills and writing writing writing to keep us safe while those old women have known something that makes all of my efforts worth nothing. It is worse than nothing because they have known all along I am wasting my time. Also this means Selene does not listen to me, does not take into account my belief in her protective goodness that will save us all. I have been lied to by the sisters, and Selene herself has done nothing to let me know my work is appreciated. It is all a lie. Standing under a tree, I have learned that I knew nothing until this moment. How dare they! And on top of everything else, Selene is going to kill us all!

I could not stand there any longer and let those two think they were going to fool me even for another heartbeat. I marched around the elm and stood before them. It must have been a shock to learn they had been overheard talking about their precious secrets. I glared at them, wanting to tell them how awful they were, but no words could leave my mouth. Sister Luka and sister Briony stared at me, too stunned to speak also, and the silence between us was so crammed with unspoken words it made my ears ring and my fingers clutch at nothing. Finally sister Luka said, 'Rory… Aurora…' but I did not want to listen to any more lies and turned away. I think I made a strange whinnying noise as I marched away with arms held stiffly at my sides and my feet going tramp tramp tramp across the yard and my mind swirling with betrayal and fear and anger so fierce it burned a hole in everything I looked at. I did not know where else to go but into the nearest refuge – the room of names, but once in there I felt trapped. Of all places to hide, I had chosen the very room where for all this time I had worked so hard for the sisters of Selene, and now I know that they and she have betrayed me. I am the Scribe, but what does that mean any more? I am the Seer, but does that mean anything if being the Scribe does not? I wanted to scream. My head was so filled with grinding and roaring I could not think any more, not even about the awful things I had learned. I could not breathe, just stood there panting and making that whinnying sound like a horse, then there was a knocking on my door. Of course I did not answer, but sister Briony came inside anyway, saying, 'Little girls that spy on their elders can get their ears burned.'

It was such a stupid thing to say, as if I was the one who had been caught doing something wrong and not them. She was talking to me like I am the fool and she is the wise one, but sister Briony is the fool for being a big liar, and sister Luka too. I screamed, 'Get out! Get out!' Sister Luka came in then and sent sister Briony away so she could talk to me like mother and daughter, but I did not want to listen.

'Rory…'

'No!'

'Listen to me…'

'Go away!'

'You have misunderstood…'

'Is Selene getting closer or further away?'

'Some things are not under our control, Rory. We are only human beings…'

'Closer or further away?'

She sighed and said in a weak voice, 'Closer, but our prayers and your writing…'

'So it doesn't work!'

'Our lady is not at our beck and call, Rory.'

'What does that mean?'

'It means we try our very hardest as sisters of Selene… to make our way as best we can, with whatever is available to us. We pray and we try to understand… but sometimes we fail. Our knowledge is limited, Rory, and we must feel our way through the darkness…'

'So being the Scribe doesn't mean anything, then.'

'No, no, child… Your efforts do not go unrecognized by our lady…'

'But it doesn't *work*. Sister Briony *said*.'

'We can't be certain of that. If not for your hard work it could be that calamity would have been visited upon us many times over. Why, the last few seventh nights haven't caused even a little quake, not even a ground tremor. It could be that our lady is preparing to spare us by moving further away, but the time for her to do that is not made by arrangement with us. Our lady is not some fellow sister, available for conversation about her plans. The thoughts and moods of our lady are for us to… to guess at, and hope we've caused no offence that might result in more disaster. Rory, all we can do is what we're doing.'

'So it's all just made up.'

When I said those words I felt like a traitor, but was too angry to care. I wondered if they were true words, or if sister Luka's words were the true ones. If I was right then Selene does not care about us any more than we care about the ants we step on, and if ants pray not to be stepped on we are not listening and step on them anyway because we do not care. The thought of being like an ant, as unimportant as that, made my head spin. It could not be true. Sister Luka's face was creased with sadness as she watched me trying to make up my mind. I am so fond of sister Luka with her funny eye and how hard she has been trying to hold the church together against these men, and her old love sister Belinda dying. It is too much for an old woman to be doing. And I have made her unhappy on top of all that by doubting our lady. And what she said might be true, that if not for my writing every day then Selene might already have come crashing down. My words might have been the only thing to stop that from happening. We might all be dead if not for that, so getting angry just because our moon has not gone further away so we can rest easy is just silly and childish. Now I can see what sister Luka means about trying our best to please Selene while not being able to know exactly what our lady has got planned for us. So it is like when sister Marion in the bakery makes a cake and it rises nicely and then falls for some reason and does not look as nice, but the cake is still all there and delicious to eat, so if it fell that is not really important, and if someone cries about the hollow in the centre of the cake then they are being childish and ungrateful, which I did not want to be or have anyone thinking this about me. And the important thing is, as the Seer I will be able to understand more deeply than the other sisters what our lady is thinking, because that is what the Seer is for. So even if being the Scribe is a fallen cake, being the Seer will explain about that and there will be a whole new cake for everyone that I can tell them about.

'Not made up, Rory, more like an imperfect understanding of something greater than ourselves. Just because we don't know everything is no reason to throw what little we do know out the window. It's all we have, and could be all we ever have.'

'Will the Seer get to see more than everyone else?'

'Why are you talking about the Seer?'

'Well, wouldn't she? The Seer sees what the rest can't see, and tells them and they change things around to make it better.'

'The Seer is someone who comes along once in a great while, Rory. It's been a very long time since the last one…'

'But that's what she does when she comes.'

'Yes.'

'And she has come.'

'Why do you say that?'

It was foolish of her to deny that I have come at last to deliver a new message. Sister Luka and sister Ursula were worried about me being so young, but it does not make sense for them not to be admitting that I am here anyway.

'Is the Seer here among us or not?'

I was very firm, asking that. It was time to stop the secrecy and say what was true now. Sister Luka's face changed, became calmer. 'Rory,' she said, 'I want you to avoid all talk of the Seer until we're... sure what is happening. If you tell the little sisters that the Seer has come again they'll get too excited. This matter has to be discussed further among the big sisters, so we're sure we know what we're talking about. Sometimes the things that come to us from Selene are hard to understand. If the Seer is among us her message will be studied and announced in due course, and not before. There are ways of doing things and these must not be rushed. The return of the Seer is a special event. Of course, the message she brings may be difficult to understand, or even frightening, but we must simply do our best as our lady decrees, trusting all the while that she would never allow us to make the wrong decision. It all takes time.'

I could tell she was trying to make peace with me, and at the same time asking me what kind of message I have brought, but I could not tell her yet because I do not have the message. What sister Luka says about it all taking time is true, so I should do as she says and stop being angry because everything is not exactly how I want it to be. I may be the Seer, yes, but I am only twelve and cannot be expected to understand. When the message comes I expect sister Luka and some of the older sisters will have to examine it and talk about it and make up their minds what it means and what should be done about it.

'I'm sorry...' I said, and started to cry. I did not mean to but it happened anyway because it has all been very hard. If the Scribe's work is not able to do exactly what it should, does the Seer's message need to be much clearer to make up for that? So much was being asked of me because I am both Scribe and Seer now, that I am not able to carry it all. Sister Luka came and put her arm around my shoulders to hug me, and I put my face between her flat old breasts and cried some more, but I am not ashamed about this. And I felt guilty too, because it may be that Selene has come closer because I have not been fully attending to my duty as Scribe but have wasted time writing in the secret book when I should have been writing down the name of our lady as usual. But I did not want to say this to sister Luka because she already has too big a burden to carry with all these things happening at once. I will say a special prayer to Selene apologizing for what I did, and wait for the message. Maybe it has been delayed to punish me for being neglectful. I have so much to be grateful for and have appreciated none of it.

'Sister…? Is Willa all right? I've hardly spoken to her.'

She stroked the top of my head. 'Willa is fine. The wasp hurt her more than you might think, but she's beyond harm now.'

'I gave her an apple but it was old.'

'I know about the apple.'

'I thought she might die.'

'And now we know she won't, so everything will be all right.'

'Yes, sister.'

'Tomorrow night is seventh night. This will be the second one since your blood. Are you able to believe in our lady again, Rory? Coming as close as she will tonight, Selene will know your mind.'

'I do believe, truly.'

'Then all will be well.'

She gave me a final squeeze then released me. I was so happy I almost cried again. Sister Luka left me to get on with my work, which I did for a little while, then got out my secret book and have done that too, because I should not feel so guilty after all about doing this, writing in the book, because everything I write down will be studied later on by all the sisters, and parts of it read aloud to the newest little ones to show how devotion to our lady can be done in different ways.

20

Willa was at supper, which I arrived late for because I had so much catching up to do, but she had saved a seat next to her for me and was looking like her old self. Some of the little sisters asked how much the wasp sting hurt, and she opened her arms wide and told them, 'This much,' which made them laugh, even Sarah. I ate a huge amount of sister Kath's food because I am happy again, and only a little bit sad because I cannot tell Willa I am the Seer. She would never be able to keep it a secret and would tell everyone, and that would reach sister Luka's ears very fast and then I would be in trouble. The notion that a Seer can get herself into trouble by opening her mouth was just too silly for me to risk it, so I said nothing and enjoyed watching my lovely friend being funny to make the others laugh. Sometimes I wish I could do that, but a Seer who cracks jokes would also be just too silly, so I must be content with my own kind of quiet work and let the ones like Willa entertain the others.

Then it was bedtime and we left together, wanting to be alone. We sat on Willa's bed and hugged for the longest time, then took off our clothes and very tenderly rowed the boat without making too much noise, then cuddled for another long while. I asked her to show me the hand that had been bitten by the wasp and looked for a mark there on her palm, but the candlelight was so dim I could not see anything, and anyway Willa told me there is nothing to see so I just kissed it instead. Then I remembered the apple that was still in the pocket of my smock. It was no good for eating now, but I wanted her to know it was me who brought it to her in the infirmary, in case she had already forgotten. I got out of bed and fetched it back and told her how I had wanted her to have it while she was sick from the wasp sting. She laughed when I showed her, then said, 'I had a dream about an apple.'

'It was right there in your hand in the infirmary. Sister Luka and sister Ursula watched over you all night, and sister Belinda died in the bed right next to you.'

'Poor sister Belinda.'

'And the men in the valley are trying to change everything around, but Selene will stop them.'

'How?'

Well, I did not know how, not yet, but could not tell Willa about the message that soon will come. If I told her I am going to be the messenger she would not believe it. She will be so excited when it all comes out, and proud to be the Seer's bedfriend so soon after getting to be the Scribe's bedfriend. Really it is all just falling into her lap. Willa does not know how lucky she is to know me because she does not know the secret thing about me, not yet.

I told her, 'That fire where the berries grow, the men made that.'

'With the goat's head?'

'They made a sacrifice like in the old world, a blood sacrifice.'

'I've heard about that. It's just a waste.'

'No, they ate the goat after they sacrificed it to Sol.'

'So now Sol's going to go hungry, too bad.'

We laughed into each other's face, then started kissing and ended up rowing the boat again, then fell asleep.

Early in the morning, during prayers, Grover Styles came to the church along with Buford the blacksmith's son and interrupted everything, just walked in and announced to all the big and little sisters that from now on nobody in the valley would be sending their daughters to us any more because this place is just a nest of female perversion that is corrupting the young and making girls do things they do not want to do, which makes them unsuited for marriage later on, leading to unhappiness. Both men are strong and heavy and even sister Nell would not go up against them, so really what happened was everyone just listened while Grover Styles spat a lot of foam from his lips and Buford stood there smirking, and he even winked at me several times, which made me furious that he could come here and do that to the Scribe and the Seer both and not be struck down by Selene for punishment.

'What you women got to understand from now on is, you aren't running a damn thing around here, not any more, that's all gone. The sun come up this morning on a new set of rules happening right now. There's been discussion and opinions and it's been decided. From now on there'll be men teaching what there is to teach and it won't take no more than one year to teach all of it to any child, male or female, then everyone goes to work, useful work that'll be good for the whole valley and not be wasting time with prayers to your Selene.'

Grover Styles was enjoying himself, giving little looks to Buford, who kept nodding his head to say what a good job he was doing. Sister Luka and the big sisters just stood there listening with their faces very hard and unhappy while he ranted. 'And another change around here, from now on the boys say who'll take who for a spouse, not the girls, and if they want two wives and have got the wherewithal to support them, that's what they'll get, and if a girl says she don't want to be some man's wife, she'll have to give a good reason why, so long as the man is a good man that everyone knows will provide. Also, the woman takes the man's family name from now on, like it used to be in the old world. There's not many people left in this world, just us and the sea traders come to light all this time after the stone, so likely that's all there is, and it ain't half enough, so there'll be more babies born around here when a man has got two wives, maybe more if he's prosperous. More people, that's what we need now to take the world in our hands again like it was before, then things'll get back to being the way they're supposed to be. There's been a story put into the heads of the young that it was men fouled everything up and brung down the stone, but that story come from the lying mouth of a woman, the very woman that started us here down the wrong road with her Selene. Well, that woman has been dead a long time now, and it's long past time we put her words and bad thinking to rest too, so that's happened as of now.'

He looked over at the big sisters and sneered. 'You women, you'll be taking care of your bakehouse and beehives and such, not pouring useless moontalk into the ears of these young girls. You been spoiling them and turning them bad on us going all the way back to the beginning. Well, this is the new beginning that has beginned, and my advice to you is listen hard and take it in because from now on, any man that has got a gripe against you, he'll be listened to in the village council and there'll be charges laid and acted on and punishment to follow if need be.' He let that sink in, thinking we all believe him just because he is talking and we are not, then he said, 'Seventh night is tonight. When that moon comes up it won't be no female you can send your prayers to. From now on the moon is a brother, not a sister, and his name is Sel, little brother to Sol. That's the way things ought to've been all along, and now they are. He'll come close enough to touch and make the ground shake, then he'll be heading further off when we ask him to, talking man to man, and not be needing to shake us into calling him by his right name. That's what all this is about, the wrong name all these years, but that's over now and he'll be moving back into the far sky like his big brother to watch over us peaceful through the night. All right, anyone that's got anything to say, say it now because this is the last time you'll be invited to do that.'

Everyone knew sister Luka would have something to say, and she did not disappoint us. She stepped forward and said, very calm and dignified, 'I speak for us all, every girl and woman, not just here but across the valley. You men have come with a plan for change, but you think putting things back the way they were is the answer. It is not. Selene is and will always remain female. Your words change nothing. Untruthful words are little birds carried away on the wind, never to be seen again. True words are like the mountains, unchanging. Your little birds are already being blown away across the mountains. We are the world made whole and complete. We are women. We are the beginning of life and its cradle. We are not here for you. You are here for us. Every change you have talked about will not happen. None of it will happen because it is not right. It is the result of foolish thinking, which men have been known for since before the stone. Why did the stone come if not to tear down your world and replace it with the world that should have been set in place from the beginning. We accept nothing of what you say and will do none of the things you want. You speak from ignorance. I refer to a specific ignorance that I will explain to you while you have so kindly decided to visit us and exchange views. Here is the thing you do not know. There is among us a special person. Who is she? She is the spirit of our lady made into flesh, the better to explain the wishes of Selene, who will always be called by that name and no other, no matter what some little bird might twitter and squawk about. This is the Seer. You have heard about her from your grandmothers, and from their grandmothers before them. The Seer has come again to reassure us in our time of trouble, and she is in this room taking note of those who have set themselves against her. She will not forget, and neither will they when they are punished for their blasphemy...'

'Point her out,' said Buford, these being his first words.

Sister Luka drew herself up to full height, about level with Buford's chest, and said, 'She will remain unknown to you, to avoid persecution.' Buford did not know that word and narrowed his stupid little eyes, suspecting something. Sister Luka went on, speaking very firmly, standing strong against these men that came to cut her down. 'Selene is almost with us, swooping down upon the world, and tonight will shine with a fierce light born of anger. The Seer among us has already sent word of your outrageous demands to Selene, and you will find our lady harsh in her judgement. It is too late for me to intercede. You have profaned the church of our lady with your plans, and must leave now. Go back to your work and pray hard to Selene, with humility, and you may be spared. If not, you...'

Buford pointed a grimy finger right at her face, interrupting. 'You! Old Woman! Close your mouth and quit spouting Selene this and Selene that. There's no more Selene, only Sel and his big brother Sol. That's the way it is now. You've been told, so you got no excuses for what happens after this, hear?' Then he swept his arm across the room and aimed his finger at me. 'And I say you don't need to tell which one's this Seer bitch, it's her – Spooky Clamphole! And I got this to say to Spooky – two years from now, three maybe, and you're mine. No need for you to worry and wonder about who's your husband – it's me, and I'll be reminding you once in a while so's you don't forget.'

His words were like water pouring inside me, chill and cold, but they could not be stopped until they lapped about my heart, squeezing my chest so tight I could not breathe. Nothing could be worse than the thought of Buford taking me to his bed for a wife. This could never happen, and I sent an immediate prayer to our lady asking her for strength to resist what these men wanted, and strength also for sister Luka who has defied them even if she is old now and frail. They are cowards, these men, and fools to think they can change the things that Selene has made changeless. But the look on their stupid faces did not alter at all, which means they have not listened and not learned, so now they must be punished. Buford did not really know I am the Seer, he is just guessing because he wants to point his finger at me the same way I pointed my finger at him and told him he is cursed. He was trying to frighten me, but I am not afraid, only made sick to my stomach with hatred of him.

Now it was Grover Styles talking again. 'Me, I don't believe in no kind of Seer, not till I see 'er myself.' He laughed at his own joke and Buford did too, then he said, 'All you girls, this is your last day. Tomorrow your parents are taking away the rest of you back home where you belong, doing work for the ones that brung you into the world that you owe a debt of obligation to, not these old women keeping you here to fill your heads with nonsense. You go ahead and take a good look around at what you had here, because you won't none of you ever be coming back. Selene is dead. Long live Sel.'

And with that he marched out, taking Buford with him. Only when they had gone did anyone stir, releasing their breath and looking around at others to see if they were scared too. The first word allowed into the air was from sister Kim, who is only nineteen. She asked, 'Who is the Seer?' and all eyes turned to sister Luka, still holding herself at full height even if the men had gone. I felt a secret thrill as I waited for my name to spill from her lips, but she shook her head firmly. 'The name of the Seer will not be revealed for the moment.' There was a sound from almost everyone, a kind of moaning. They all wanted to know. Willa was looking at me, as if she suspected the answer and was trying to see the truth in my face, but I did what sister Luka was doing and held my face hard and stern like a mask no one can see behind till I say they can. Sister Ursula and sister Briony were giving sister Luka strong looks that could not hide their worry, so I think they are concerned that after the visit from Grover Styles and Buford we all need to be told some kind of cheerful thing to make up for that.

Sister Luka could feel it too, so finally she said, 'Tonight, when Selene is riding proud and serene above us… the name will be revealed.'

There was a whispering of delight around the room. I lowered my eyes, thrilled beyond words. Soon they would all know. I did feel a small wave of panic, though, because I still have not received a message from Selene. With Grover Styles and the rest of the men threatening to turn everything upside down, you would think that our lady might place some kind of plan in my mind, something I could announce after sister Luka tells everyone who I really am tonight, but there is nothing. There is an empty place inside me that is waiting for the message, aching to be filled with words of encouragement that will lift our spirits after the terrible things Grover Styles has said, things that could not possibly happen the way he says. But I have the rest of the day and evening to be receiving this, so there is time yet. While writing down the name of Selene I will also pray especially hard to be made worthy.

Soon after, we all went about our daily tasks, the mood the men had left behind lightened by the promise of a great revelation tonight under Selene. I had difficulty concentrating on my names, finding I could not write down the name of our lady even though I have done this so many many times now, I am so excited about what is to come. But I am able to write down my thoughts, and these are filled with joy and certainty. How wonderful it is to know that my presence in the world is for a definite purpose, that I have been selected from among so many as the only one suitable for such a position. I am very modest by nature but I cannot help feeling that all of the unhappiness I have ever felt has been to prepare me for what lies ahead. I do not fool myself into thinking that anything will be easy, especially after listening to Grover Styles, but then I remind myself that beside that awful man stands the lowly Buford, while beside me stands a goddess. Really, I should feel sorry for all those silly men who are thinking they will be in charge from now on. Their jaws will drop when I am revealed as the Seer, and drop further still when I reveal my message. The spirit of Selene is filling me like a jug filled to brimming with clear water, cold and lovely to the taste. She will take me by the hand when my hour comes and make firm my heart, take hold of my tongue so I may tell of the many changes that will happen now, exactly opposite to what Grover Styles thinks these will be.

The church of our lady will not be torn down and her followers scattered among homes and farms to be like other women. The church will be made stronger because of my message. Our lady has chosen me to be her mouthpiece on earth, her eyes and guiding hand, the spout for her blessedness to be poured out into all those empty pots waiting for the truth. Even the men, who are stupid as cattle, will be blinded by the bright light of my message, awed by its greatness, and they will be humble before the truth I shall reveal to them. I am crying now as I write these words, overcome by feelings of blessed joy and privilege. I will not let our lady and sister Luka down. The hour of my glory is fast approaching, the time of transformation. I realize now that the reason I do not have the message is simple – it will not be given to me until after I have been declared the Seer. When I open my mouth to release the message, that is the moment it will be given to me, planted by Selene onto my tongue, and the words will flow without hesitation, holy words forming a new language that everyone will understand instantly. I must keep a certain distance from the rest because I am the Seer. I think when sister Luka says so, I will stop being the Scribe because that is too much work on top of being the Seer also, so that work will be given to someone else, someone chosen by me, and I will choose

Willa even though she is still being taught how to read and write. It is only one name over and over so anyone could do that.

It is only afternoon and the day has already been so long. I am starving but the Scribe cannot eat while she is working so I must keep on despite my poor stomach begging to be fed. I see that I am being chastized by our lady for neglecting my duties. I am still the Scribe after all and will remain so until sister Luka announces that I am the Seer. So I must close the book of secrets and open the book of names and make my mark there.

21

The secret book is open again and I must set down all of the strangeness that has happened. The first thing to go wrong was brought to my ears by a scream from far away. The last time I heard a scream so loud was when sister Loren found a snake in the storeroom and sister Nell had to come kill it with a shovel. This scream now went on and on until I could not ignore it any longer and went out to see what was wrong. There were sisters running across the yard, all heading in the direction of the screaming, which could have been coming from anyone's throat, you cannot tell who with a scream, but it was coming from behind the kitchen. I joined the rest and ran to see, and quite a crowd was gathered by the trees bordering the wall there. It is usually a quiet place because there is just the trees in a corner where the boundary wall meets the kitchen. It was Eunice doing the screaming. There was a girl floating under one of the trees, that is what it looked like, but then I saw the rope joining the girl's neck to the branch above as her body slowly turned, showing us her face. It was Sarah, who did not want her parents to come and take her away because they do not like her.

Eunice ran out of screams as sister Mattie came hurrying in behind the crowd. I watched her mouth fall open at what she saw. She clapped a hand over it but could not make her eyes stop looking at Sarah's blue face and the tongue that had come out between her lips. There was an overturned stool beneath her feet. Some of the little sisters were crying. Then sister Nell came along and took hold of Sarah's legs to lift her a little so the rope was not so tight, but anyone could see it was too late for rescuing. Sister Nell yelled at sister Mattie to go fetch a knife and she ran off, then sister Ursula and sister Luka came and stood there looking like they could not understand what had happened, just stood there looking, too old to help sister Nell, who was still supporting Sarah and crying herself now. Then sister Mattie came back with a knife from the kitchen and set the stool upright so she could get on it and reach up to hack at the rope until it parted. Sarah's weight made her slump down over sister Nell's shoulder, and that carried them both to the ground even though sister Nell is the strongest sister.

The crying and moaning went on until sister Luka suddenly told everyone to stop. She pointed to Sarah lying in sister Nell's arms and said, 'This is what happens when men try to take control. They cause death! Sarah is the first to fall, but all of us must beware! Something has changed…' She seemed to take a step sideways and fell against sister Ursula, who could not support her and both sank to the ground. I think sister Luka fainted. Seeing three big sisters and one little sister on the ground made everyone start to wail again, then some of the little sisters took it into their heads to faint also, and down they went, one after the next. Only Willa and myself stayed upright, looking at the others and at each other and wondering what would happen now. Then sister Alicia came up and started getting people to their feet, and soon the only one still on the ground was Sarah, her blue face staring up into the sky.

Sister Alicia took several of the big sisters aside and asked which ones would offer to be the bearer of bad tidings to Sarah's family, but they did not want to because they were afraid the family would attack them. Until today nobody would have worried about that because people in the valley just did not attack the sisterhood. It was the sisters who started everything here and they have respect for that, or used to. By now Grover Styles would have told everyone in the village and maybe even spread word to the farms that from now on nobody needs to show respect for the church of our lady because we have fallen and are just a bunch of females that have no special knowledge and now our time to rule has passed. I waited for one of the big sisters to put up her hand, but nobody did. Sister Luka was not doing anything except getting looked after by sister Ursula, who was looking very old and confused herself now, and the younger big sisters had all turned cowardly it seemed to me, and it was interesting to watch and wait to see what would happen.

Willa came over to me and asked, 'Do you know where they live?'

'Who?'

'Her folks. Sarah's.'

'They've got a farm over that way.' I pointed.

Willa went to sister Alicia and told her we would go tell Sarah's parents, even though something like this should have been done by a big sister, but they all seemed to have become helpless somehow. Sister Alicia simply nodded and turned away to ask someone to begin organizing another funeral pyre. And that is how Willa and I became the bearers of bad tidings, which is an important task for little sisters to have. I would not have offered, but Willa spoke for us both and I did not want to argue with her.

In a way it was a relief to start walking away from the church and down the road to put all that weeping and confusion behind us. We held hands and did not feel sad at all, although I did feel awful about not feeling sad. The sun was warm and the sides of the road were filled with flowers. I should have been in the room of names writing down the name of Selene, and Willa should have been in class learning her ABCs, but this was better, even if it had been caused by Sarah's death. I tried very hard to be sad but could not make myself. Really, all the excitement of finding her body and the screaming and crying and all the big sisters acting strange made me feel almost carefree, I do not know why, and it was plain Willa felt the same way.

The road to Sarah's farm was long and we got very thirsty along the way. There were orange butterflies rising and falling in the fields, too many to count even if you had a lifetime to count them. We stopped holding hands after a while because it took too much effort just to keep our fingers together, that is how tired and hot we felt by the time we came to the gate. Sarah's father was working in the field a long way away. We opened the gate and went to him. He saw us coming and stopped making his horse pull at a tree stump he was removing. When we were close enough for him to hear, Willa said, 'Are you Sarah's father?'

He took off his hat and wiped sweat from his brow, then nodded. He was not friendly.

'Well, she died.'

He seemed not to have heard, so Willa told him again, and I added, 'We're getting a fire ready if you want to be there.'

He put his hat back on and said one word – 'Git.'

We did not know what to do. He said, 'Go on now, git!'

'Don't you care?' Willa asked, being very reckless. I wanted her to shut up, and pulled at her sleeve. 'She's your daughter.' The man glared at us like we were snakes to be hated and killed. He said, 'You go tell her ma, then git.' He jerked his head in the direction of a farmhouse way over at the edge of the field, then turned his back. I pulled again at Willa's sleeve and she let herself be led away, saying, 'He doesn't care.'

'Sarah always said they didn't like her.'

'I wonder what her ma's like.'

The farmhouse was small and low, like most of them, with the window shutters opened wide to catch some air. A dog with stiff hairs along its back came running at us, barking and snarling, making us walk closer together, but it was not a big dog you would have to be afraid of, just a nasty one. It kept running in circles around us and would not quit barking all the way to the front door. Willa knocked with a very firm fist. The wife must have been right behind the door because of all the barking, and she opened it straight away but only a little bit, just enough for us to see her long face staring out. Willa told her, 'Sarah died this morning. We've come to tell you.' The door closed softly. The dog was quiet by then, watching us. 'She hanged herself!' Willa shouted, to be heard through the door, but it did not open again so we started walking away. The dog followed for a little way then stopped. When we got to the gate we looked over at Sarah's father and he was yelling at the horse to pull harder at that stump. Truly, they did not care.

'We should have asked for a drink of water.' My mouth was very dry.

'She wouldn't have given us any.'

'She might have.'

'Nobody's going to give anything to the sisters any more.'

The way she said it made me believe, as if she had pointed to the butterflies and told me, Those are butterflies. If nobody was going to trade with us that was a bad thing, because we do not butcher our own meat or tan hides for making into moccasins, but those things can be learned. We will just not have anything more to do with the villagers and farmers now that the men have decided we are only a bunch of women and not deserving of anything, but we will show them, those big idiots. The sun was very hot now, standing high in the sky, and my head began to ache for lack of water. I wished we had not come so far to do this, especially since Sarah's parents did not care. I knew they would not come to the burning.

When we returned at last to the church a long time had passed and Sarah had been taken to the storeroom, which is the coolest room apart from the cellar, and there was already quite a lot of wood taken from the pile out to the field where sister Belinda had been burned. We went looking for sister Luka but sister Mattie told us she was lying down and feeling poorly and not to bother her. I told her about Sarah's parents and she just shook her head, like this is just one more thing that is not good today, so then we went to the well and drank from the bucket and dipper, two scoops each. That took care of our thirst, then we went to the kitchen and asked sister Kath for something to eat. She told us supper was still a long way off and we could share one of yesterday's bread rolls that was left over but that was all. While we were eating, some more of the little sisters came in wanting something too, and sister Kath got annoyed, telling them it had not been that long since lunch, which made them start to cry. She told them, 'Go look at the sun if you don't believe me,' and they trailed out, then sister Kath told us to go too and leave her in peace until supper, which she had to prepare the same as usual even if everyone was running around like chickens with their heads cut off.

The classroom was empty, just like the yard, so most of the sisters were in their rooms if they were not helping build Sarah's pyre. We wandered into the herb garden and saw sister Briony standing by the sundial at the centre. She was looking down at the dial, which is very old and has always been here, then she looked up at the sun, still very high in the sky, then down at the dial again. When we joined her she seemed upset, but everyone was upset today so we did not take much notice until she said, 'What time of day would you say it is?' She is the only one who knows how to read the sundial because we do not have to know what time of day it is to go about our duties. Morning, afternoon, evening and then night – those are the four times of day. Willa looked up at the sun and said it was noon, but then sister Briony said, 'And how long has it been noon now, would you say?'

We did not know how to answer that. I knew it was still a long time until darkness would bring us seventh night, which is when sister Luka would tell everyone I am the Seer come back after all this time to deliver a message. Sister Briony pointed to the sundial on its stone column and said, 'According to this, it's been noon for most of the day.' She said this silly thing with a crooked smile, as if apologizing for saying anything so ridiculous, but the smile was not funny, and her voice was the same. 'Ever since late this morning when… we found Sarah, I've come here more than once to think a bit and pray, and the shadow has barely moved at all.' She meant the shadow of the sundial's metal finger that points to the sky. It did not make sense because even if I do not know how to read the sundial I do know that the shadow moves across the lines fanning out from the finger, and the only way this would not happen is if the sun stood still. She kept on staring at it, as if this would make the shadow move. I think she forgot we were even there, so Willa and I went away. She said she would help with the fire, and I went to the room of names, where I have set all this down. It should be suppertime soon, my stomach is telling me, but the light coming through my window is strong and bright.

22

I do not know how it has happened, but the sun will not go down! Now everyone knows what sister Briony knows. The sun has come up today and then stayed high in the sky, a noonday sun that is still burning in the same place above. We knew time had passed because we were all hungry and sister Kath had supper ready. While we ate we could not stop talking about how the sun has stopped in the sky. The best reason anyone offered was because of Sarah. Our lady was so sad to see one of her little sisters die that way because of what those men said this morning she had made Sol stop moving out of respect for little Sarah the mouse. Sister Marion said she had been told as a girl that in the old world one of their gods had done that, stopped the sun in the sky, so if an old world god could do that, why not our lady who is more powerful.

After supper Grover Styles and some other men came out to visit again, and they said Sol was showing who is boss around here, making himself shine long into what should have been twilight and evening or even full dark by now. 'You take yourselves a good long look up there,' he said, 'and tell me if you ever seen the like. It's like I said, your moonlady's time is over. Sol, he's the one rules the sky now, not your Selene, which is called Sel the next time you see him.'

He was telling this to sister Luka, who would not answer or even look at him, only at the bright blue sky. The little sisters should all have been in bed but no one was, it was all so strange and mysterious. What Grover Styles does not know is that it is Selene making Sol stand unmoving above us to teach the men a lesson, and she will hold him there until Grover Styles and the rest apologize to sister Luka for the bad things they have said. Now he was saying, 'It's on account of the real sacrifice we made, the blood offering. No god that's real would be happy with sheaves of wheat and apples and such. A real god needs blood, but I guess that's too messy for ladies like you. Well, it works, I'd say, just take a look there.'

He was very pleased, strutting in front of his menfriends and grinning like a fool. I hated him and felt sorry for him at the same time because he has misunderstood everything but thinks he is smarter than us. He will look like such an idiot later on when Selene rises to fill the sky and tells Sol to go to bed around the other side of the world so we can all get some sleep in the darkness. It is hard to say when that might happen because there is no way now of telling what time of day it is. Having the sun stand still in the sky is Selene's greatest show of power, but only women can understand this.

Sarah's pyre had been ready for a long time, so sister Luka gave the order to bring out her body. Willa and I helped carry Sarah from the storeroom, but as we were crossing the yard Grover Styles saw what was happening and wanted to know why this girl died. Sister Mattie explained that she hanged herself because she did not want her parents to take her home. When he heard this Grover Styles got very furious and said it was a lie about Sarah not wanting to go home. Her folks were good people, he said, so why would Sarah not want to be with them? He pointed a finger at sister Mattie, saying, 'I'm holding you responsible for this,' which did not make sense, then he said, 'If you take this girl and burn her, you'll find that won't be the only thing that'll burn around here.' Some of the other men muttered agreement and made us put Sarah down. 'She stays right here till her parents come get her.'

'We already told them and they don't care,' I said.

Grover Styles turned and studied me for a long time, as if I was some kind of interesting spider he had found. 'Girlie, in this place they treat you like something special, but you're not, I don't give a damn what the rules are here. All those rules, they're gone now, so you better learn to mind your elders and show respect. There's a new day coming and this place is nothing.'

'Is that so?' I told him, then looked up at the sky. 'Well, it's starting to be a fairly old day now, it seems to me.'

Some of the men laughed, which he did not like. 'If you had a father,' he said, 'he'd give you the spanking you just earned. Too bad your father's a murderer that went away and died in a hole somewhere.'

'I'm glad he died. He killed my mother.'

That made them go quiet, then one of the men said, 'The reason he killed her, she was whoring around. You're not even his daughter, the whole valley knows that.'

Now I have heard this lie before and do not believe one single word. It is something to make me feel small and unclean, but they do not know I cannot be hurt by this since I do not accept it. My mother was remembered by sister Luka and sister Ursula as a good girl who stayed with them until sixteen and then chose to marry, but she chose unwisely a man who was good-looking on the outside and ugly on the inside. It was his ugliness that murdered my mother for no reason, but fools like Grover Styles will always invent a reason that makes sense to them and makes the murdering man the one to feel sorry for.

'Liar!' I said, then sister Mattie took hold of me and made me go to my room. She did that to keep the men from getting angry, which was a mistake in my opinion because it just makes them think we are afraid. She told me to stay there until someone came to say I could leave. I did not want to, but sister Mattie is not to blame for anything so I told her I would. A little while later Willa came in and said the men had gone but would be back later with all the parents to take away the little sisters that have not been taken already, and Grover Styles said Sarah's body should be put under the elm tree to wait for her parents. If we burned her, he would burn down the church! So Sarah was put where he said and now no one will go near her, which is a disgrace.

I do not know how late it was by then, but Willa said some of the littlest sisters had gone to bed after being worn out by a longer than usual day in which many strange things happened, but she and I were too excited to sleep and sat on her bed talking about it all. And then I told her I had something special to say, about what would happen later on when Selene rises and sister Luka tells everyone I am the Seer. Willa was impressed, I could tell, after I explained to her about who the Seer is and what she does. 'All this with the sun standing still,' I said, 'is just to get everything ready for the announcement. Selene is making a show to help sister Luka.'

'And then what'll happen?'

'I expect the sun will go down very fast and obedient to Selene's wishes.'

'I mean to you.'

'Oh, I'll tell Grover Styles and those others they were wrong, if they haven't worked that out for themselves, and then we'll take Sarah to the fire. By the time she finishes burning everything will be back the way it was, and if the men try anything again like today I'll just have to ask our lady to punish them, to set an example.'

'What would she do, set them on fire?'

'No, twist their silly heads off!'

'No, hold them upside down in a bucket of shit!'

'No, wait... she'll shrink them down to little men you have to be careful and not step on them!'

We rolled about on the bed, laughing at how stupid the men will feel soon, then we heard a knock at the door. Willa went to open it and there stood sister Luka trying not to look worried and old and frail. She asked Willa if she would mind leaving so she could speak with me. Well, it was clear what this talk would be about, getting me prepared for the announcement later on, so Willa winked at me and went away. Sister Luka sat on my bed and worried the moon pendant on her chest with anxious fingers, she was so concerned about having things go exactly right and turning this long day back into night the way it should be.

'Aurora, we must have a little chat together while there's time.'

'Before our lady rises.'

'Yes.'

'And you tell who the Seer is.'

'I may have made a rash promise this morning... how long ago that seems now. I was angry with that man and wanted to put him in his place, but he won't listen so I shouldn't have bothered. The Seer, yes...' She fiddled with the pendant some more. 'It isn't right that Sarah is lying under a tree out there.'

'Her parents will never come. They weren't even upset or anything.'

'We'll see, but about the Seer... are you very attached to Willa?'

'We're bedfriends,' I said, which sister Luka already knows but I felt I had to remind her, she is in such a state of distraction over everything that is happening.

'And can you bear to be separated from her? There is a tradition of the Seer having her own room. The previous Seers wanted that, but they were older women... I really don't know quite how to do this...'

I wanted to go over to the other bed and sit beside her, maybe take her old wrinkly hands in mine and tell her there is nothing to worry about, our lady is in charge and everything will be put back the way it should be after the Seer is announced. But of course there was still the problem of the message that I had not got yet, so I asked, 'After you say who she is, does the Seer have to say what her message from our lady is straight away, or can she wait a little while?'

'The message? Oh, that has already been given. That's how we know who the Seer is, when she makes a pronouncement of an unusual type.'

I could only look at her and feel sorry that sister Luka was so distracted that she thought I had already given her the message, when Selene has not even given it to me yet, so I could not have given it to sister Luka. I said, 'What was the message?' thinking this would remind her that she did not have it yet but soon will.

'The apple,' she said, and gave out such a long and weary sigh I felt even sorrier for her age and confusion, because this did not make sense.

'The apple?'

'That you gave her.'

'Gave our lady?'

'Gave to Willa.'

Now I was very confused myself, which is what happens when someone who is confused talks to someone who is not.

'I don't understand, sister. About me giving the apple to Willa I mean.'

'That was what started it,' she said, 'the apple. She told us it would fall over and its stalk would point at the sun. I don't think she was even properly awake when she said it. Her eyes were open as she spoke, so she could see us, sister Ursula and myself, so there are two witnesses.'

'Witnesses?'

'To the message Willa gave. With your apple in her hand. It would fall over and its stalk will point at the sun, and that has happened. We didn't know how to make sense of the message until today, when the sun stopped at noon.'

I could hear a faraway roaring in my ears. The message had already been delivered? By Willa? She said something to me about an apple dream, but this was not right and sister Luka of all people should have been able to see this. I asked her, 'Who is the Seer?'

'Willa,' she said, a little bit exasperated with me, but I could not allow her words into my heart because they are not true words. 'I'll announce her presence among us when Selene rises, but sister Briony says if the earth has laid itself over so the stalk – the top of the world, you understand – is facing the sun, then our lady will rise in a different place than usual, assuming she still follows the same path around our world... and sister Briony is our expert on the heavens. She was the one who observed our lady coming closer. The instrument has settings for distance, and there was one setting that allowed Selene to fill the lens perfectly, but that was many years ago. Now the setting has to be adjusted back because our lady fills the lens too much, and that is the proof. What it will mean if the earth has laid over permanently is beyond anyone's guess...'

'It hasn't. Selene has made the sun stop still in the sky, that's all...'

'Rory, you must face the facts. This has happened. The world has laid over and now the top half is spinning directly under Sol, so there will be no more night for us... and the bottom half will have no more daylight at all, only night and stars, never the sun... If there are people there they'll freeze to death. Everything down there will freeze forever...'

She put her face in her hands and gave another of the long sighs. I wanted to slap her, slap her face so she would wake up and not talk this nonsense. The world had not laid itself over so the top faces the sun. How could it ever do that? Our lady has made the sun stand still until those men have learned a lesson, that is what has happened and I am the Seer, not Willa! Why would Selene choose Willa to be the Seer? It did not make sense that our lady would do this because Willa was not even born here and was not even connected to the church before the traders came. We gave them beef and they gave us salt and salt fish. And they also gave us a Seer? No! No they did not!

'…and as for us, we'll burn… Can you imagine one endless day with the sun standing at noon… forever? That is what Willa foretold, and now it has happened. We didn't want to accept it at first, but Willa had already told us sister Belinda would die that night. How could she know such a thing if she isn't the Seer?'

'But sister Belinda was dying anyway. Willa didn't say anything we all didn't know!'

'She told me very soon after arriving, and gave the exact number of days until it would happen, and it came to pass just that way. She *knew*. Willa told me she has seen this before in people, and has been punished for it, but she felt she must tell me because she knew… she *sensed* that sister Belinda and I were close, so I should be told.'

'It's not true! It just *isn't*…'

'Rory, aren't you proud your bedfriend will hold a special place among us?'

'No! She isn't the one!'

'Rory…!'

'She isn't! *I* am!'

Sister Luka's mouth fell open as she finally understood what I am saying. 'You…?'

'Yes!'

'Now listen to me, Aurora, you already have a special place among us. You are the Scribe, and that will be your position for life, which you should be justly proud of. You can't possibly imagine our lady would choose you for *two* important positions…'

'Yes!'

The look on her face was infuriating, a kind of sad expression that also said I was completely mad or getting above myself, which I was not, I was not doing that, I was just trying to make her see she had made a mistake that would offend our lady if she did not see the mistake and tell everyone I am the Seer and not Willa, never Willa who is not one of us and has no sense of correctness about anything, no special link to our lady like I have. I knew this was true and not what sister Luka was saying, she was just an old woman who was not able to handle things properly any more, not with so much that is new and strange happening, and now she would tell everyone Willa is the Seer.

'Oh, Rory…'

'Shut up!'

Her mouth fell open again. She was truly shocked and hurt, which I wanted because she has shocked me and hurt me with her old woman nonsense that was not correct, not correct at all and she better take it back before she tells anyone else about this not correct thing, but I could see in her stupid old face she would not be doing that because she thought I was a spoilt little girl who needs a spanking just like Grover Styles said.

'Rory, that is uncalled for…'

'Shut *up*, shut *up*, shut *up*… stupid old cunt!'

Her eyes were fixed on mine and filled with sorrow, but I could not call the words back into my mouth. I had done something so bad I could not see how bad yet, but very bad because nobody in the church has ever said that to the High Sister and I wondered what my punishment would be. But then I made myself turn everything around and wonder how soon our lady will punish sister Luka for getting everything wrong and saying Willa is the Seer. It was easy to do that, turn everything around, I just made myself into sister Luka and made her into me, so the next thing to do was stand up and go to the door and say to her, 'You're not to leave this room until you change your silly mind.'

I went away to the yard. I would give her plenty of time to see where she had got everything wrong, then I would go back and accept her admission that she has been a foolish old woman who was confused about all the important things. It was not too late for her to admit this and apologize because Selene had not come up yet over the horizon out beyond the village where the mountains are lowest. Sooner or later our lady would rise from the peaks to show herself and let everybody see that she is able to send the sun limping down the sky in disgrace and all this confusion and nonsense will be over and done with. I saw Willa over in the corner, looking at Sarah who is propped against the elm's trunk and waiting still for her parents who will never come. I will make Grover Styles pick up her body himself and carry it to the pyre and set it down with tenderness to punish him for the bad things he has said and done. I did not want Willa to talk to me or come anywhere near me until sister Luka had changed her mind and told everyone I am the Seer. Everything that is good and true would start from that moment. This I knew.

Behind me I heard moaning, and turned to see some of the big and little sisters looking over towards the forest. There above the trees was a pale arc drawn in the air like the line an arrow would take if it could travel for miles and miles, the topmost part of Selene. She should have been rising above the village, not the forest, but it was her, it was our lady rising quickly now where she should not be, with the light from Sol blasting her face as it was lifted into a new place in the air. And when I saw this I knew the end had come to our world, because if the earth can lay down and offer just one half of itself to the sun forever, it means our lady is powerless. She is just a bird flying around and around the nest where she cannot land, and we are the eggs in that nest that she cannot protect, so now the egg thieves will come and take these away for eating. I could not breathe, could only stand like the rest and watch the moon rise with all her silent majesty washed away by pale blue light that should not even be there.

'What does it mean?'

Willa was standing beside me. I could not turn to face her. She knew this would happen, saw it in the apple I gave her, and yet she does not understand anything. How could Selene have made this one the Seer? She is able to see the face of death behind the face of life, and she has seen the new face of Selene behind the old just by handling an apple while not even fully awake, just a wasp-bitten girl being tended by two old women, but her words have been proven true, she has seen the shifting of worlds without knowing what she has seen, and all of it happened while everyone was looking the other way, going about their chores, concerning themselves with this and that and all the while our earth was tipping over, bowing to Sol because Sol is the real ruler, just as Grover Styles has said. Truth should not come from the mouth of such as him, nor should it come from the mouth of someone all unknowing of her gift like Willa. She is the Seer and I am not, even though I should be. Selene has whispered to me of what is to come, the positions of rule that should be mine as I become a woman, but those whispers were lies. I am the Scribbler, and my scribbles have not kept our lady further from the earth after all, and this has been known to sister Luka and the other old ones who have kept this a secret from me as they watched our lady through the instrument. They saw how she came closer and closer no matter how many times her name was written down by myself and the Scribblers who came before me, a long line of Scribblers, each one thinking herself important as she dipped her quill and scratched away on sheets of paper made in the old world, fragile yellow paper filled side to side and back to back with nothing but wasted ink, just as the prayer hall has been filled all this time with wasted prayers. Our lady will do what our lady will do, but she will never do anything to defeat Sol, who rules supreme over us, the burning god of men. It has all been a joke, but who has played it?

'Rory, what does it mean?'

'It means we are fallen leaves and will be blown away now.'

'What does *that* mean?'

'Ask our lady to tell you.'

'Why would she do that?'

'I don't know!'

I walked away from her. If I went directly to my room I might be able to beg sister Luka's pardon for what I did and not be punished, although I do not know why I should be. I have been very rude, nothing more. Secrets were kept from me and I was deceived. Sister Luka has no right to punish me. I believed what I believed because of her teaching, and the teachings of our church are hollow. But I must go to her and beg her pardon just because she is the High Sister, even if this does not mean anything to me any more. She is just a woman, the last leader of a flock who have lived here, spinning llama wool, spinning lies and fabulations, spinning in circles around the one god, Sol, while the pretender Selene spins in her useless loopings above.

Passing the room of numbers, I went inside to stare at the piles and piles of books that are filled with nothing, years and years of wasted effort, duty done with a willing heart because we all believed, and now I do not. These hundreds of books are from the old world, we cannot make them now, and I am wondering why sister Winona had them here, or were they part of the building that she moved into before the great stone? It may be that in the old world there was a purpose to books of empty pages, a purpose that has not been passed down from the old world to the new. I will never know, but I am not alone. Where I am alone is in knowing that everything is a lie. Piles and piles of bound pages covered in just one name, the name of the liar, and all of us believed there was power in that name, and truth and mercy and other fine things my mind might bring forth. On top of the nearest pile was sister Ursula's book of numbers that is filled with name counts so we know after all this scribbling exactly how many times our lady's name has been set down. Somewhere in this room there may be a book containing the number of books that are here containing the number of numbers of times the word has been set down. For this and this alone we have learned our ABCs, to set down more lies to follow the lies that came before. We are a gathering of fools, and we will never see the stars again.

Sister Luka was still on my bed, lying on her side. I went to her and stood where she could see me. Her breathing was shallow, her eyes half-closed. I said to her, looking down at my feet, 'The moon has risen. It came up from behind the forest, not the village. The earth has fallen over. Willa... Willa is the Seer. I'm sorry.'

Her lips parted a little but no words came out. I waited to be told I was forgiven. I had made myself humble and apologized and recognized Willa's position. I am not the Seer, not even the Scribe any more because I could not bring myself to pen that name again, that name our lives have been built around. Now I will become a weaver like sister Loren and sister Amanda, the sister-sisters. They are not clever and I have not spoken with them much, but they are the company I need in which to make myself useful. Or I could devote myself to the flock of our lady, watching over the llamas and talking with Brindle, who will listen patiently to everything I say, truth or lie or fabulation, it will make no difference to her. I waited for sister Luka to say something, anything at all, forgiveness or chastizement, but all that passed between her lips were tiny sips of air. I asked her, 'Should I fetch sister Ursula?' There was no reply, and I began to wonder if sister Luka is very sick, and went away again to find sister Rose, who would know.

All the sisters, big and little, were clustered here and there talking among themselves and looking worried, as well they might. The difference between them and me is, I have seen further than them into the truth. They will be sending their prayers to Selene even though we will never again see her riding all silvery and serene across the night sky with twinkling stars all around. Night has been banished from our sky forever by Sol. Our lady, pale and blue as watered milk, lifted clear of the forest and rose like an inflated cow's udder set adrift in the air. I was ashamed for her and ashamed for myself, the two shames linked somehow. Everything that has kept us separate from the village and the farms is gone. We are husbandless women, and we are girls about to be returned to their parents. We are nobody now, and the men of Sol will tell the sisters of Selene what is what in this newest world. We have been cast down from power, our spirit wounded and soon to be crushed completely. I am not the Seer, but I see this. They will have their revenge, Grover Styles and Buford and some of the others. They will want to see us humiliated because it suits their brute nature to make this happen for their amusement. No one will be safe. The other sisters do not know this yet.

I found sister Rose with sister Ursula and told them sister Luka was feeling poorly and resting on my bed. 'I'll see her directly,' sister Ursula said, but kept on talking to sister Rose about Sarah. They did not know what to do about her and were arguing over whether to shift her back into the storeroom or onto the waiting pyre despite Grover Styles warning us against this. 'He wouldn't dare burn down the church,' sister Rose was saying, but sister Ursula, who is older and wiser, did not seem so sure. Anyway, they were not alarmed by what I told them about sister Luka, so I went away to the field of Selene to stroke Brindle's ears and be comforted by her placid affection. I should have gone looking for Willa but was not able to stand the thought of her holding my hand now that I am nothing. She is nothing too, and all the rest as well, but they do not know this yet. Being the first to know that we are all nothing now is so hard because I am alone in knowing what I know. I should be called the Knower, but what I will be called from this time on is Spooky Clamphole, the used-to-be favourite of sister Luka. Now that fool

Buford will be watching me for a few short years, proclaiming me his bride-to-be and talking filth to me about our wedding night. There will be no more weddings conducted by sister Luka. These will be replaced with something made up by the men, some new ceremony that makes the bride her husband's possession, to be used as he sees fit, as it was in the old-old world. Everything sister Winona wanted for her fellow sisters has been overturned just like the earth, and now we are spinning in a new way through a new world of sunshine without end. I suppose we must be grateful we are on the shining half and not on the dark half, where our crops and herds would die from lack of sunlight to keep them alive, and we would die also from freezing cold and not enough food and a longing for something brighter than starlight. Imagine waking up in the morning and there is no morning, just more night, and the night will be there forever. If I lived in that world I would do what Sarah did. But we are the lucky ones who will live in sunlight and plenty, even if we are made slaves again by the men Sol has placed above us now.

Stroking Brindle's lovely ears while her nose went searching for a carrot in my sleeve, I began to cry. I do not know who or what I was crying for. I felt I was crying for everything and everyone, but most of all for myself, because I am the only one that I really know, and I know how truly sad I am now, and crying also for shame because behind all my sadness is the picture of sister Luka lying on my bed, dying maybe, and I wanted her to do that because she is the only one who knows what I said to her, the only one who knows I thought I was the Seer, apart from Willa, a witness to my shame, and so I wanted sister Luka to die. Yes, that is what I thought as I cried and cried and Brindle lost interest to wander away and nibble daintily at some grass. Knowing my wishes, knowing them to be bad and selfish, hurt every bit as much as knowing that our lady is a flying lump of rock and nothing more. This has been a very long day, the first day that will become the one and only day this side of the world will know from now on, but it is not long enough yet to allow for everything I have lost. Before Sarah hanged herself I was filled with pride and expectations of wonder, anxious for these things to be bestowed upon me by Selene and sister Luka, but now I have no expectations that are not as dark as our new day is bright. And it will always be this way because once the true truth is known there can be no shoving it back into darkness, not in a world where such a thing no longer exists. All that was good has fallen, and now all that is bad will rise about us and smother those unable to resist.

It should have been dark long ago. I should be asleep, but I have returned to the room of names and set down the end of that name's time as I have seen it happen. Now I will sleep.

23

Willa was sitting crosslegged on her bed when I woke up, and the smile that opened in her face as our eyes met made me cringe. I have no idea how to deal with Willa now. It is not her fault I am not the Seer but I blame her anyway, her and sister Luka. As if reading my thoughts, she said, 'Sister Luka died. They took her away to the pyre. It's hers now.'

My heart soared hearing this, because it means my secret is safe. When I came to my bed to sleep it was empty, the room too, and I imagined, in my weariness, that sister Luka had recovered. They must have taken her away while I was writing in the room of names. Why had no one come to find me there and tell me? I think there will be much more of this, people not doing the obvious thing, because now there can be no ordered way of living. If our world is to be filled with light forever, how will breakfast be made if sister Marion and sister Kath are not woken at dawn by the rooster that crows for the breaking of each new day? With one single day in which to live, there is no morning or afternoon or evening, only noon, now and forever, so the schedule of events we have always followed will be broken and made meaningless by everlasting sunlight. In the old-old world there were mechanical instruments for measuring time, but that knowledge was lost long ago. Now it will be anybody's guess what part of the day it is, and we will be guided by our stomachs alone, not the rising and falling of Sol any more.

Willa unfolded her legs and set her feet on the floor. 'I'm hungry. I was waiting for you to wake up.'

'Is it breakfast time?' My own inner growling told me it must be.

She shrugged, giving me an impatient look. I sat up, feeling dizzy for a moment. On the blanket beneath me sister Luka had died. That did not seem possible. For all of my life sister Luka has been a part of it, and now she is cold flesh like Sarah. And I had wished it so for my own reasons. Now that these can be kept hidden, I am safe. My only shared secret is with Willa, about my bleeding that was really deer blood. For just a moment I asked myself if that little lie had started everything else happening as punishment, but why would the whole world be punished for what I did, so I made myself not think such things. Had it been my cruel and ugly words that killed her?

'Are they going to burn Sarah at the same time?'

'They're too scared. Nobody's in charge now so she's still under the tree.'

'That shouldn't be.'

'Someone covered her from the flies. Her folks didn't come.'

'They never will.'

'Are you hungry?'

We went to the kitchen and found sister Kath making soup. She set down two bowls, telling us most of the other sisters had been coming in for food every now and then as hunger overcame them, but there had not been a proper mealtime since the world tipped over and most likely never would be again. She was holding back tears telling us this, and began crying when I asked how sister Luka had died. 'We don't know, but sister Rose thinks it was her heart. It just gave out under all the strain. Sister Ursula is poorly too. There's nobody now to tell us what to do.' It was strange to see a grown-up crying, and I expected to see more as it dawned on the sisters that everything has already ended for our church. 'You girls better finish up if you want to see the burning. I think it'll be soon.' Sister Kath's tears were sniffed away as she arranged more soup bowls for anyone else with an appetite. We spooned up our breakfast in silence, knowing that any more talk might set her off again.

I felt sorry for sister Kath, but to be honest, not as much as I felt for myself. Sister Kath and the rest had lost their sense of belonging to our lady, just as I had, but my loss was bigger because I had also lost expectations of glory as the Seer. Nobody has mentioned the Seer since sister Luka announced she was among us at morning prayers, when Grover Styles came and caused all that disruption. That was the last time we all ate together after getting out of bed thinking it would be a normal day, but the apple had already fallen over and pointed its stalk at the sun by then, we just did not know it. I do not understand how it is possible for a huge thing like the earth to fall over without even a rumble from under the ground or a tearing at the clouds as the falling happened. I think the sky must be joined to the land somehow and it all moved as one, and there was no rumbling because all the noise that has come from beneath us down through the years, especially during seventh nights when Selene is very close, was the sound of our earth getting ready to fall over, but the getting ready went on for a longlong time, maybe even back as far as the great stone. If a branch fell out of a tree and hit a man he would fall down straight away, but the earth is so big that when it was hit by the stone it had to wait a long while, making up its mind if it should fall over or not. It thought about this for years and years while people got born and grew old and died and their children and grandchildren did the same, and then, while we slept all unknowing about this, it happened at last in silence and mystery. Now we are all presented to Sol like seedlings in a garden, and he will pour his light down upon us to make us grow, but will there be too much that will burn us to a crisp with no nighttime in between the days any more? And what will seventh night be called now that Selene will visit only during daylight? And do crops need the darkness in which to sleep and rest like we do? The wheat and corn might not like all this daylight now. They might hang their heads and die from too much heat and light. This has not happened before, so nobody knows. Except maybe the Seer. If anyone can see what is coming for us all in this newest world it will be her.

Willa set down her empty bowl and made a small sound of satisfaction now that her stomach was filled. She did not look worried about anything, was not even aware that she was to have been declared the Seer when Selene appeared. Only three people know — sister Luka who is dead, sister Ursula who is poorly, and me. This had not struck me until that very moment. If sister Ursula dies then there will be only myself who knows, only myself with knowledge of my disappointment and shameful behaviour, which could then become a secret known only to me, which is the best kind. Knowing this made me feel better about everything, and I could set aside the jealousy that took hold of me when I learned the Seer would be Willa. Now I could love her again because there would no rivalry between us. All of that would just be a bad memory inside my head where no one can see. I wanted to love Willa again. I had not had time to begin hating her, so it seemed that it should be easy to put everything back the way it was. She did not need to be told anything, that way she would think nothing had happened, and in a way nothing had. But in that case I would also have to live with some other bad memories inside my head, like saying those things to sister Luka, and just now thinking that it would be good if sister Ursula died. How can I make things like that go away? Why could I not just finish my soup, thank sister Kath for her effort, then go visit sister Ursula and pray for her recovery, then put my arms around Willa and tell her I love her? She closed her hand around a wasp to prove she loves me, but I have never done anything like that for her. Am I a very bad person? Are these the signs?

'We should go to the fire now,' Willa said.

Leaving the kitchen, we went across the yard to look at Sarah. She was covered by a blanket but her bare feet were sticking out. I covered them, breathing through my mouth because Sarah has already been here a long time and this day we have now has become very warm. She should not be left there any more, it is just not right, but if Sarah is taken to the pyre Grover Styles has said he will burn down the church, so what can we do? Over by the gate were two people with a little sister they had come to take away with them, and a wagon was coming up the road to take away more. We watched it come inside the gate, the horse looking weary in the heat. The man stayed on the driver's seat while his wife went into the church to find their daughter. When they came out I saw it was one of the youngest, Lena, who has only been here less than a year. She broke away from her mother and came running over to give Willa and me long hugs with tears on her face. 'You have to visit,' she said, then went over to the wagon and was taken away. The other parents and their girl were already walking down the road.

'Do you know where she lives?' asked Willa.

'No, and if we visited we wouldn't be welcome.'

'We'll be the last ones. No parents.'

'Sarah will be last.'

Poor Sarah had been rejected twice by her own mother and father, in life and in death. It was not fair. I had never liked her much because she was so silly and helpless and sad, not a person ready for even a little bit of trouble or disappointment. But the funeral pyre had been built for Sarah, and it was not right that she could not be placed on it beside sister Luka just because of some stupid man who said otherwise.

'We're going to take her there,' I said.

'To the fire?'

'It was supposed to be hers in the first place.'

'What about old whiskers?'

'He can jump in too if he wants.'

Willa laughed, daring me to do it. 'Come on then.'

We fetched the funeral wheelbarrow from the garden shed and loaded Sarah onto it, gasping at the smell. The blanket would have to be washed and then dried in the sun to get the stench out. I folded Sarah's skinny arms across her chest but her legs had to dangle over the front, either side of the wheel. It has never been a dignified way of taking someone to their own funeral, but this is how we do things here. We took a handle each and began trundling Sarah across the yard and around the church, heading for the field. It was awkward work and we had to stop twice to rest. I knew why I was doing this. It was to make me believe I am a good person who wants to do the right thing. This would make up for some of those things I have thought and done just recently, so I could think well of myself again. There were three sisters standing by the pyre, Loren, Amanda and Frieda. They did not offer to help, but they had already worked hard to get sister Luka's body out there, which they must have carried or the wheelbarrow would already have been with them.

'You shouldn't have brought her here,' sister Frieda said.

'She has to be burned.'

'Not if it means the church is threatened. Take her back.'

'No.'

'Yes!'

I could not let sister Frieda have her way and still feel good about myself. I asked the other two, 'What do you think?'

They said nothing, just stood there looking uncomfortable, and I saw that a change has come to the church of Selene. All the sisters are afraid now. With sister Luka gone and sister Ursula poorly they have nobody to stand behind, nobody to give them courage to go on despite everything being changed around and made different than before. This was a shock. I looked at Willa, who was looking at me. I said to sister Frieda, 'It isn't right.'

'Isn't right!' she snapped back. 'Isn't right! Nothing is right! My bees have gone…' She started crying, like sister Kath, her face all twisted. 'I went to the hives and they're all gone and… the queen is dead. She's dead! They'll never come back! No more honey…!'

She suddenly dropped to the ground and began howling, then screaming, then fell over in a faint. Sister Amanda and sister Loren held each other and stared at sister Frieda with horrified looks on their faces, but they would not touch her to help her up, and I saw that theirs was another kind of fear, the kind that paralyses, and these were all grown-up women. This was the thing that made me feel afraid too, because if the grown-up sisters are falling apart and not knowing what to do, then there is no chance for any of us to stand up against Grover Styles and the rest. Sister Luka was the one holding everyone and everything together, so without her to organize things on behalf of us all there will be no more church, just like Grover Styles wants. So really that has already happened. And where will it leave Willa and me? We are just two girls with nowhere else to go. And I think I killed sister Luka by talking to her that way and making her tired old heart give out. This is my fault. I did not make the world fall over but I did shout at sister Luka and make her heart stop. I have done this and now I am so sorrysorrysorry and wish I could make time go backwards and not do what I did. There she lay in front of me on a bed of kindling, ready for burning, and it was me who put her there.

Willa said, 'What should we do?' She saw that it was pointless asking the sisters, they were no good now for anything but giving in and weeping about all of this. 'We could take her home,' she suggested, but not with much hope, because from here to Sarah's parents' farm is a long way to trundle a wheelbarrow with a dead girl in it. We were both worn out by walking there yesterday without a wheelbarrow. Yesterday! It was not yesterday, even if it was a while ago, because there are no more yesterdays and there are no more tomorrows, there is only today stretching out forever, and I wonder why the bees flew away leaving their queen behind. Where would a bee go if not back to his hive? Where would we go if we have to leave here? Not knowing what to do and feeling guilty made me very angry. I took hold of Sarah and tried to lift her out of the wheelbarrow. Willa helped and we carried her over to the pyre and lifted her onto it beside sister Luka. There was not much room there because the pyre was made for just one, but with everyone as upset as they are, building another pyre would be hard to get them interested in, so Sarah must burn along with the High Sister, which just a little while ago would have been an honour, but today it is just killing two birds with one stone. Frieda was moaning softly and the other two could do nothing but hold each other while watching us work. Then of course we found out they had not brought the flint striker with them when they brought sister Luka out to the pyre, so we would have to do that also.

Walking back to the church together I felt Willa's hand slip into mine, and that made me feel guilty too, because I hated her when sister Luka told me that she is the Seer. I must put all that behind me or I will go crazy. We did not know where sister Luka kept the flint striker so we went to her room to look, but it was not there, even though we opened every drawer and poked our noses into places we would not have dared to while sister Luka was alive. Willa found the metal thing that I found when I was snooping before and held it up. 'What's this?'

'Something from the old world, I think.'

'Is it a hammer?'

'I don't think so. It isn't here.'

'It might be in the kitchen to light the stove.'

'The stove fire never goes out, it's too much trouble getting it started again.'

'Well, it must be somewhere.'

We went to the infirmary to ask sister Ursula. She was lying in the same bed sister Belinda had until she died. She looked very old, almost as old as sister Luka, and turned her head very slowly when we stood beside her. She asked, 'Are they all gone?' meaning the little sisters I expect. 'Not all,' I told her, even though I was not sure. It would make no difference in any case, because soon enough they all would be, apart from Willa and me.

'Sister, we can't find the flint striker so sister Luka's pyre can be lit.'

'Take some coals from the kitchen in a bucket. Has everyone gathered there?'

There were only three sisters waiting to witness the burning, but it would serve no purpose to tell sister Ursula this. I had not seen any of the other sisters for a while, so they must have been in their rooms trying to think what they should do next, or else weeping like sister Frieda, or waiting for Grover Styles to come back and tell them what to do.

'Yes, sister, they're all there.'

She sighed. 'Good. You girls will represent me. I can't seem to catch my breath.'

'Yes, sister.'

'Willa, you go and find a bucket and put some kitchen coals in it. Use the fire tongs or you'll scorch yourself.'

Willa went away. Sister Ursula looked at me steadily, then said, 'Luka went to your room to tell you about the Seer, to prepare you. Are you happy that your bedfriend is the one?'

'Yes, sister,' I said, but my lips were squirming.

'She is the future now. Did Luka tell her?'

'Not yet. I mean… no.'

'Send her to me after the burning. She must be told.'

'Yes, sister.'

She stared at me some more, her breathing very shallow. 'Luka thought you might be jealous, so she went to chat with you about it, and died…'

'Why would I be jealous?'

'Because it is in your nature, Rory.'

It made me very angry when she said that. Sister Ursula does not know me well enough to say such a thing. She said, 'You have always been too proud, Rory. Even when Luka made you the Scribe you seemed to think you deserved it. You have a way about you, child, that is not suitable.'

'What do you mean, not suitable?'

'I mean you carry yourself above the rest. They all came to us at six years old. You came earlier because of what your father did. You were always different, a strangeling from the beginning. We worried about you. Luka made you Scribe to give you something extra, something just for you.'

'I was her favourite.'

'There's that pride again. Luka had no favourites. It was to give you something that would allow you to be on your own for most of the day. You do like being alone, don't you?'

I do, but it was not fair for sister Ursula to be saying how I am. Nobody knows how I am except me. She went on, 'You would not have been given the position if your penmanship was not better than most. Our lady's name must never be scrawled carelessly.'

'Does it matter now?'

I did not mean to ask that, it just slipped out somehow.

'How could it not matter? What a thing to say. Are you too proud to follow the teachings of Selene without questioning everything?'

'I never did that.'

'Do not contradict me or you'll be sent to your room for reflection and reconsideration.'

That has always been the remedy for any little sister who causes a fuss or does not obey the rules, never smacking or punishment chores, only being sent to think about your naughtiness alone. It never happened once to me, so how can I have been too proud the way she says? Sister Ursula was not being very nice to me today, which is not like her, but then it has been a very bad day so far so I tried to forgive her, but that was hard too.

'Sister, what's that thing in sister Luka's room, the thing in her drawer?'

'You have no right…'

'We were looking for the flint striker. There's a thing there all rusty.'

She sighed. It was too hard for her to keep on looking at me with her head turned just a little bit sideways, so she stared at the ceiling, at the same patch sister Belinda would have stared at a lot if she had not been blind. 'That is our secret,' she said, so very softly I wondered if she was about to fall asleep or even die.

'A secret?'

'She killed him with it.'

'Killed? Sister Luka?'

I pictured her attacking Grover Styles with the hammer thing.

'Sister Winona. Maybe I shouldn't tell you…'

'Sister Winona killed someone?' I was thrilled by this as well as shocked.

'Only a man, a bad man. He wanted to take over. That could not be allowed to happen. Sister Winona did what she felt she must, to keep her dream alive. Imagine some man taking over…'

'Was it Ranger?'

'Yes, Ranger. He had a weapon. She took it from him.'

'I thought she told him to leave.'

'He would not be told. He was a typical man, and he paid the price. Sister Winona stopped him, blessed be the name of sister

Winona. Sometimes bad things have to be done to save the good things. You might be too young to understand.'

But I do understand. I understand that the moon is coming closer, not further away like it is supposed to because I have been writing down the name of Selene over and over, and I understand that our way of life here did not begin in a spirit of cooperation, which has always been an important word here, it began with a murder, just as my time with the sisters of Selene began with a murder. And there are no invisible gardens of Selene on the moon. And I do not believe Selene is there either. When that thought came into my head it made me dizzy, like if you suddenly found out your head was not your own but had been stitched onto your neck from someone else's body that died. Anyway, now I know what the secret is in sister Luka's room, it is a weapon. Now I could picture it in use for what it is, a war club for smashing people's skulls in. I wish I could use it to smash Grover Styles's skull in, which he deserves.

'I'm not too young.'

'Whatever I say, you contradict me. This would not have happened a little while ago. You're not yourself, not obedient. I may have to talk to Luka about you if it continues. You aren't above suspension from your duties if that's what it takes…'

She puffed and panted through dry lips, trying to sound stern, but how could I take her seriously when she was calling sister Luka just plain Luka, which is disrespectful, and threatening to tell on me to a dead person? I think she is dying inside her brain. When Willa came back I wanted to have her look for the face of death behind sister Ursula's ordinary face. She is the last of the very old sisters now, and none of the younger ones are ready to be the High Sister.

I said, 'If you suspend me from my duties, who'll write down the name of Selene?' She said nothing. I said, 'And if that happens then the moon will come crashing down.' She would not reply because she could not overturn that argument. I said, 'But it really doesn't matter any more, because it didn't mean anything in the first place. It's all a lie. There is no Selene now, only Sel and Sol, and Sol will burn us for punishment for worshipping the wrong one! You did everything wrong…!'

Her mouth was gasping, her eyes opened so wide I thought they might fall out. 'Stop… stop!' She panted for a moment, then said, 'Now we see the real Rory… the unbeliever. Something happens and you abandon your faith… Shame on you… but you can redeem yourself.' I said nothing. I do not need redeeming just because I have found out the truth. She is just saying this because she thinks I am a little girl who she can tell what is real and what is not, but I will make up my own mind about that from now on thank you.

'You must… protect her.'

'Protect who?'

'The Seer. She will be the one who leads us out of this… misfortune. If you love her, protect her.' She was looking at me again, not at the ceiling. 'Will you protect her?'

It was something I would do anyway because I love Willa, I think. Loving her would have been easier if sister Luka had not picked her to be the Seer. Everything has gone bad because of that. But that is not Willa's fault. She has not even been told yet. It would be better if she never got told, because then we are equals, or no, I am a little bit above her because I am the Scribe, but that means nothing now too, so really we are just girls. I do so want to love Willa again, but it will be harder if she knows she was picked to be the Seer.

'A long time ago sister Marion told me something about you, Rory. She said you told her you would be High Sister someday. You were not even Scribe then. Why would you imagine something like that?'

I do remember telling sister Marion that. It happened just after I came to know that this would be my future, like a voice whispering in my ear, telling me of things to come. I should have kept it to myself, but I was very excited. Sister Marion had just laughed and said I might be if I was very good. She should not have told anyone else.

'That would not have happened, Rory, do you know why?'

'No.'

'Because you are not likeable. The High Sister must be someone who is able to get along with people. That has never been your strength. Being made Scribe kept you out of everyone's way…'

'No it didn't…'

'… because you have a habit of telling people what to do, young as you are. Your father was a murderer. We always wondered if some of his badness would come out in you.'

'No you didn't…'

'And until today, nothing did. Shame on you for doubting our lady. And you… *you* of all people thought you were suitable to be High Sister. Too much pride…'

'I'm not like that…'

'You make me weary… Go.'

How I hated her for telling me that. A dying old woman and I hated her.

'Yes, sister.'

Outside, I saw two things. The first was Willa coming from the kitchen with a bucket, and the second was sister Amanda and sister Loren struggling to tip Sarah from the wheelbarrow onto the ground under the elm tree. They had brought her back! They are such cowards! Sarah fell from the barrow in a heap, then the sisters saw Willa and me watching and shrieked, clutching at each other for support, as if we were men come to do them harm. I think everyone is losing their mind today, so I should not be so hard on myself about there being someone else inside my head, whispering to me. The sisters ran away in the direction of the pyre, still making shrill sounds of alarm. Willa started laughing but stopped when she saw I was not. We went over to Sarah, who was lying on her face. The wheelbarrow had fallen over too. Willa was carrying the bucket of coals, so I pulled the blanket back over Sarah, not wanting to do again what we had already done. Sarah can just stay right there, and when Grover Styles came back he will see that his order not to move her was stupid, because there she lies, not picked up by her parents and stinking nicely. All kinds of things are going to be done now that are stupid, just because everything has changed.

We carried the bucket between us back to the pyre. When they saw us coming the sisters stepped away from sister Luka and did not interfere when we tossed our bucket of coals onto the firewood beneath her. Some of the smaller kindling caught fire straight away and we knew it would burn now with no more help from us. Smoke began rising around sister Luka's body. The air was very still and hot. Every stick beneath sister Luka seemed to give out a loud crack as the flames began taking hold. Then I noticed that nobody had bothered to remove the moon pendant from around her neck. The pendant was worn by sister Winona, they say, so it is important and should have been taken off before they put her on the pyre but the sisters are like headless chickens today. I reached through the smoke and took it off, almost burning my arm. The pendant went into the front pocket of my smock. I waited to hear at least one of the sisters protest, but they just watched the fire begin burning fiercely, Willa too. The heat drove us back away from the blaze. The pyre was roaring now, the wood cracking and splitting, sap oozing out in bubbles and hissing as it burned. Sister Luka's smock and vestment caught fire, then her hair. It was a much louder fire than sister Belinda's, and hotter too, but that might be because the air is hotter under a sun that never goes away. Soon we could smell that special smell of burning flesh as sister Luka became part of the fire. I felt angry and sad watching her burn. Soon it would be sister Ursula's turn. I was supposed to tell Willa to go to her after the burning so she could be told she is the Seer, but I made up my mind, watching the flames twist and crackle, that I would do no such thing. I wanted to love Willa again like before, when I was the Scribe and she was the newcomer, the latest little sister and nothing more. That way works best so far as I am concerned, and Willa would not miss being someone special because she is really not interested in those things anyway.

We moved further back from the heat, held hands and watched the last High Sister of the church of Selene get burned to cinders, then Willa said she was sleepy and would go to bed, and I have come to the room of names to set down what has happened.

24

The men came back, led by Grover Styles, and went through the church to get everyone out of their rooms and assembled in the yard. All the little sisters were gone by then, leaving thirteen big sisters, including sister Ursula, who seemed to be sleeping and so was left alone, and Willa and me. Grover Styles did not even look over at Sarah, still under the elm like a bundle someone has dropped and forgotten. He ran his eye over us and began talking, pulling at his shirtfront now and then to try and get some air to his armpits. Everyone's face was sweating and worried, among the females I mean. The men had eyes shining with power and determination. Everyone knew they were here to take wives, and I saw, searching among their eager faces, that they were not all bachelors. Buford was there but I would not look at him, not wanting our eyes to meet.

'You women have been told there'll be changes happening now that Sol is watching over us like he is, a whole new way of doing things around here that's different to before. Sol wants that and he'll be staying right about where he's at till everything has been figured out according to the new ways and we can all start over. I can see you women are as hot as I am so this won't take long and we can get back to night-time again, if that's what it is right now, only Sol knows. So what I'm saying is this – for a good long while now you been doing things your way, only your leader, she's gone and there's no replacement, so you have to be asking yourself what are you if you ain't a Selene sister, not any more, and the answer is, you're about to be a bride to some good man that's needing a wife, or maybe a second wife if he can afford to keep her, which some here have got that ability. Now I know you think you don't want a husband, but that's where you're wrong. A woman needs a husband and a man needs a wife so they can have children and the human race goes on. That's the natural and obvious way it should be, only it hasn't been that way for too long now. Well, that's over and done with.'

He swept his hand across the dozen or so men with him. 'These will be your husbands pretty soon. They'll be making their selections and taking you to a real house that's yours to live in alongside your man and be raising his children like you should, and he'll protect you from harm and treat you right so you can be happy. You can't tell me you been happy here with this Selene nonsense getting in the way of your natural feelings. Some of you are so mixed up you think it's all right to be sleeping with one another, but that's something you been told by liars. Women are for men, not for other women, not here on earth and not on the moon.' He laughed and some of the men did too, but we did not.

'Now I guess you might be worried about all this, but you don't need to be. This is a good thing, this change, just a way to get you away from something bad you never should've been doing, and now you can be true women after all and be happy doing that the way it's intended between men and women. Now, ladies, when one of these good men here picks you out, and he's known to be a good provider and hard worker, I'd advise you to accept him. If you don't, you have to have a good reason. I can't think of a single one myself, the situation being what it is. So now you men are going to move among these ladies here and make your selections, and you'll be nice and polite doing it, no grabbing and you have to ask, you don't just tell her she's yours. Women like to be treated gentle for courting so that's what you'll do, you hear? Go ahead.'

The men moved forward slowly, almost shyly, looking very awkward but that did not hold them back. Grover Styles was ahead of the rest and went directly to the sister-sisters, Loren and Amanda. His wife had died last year from something wrong inside her, and it was clear that as the man who milled almost everyone's wheat into flour he had a bigger house than most and three children needing a mother, or two mothers if he had his way. I watched their faces as he spoke to them and saw their expressions turn to wood. It was the same with the other sisters as the men moved among them, smiling and trying their best to seem pleasant, but there were no smiles on the faces of the women. Two young men started a fight over sister Alicia, who is pretty and only nineteen, until Grover Styles stepped in and told them the woman could choose so there would not be any fights. But sister Alicia would not pick either man, just stood there hiding her face in her hands and sobbing, which got the men more irritated with her than with each other. They started shouting to make her choose between them until sister Nell marched up and put her arms around sister Alicia and tried to soothe her. That got the men angry and they told her to step away, but sister Nell would not, and she is our biggest sister with plenty of muscle so they did not lay a hand on her, just made comments about how the one they want has gone and disappeared behind a wall of flesh hiding her from them, but sister Nell and sister Alicia ignored them still. Then one of the men got tired of this and yanked sister Alicia away, and when sister Nell tried to stop him he punched her hard in the stomach. Sister Nell grunted and slumped to her knees, gasping and holding herself. Grover Styles roared at the man to quit that, then he told sister Alicia she better choose one and settle things before any more fighting happened, but she would not, so the men decided to arm wrestle for her and the fair-haired one was the winner. It was the loser who hit sister Nell, so in a way this was the best result really for sister Alicia. Poor sister Nell sat on the ground and wept silently, ashamed to have been hit like that.

I watched Buford from the corner of my eye, half-expecting him to choose me even if I am not old enough for marrying, but he did not, and he did not pick some other sister, so I could not see why he was there, then he caught me watching him and came over with a half-smile sitting crooked on his stupid face. 'Hey there, Spooky, who's your friend?' I did not answer, just stared between his eyes, a narrow target because they are set so close. He said to Willa, 'You run along now while me and Spooky talk awhile.' When she told him, 'No,' he did not get upset, just ignored her the way you might ignore someone's dog while you speak to its owner. 'Spooky, just to remind you, a year or three from now, you're mine, see? That gives you plenty of time to get used to the idea. I don't want some other wife today, I'm just here to remind you.' The reason he is not looking for a wife today is because he shares his stepmother with his father, I have heard from sister Kim, who went to the village more than most of us to barter for goods and heard gossip from the women there who were kindly disposed towards the church. He looked again at Willa, at her breasts mainly, then said, 'By then I might be in a position where I can maybe take two wives. You girls take good care of each other for me, all right?' We would not speak to him, not one word, which struck him as very funny and he went away still smiling.

Sister Nell and sister Briony were the oldest sisters, so they were the last to be chosen. Sister Nell had not spoken a word since being punched in the stomach, but her face was like a thundercloud just waiting to release rain. As they were being picked, not one of the sisters had given a reason for refusing any man, and that told me they were defeated, because their only reason would have been they just did not want to. Grover Styles would not have accepted that, and they all knew it. Sister Briony was chosen by an old man and sister

Nell by a man much smaller than herself, so they did not look like a good match. None of them did. The sisters stood looking at the ground or off into the distance, ashamed to have been made to do this, but what else could they have done except start a battle with the men, which would be ridiculous for sisters of Selene because the church is against violence as sister Winona decreed. Of course, I know now that sister Winona killed a man to avoid violence of that kind. The sisters will be taken away from the place they want to be and made to live somewhere else, in the village or on one of the farms, with someone they do not know or like, so I cannot see how this will bring happiness to anyone, but it has been done.

The sisters hugged each other one last time, most of them crying, then the men began taking their new wives away by wagon or on foot until there was only Willa and me and poor dead Sarah left, and sister Ursula in the infirmary. Grover Styles told his wives to get in his wagon and they did, then he came over to us and said, 'You two girls, you'll stay here and take care of that old woman in there, and when she dies you'll get adopted out to good families. Or if you're too scared to be here on your own you can get adopted right now, it makes no difference to me.'

I pointed to the blanket under the elm. 'What about Sarah?'

'That's the one hung herself? You can burn that one.'

'You said not to.'

'And now I'm saying something different.'

'Her parents won't ever come,' said Willa.

'Well, I don't blame them, do you? A girl so far gone with bad influences, she'll end up doing something her folks don't approve of, like what she did. Likely they don't want nothing to do with her.'

'You've got a wagon, you could take her home.'

'You're the one they call Spooky, ain't you? There's folks saying you're a bad seed and I can see why.'

'Please…' said sister Loren from the wagon.

Grover Styles was in a good mood because he just got two new young wives. That is the only reason he swore some bad words and then picked up Sarah to put her in the wagon bed. He made sounds of disgust over the smell, but it is his own fault for not letting us burn her before. Picking up the reins, he told us, 'You take care of things here, shouldn't be too long before you can be with a real family.' He clucked at his horse and the wagon began rolling. We watched it pass through the gate and turn onto the road, then it was gone and the sound of its creaking and rumbling was replaced by cicadas, which seemed to be liking the heat and were rasping away happily. Staring at the empty gateway, I did not know what to do next. I felt lucky to have been left behind and not taken away like the rest to be a wife. I knew I would never let Buford be my husband, or any other man.

Willa said, 'We should ask sister Ursula if she wants anything.'

'I'll do it. You see how much food is left in the kitchen and storeroom.'

Willa was happy to do that, not knowing I do not want her to get told by sister Ursula she is the Seer. I think this is the best way to keep us friends. Sister Ursula was not awake when I went to see, so I stood quietly and listened to her breathing for a little while, trying to hear the sound of death coming, but there was nothing, so I joined Willa in the storeroom. There was quite a bit of salt fish and some dried beef there as well as a few preserves, and the kitchen cupboards, when we looked, were far from empty, so feeding ourselves and sister Ursula would not be a problem for some time yet. Then we went to the field of Selene to look at the llamas and make sure the sacred herd was not suffering from all this daylight. They were standing under the trees along the field's edge for shelter from the sun, but did not seem sick or unhappy. Brindle came over but I had forgotten to bring a carrot again. She kept nudging at me anyway, not believing I would visit without bringing a treat. What will happen to the llamas now? Who will clip their wool and spin and weave it? Who owns them?

'I don't want to get adopted,' Willa said.

'Me neither. I don't like anyone around here. We'll just wait and see what happens. The sun might go down again.'

Looking across the field I saw heat lifting into the air like ripples in water. The sound of cicadas was ringing in my ears. To my mind, it did not seem likely that Sol would do anything but stay where he was. It took a longlong time for the earth to tip over after the great stone hit, generations of people long, so it will probably take just as long, or maybe longer, for it to go back to the way it was before. We will be dead and turned to dust by then, but if Willa wants to believe everything is going to be put back like it was, I do not want to upset her by disagreeing. There is only her and me now, so we must be nice to each other, and protective the way sister Ursula said.

'They're all going to be so unhappy.'

'The llamas?'

Willa shook her head. 'The sisters. They shouldn't have been made to do that.'

'We're the lucky ones, getting left behind.'

'I know, because we have each other.'

I could not stop myself from hugging her, and she hugged me back. I almost wanted to cry, I do not know what about. It is all so sad what has happened to the church of Selene, even if it is not as real and true as we have been taught. The sisters meant nobody any harm and should not have been taken away from the church like that just because there are some men who are needing wives. Brindle put her nose right up against our heads and huffed loudly, which made us both laugh, so then we stroked her nose and ears until she finally accepted that we did not have any carrots and went away.

25

I have not written the name of Selene since the change. I do not believe any more so it is a waste of ink, which I need anyway for my secret book. Life here is so strange now, with no night and no darkness to let us know when it is bedtime. We eat when we are hungry and sleep when we are tired and row the boat very often because we have nothing much else to do except going to see sister Ursula whenever I think of it. I do not want Willa to go to the infirmary and talk with sister Ursula, so I told her I would take care of her on my own because this is one of the Scribe's duties. She was happy enough to believe me, or pretended to, and I do not blame her because it is not easy to look after a dying old woman whose mind is wandering a lot. Sometimes sister Ursula asks me where Willa is, and I tell her something made up, like Willa is busy making supper or has gone to the village to fetch something we need, which was the biggest lie because we would not go anywhere near the village. None of the sisters has come back to visit us or ask if sister Ursula is all right, so they are under the thumb of their husbands I think and not allowed. Sister Ursula does not eat very much, just a mouthful now and then, and she sips water but I only have to bring a bucket for her to piss in once in a long while, and she has not shat even once, so that shows how little she has been eating. I think she is dying. Once she demanded that Willa be brought to her, and I said I would get her, but then I just stayed away for a long time, and when I came back to see if she wanted anything she did not ask for Willa, so she is forgetting things, which makes it easier to fool her.

One of the good things about being on our own is we can use the instrument in the tower as often as we please, so when we feel like it we go up there. In all the time that sister Briony's instrument has been aimed at the sky, nobody ever once thought to use it in daylight and turn it around to look at the village, but Willa and I do exactly that. Our view across the village is good because the church was built on a slope and is the highest building in the valley, which we can see the other side of easily. It is peculiar to see people so close when you know they are a long way away, and we spent a lot of time watching out for any of the sisters who were taken to the village. Grover Styles's house was in easy view and I did see sister Amanda once, going from the back door to the outhouse, but I could not see her face closely enough to tell if she is happy or sad, but I would be sad if I was Grover Styles's wife, and Willa has seen sister Kim going inside the butcher's and just walking from one place to another, so they have not been murdered yet by their husbands.

It is so hot now that every window is kept open all the time just to get a breath of air, but the air outside is just as hot as the air inside. We have kept the kitchen garden going with many trips to the well, but we have not done the same for the herb garden, which would make sister Ursula angry if she could remember being in charge of it, but she does not.

A little while ago some men came from the village with wagons and took away all the beds except the three being used, but I did not feel I could stop them because they are empty beds and someone else should have the use of them. They took things from the garden shed and kitchen and two sacks of flour from the storeroom and our chickens. I wanted to hit them or drive them away with screeching and screaming, but it would not have worked. This is the bad thing about being a child, the way any grown-up who wants to can do anything at all and you cannot stop him, being too small. But then sister Nell was big and strong and she was punched in the stomach, so really it is because we are female that the men can do this. How I wish Selene could float down from the sky and point a finger at these thieves and turn them into lizards or owls. That would be so much fun, to see them scurrying around or flapping their wings and wondering what happened to them. But there is no Selene or she would have stopped them from taking the empty beds from the infirmary. They just went in and took them while sister Ursula was lying there almost dead. Their ringleader took a close look at her face and said to me, 'Not much longer for this one. You and that other girl, you can come live with me if you like. My wife, she's a good cook. We've got just the one boy and she can't have more, so a couple of sisters for him to grow up with, that's better than nothing.'

'No thank you.'

'You'll think different when you start getting hungry.'

'Which will happen faster now that you stole our food.'

He did not like hearing that and narrowed his eyes at me. I do not think he is a bad man, he just did not like to hear the truth from a girl. He said, 'Before you quit this place you better try hard to make yourself more polite. Nobody wants a smartmouth.'

'Well, I don't want them either.'

He laughed at me, trying to make me feel worthless. He said, 'I changed my mind. You'd be trouble, and ungrateful too.' Then he spat on the infirmary floor and left. I went out to watch them drive their wagons away, and someone had taken a big load of firewood too, so fairly soon we will run out of this and the stove and oven will go cold.

I know they will come back and steal other things now that they have done it once. We need to make a plan for when sister Ursula finally dies and the villagers come to take away everything else. But what plan? For all we know there are no other places with people in the whole world except Willa's village and the valley, with a long and broken trail in between. If we leave here and go in another direction, who knows what kind of death we would find in the mountains? But we cannot be adopted, it would kill us, I know this. So we must think harder for a way out as we go about our duties. When we do not worry about these things we are happy just to be together.

26

Seventh night has come around twice since the change, with Selene riding across the sky as big as before but seeming less big because now she can only be a washed-out blue unless she comes between us and Sol, which will make her turn black. There will be no more silver Selene, but it is a good thing that she has kept her long looping path around the earth like before so we can at least know when seven days have passed. Without Selene there would be no way of measuring time at all in a place where the sun always shines. I have been studying the sundial in the herb garden and have noticed that the shadow of the metal finger does move a tiny bit back and forth, so the stalk of the apple does not point exactly at Sol and there is a wobble. If I could stare into the sun for a long time without being blinded I know I would see it move in a small circle up there, its path a golden halo in the sky.

27

Grover Styles has come again but he did not bring sister Amanda or sister Loren with him for a visit. I think the men want their new wives to stay away from the church so they do not get sad over what they have lost, which might make them less obedient than they have been since they were taken away. He came alone in his wagon and took almost everything left in the storeroom and kitchen, including all sister Kath's pots and pans, leaving us with next to nothing, the thief. I followed him around while he took things out to load into his wagon. He ignored me until I followed him into the infirmary, which has been a hospice really since sister Ursula began dying.

'What keeps that old body going?' he said, staring down at her. Sister Ursula's eyes were staring up at the ceiling. I think she did not even know we were there.

'The power of Selene.'

He snorted and leaned closer to peer into her face. 'Does she still eat?'

'Only a tiny bit, which is just as well because you took everything.'

He gave me a long look that was meant to make me shut up, then picked up the bucket I use to carry sister Ursula's waste to the outhouse. He knew what it was because of the smell. 'I'll take this,' he said, daring me to say he could not. I said to him, 'What would I use in place of it?'

'Whatever you like.'

'You're just a thief.'

I had not meant to tell him that, but I was angry.

'Little as you are, I'll take my belt to you, you ever talk to me that way again. The sooner you leave here the faster you'll learn that other folks don't see things the way you do. Useful work and having babies, that's what you women should've been doing, not praying to the moon and diddling each other. Now it's gone hot as blazes out there and Sol won't go down to give us some relief. People are asking me why that is, getting all worried about the ground drying up. Seems to me the reason's lying right here.' He looked at sister Ursula. 'Sol, he won't go down till the last of those old women that taught you that shit has died, so whatever it is that's kept her alive all this time, you better stop doing that and let her go. It's too hot now, hear me?'

He drove his wagon away and I went to find Willa, who always stays clear of him when he comes, as if she is frightened by him, but it is hard to imagine Willa frightened by very much. Maybe she just does not want to look at his stupid face, but someone has to or he will go ahead and take every last thing from us and make us starve. And I cannot just quit giving food and water to sister Ursula, that is not right, even if it would make Sol go down and give us cool night and darkness again, which I doubt. Willa was in the tower, watching Grover Styles and his wagon get smaller through the instrument. When I told her what he said she agreed with me, but then we had to admit we still do not have a plan for escape, so we do not know what to do. This has made us different somehow, so that when we row the boat we sometimes stop halfway through and just hold each other instead and cry, because we are only young and there is nothing good to look forward to apart from being with each other.

And the well is going dry. We did not have any rain for a long time before the change, and none since, so the ground is cracking here and there, the soil gone all crumbly from lack of moisture. To get anything from the well we have to let the bucket all the way down to reach water, and we can hear it bumping against the bottom before it comes up only half full. We are asking ourselves which will give out first, the water or sister Ursula's will to live. When either one ends we are going to be in a lot of trouble.

We are finding dead birds on the ground and do not know if they have died of thirst or because they can no longer roost in the trees for rest during the night and have stayed awake and exhausted themselves until they died. It is a mystery and very sad. The cicadas are still happy and making lots of noise. I go to the creek that flows through the long meadow for the llamas to drink from and it is not so fast or deep as before but still enough, although their grass is getting very brown and dry. We have fed them the last of the carrots from the kitchen garden, which we cannot water any more, having to keep what is left for ourselves.

28

Willa saw a terrible thing through the instrument. Sister Nell was in the stocks beside the trading field and getting pelted with garbage! Willa yelled at me to come look, and I was so angry when I saw what they were doing I went down and started running along the road to the village with Willa hurrying after me. When we got to the trading field the crowd went quiet, about twenty people, and they watched as we went to sister Nell, who has always been the strongest and bravest sister. Her face was filthy and we wiped it clean with our hands while some among the crowd jeered and made comments, but nobody stopped us until Willa tried to knock out the peg that kept the stock boards fastened around sister Nell's neck. That got them shouting, and sister Nell told us, with tears in her eyes, to get away and not make trouble for ourselves, but we would not until a man came over and yanked us away by our hair, which made both of us scream as we were dragged away. The man let us go and I saw sister Mattie in the crowd wringing her hands and crying, but there was nothing she could do either. I asked her what sister Nell did to deserve this, and got told it was because she slapped her husband after he told her to do something and she did not want to, so he hit her and she hit back. Her time in the stocks is to let the other sisters know they had better not do anything like that or they will be punished too.

Willa and I stood watching as poor sister Nell had more garbage thrown at her head. Her eyes were closed and her lips moving, so I think she was praying to Selene, which I knew would not change anything and might even make it worse if they knew what she was doing. Sister Mattie whispered that we should leave while the crowd was still distracted, then she hurried away, not wanting to see any more of this awful thing. We did as she said, moving back through the crowd until nobody was watching us, then we slipped away and began walking back to the church very slowly. This would be the very first time since the beginning that a sister of Selene has been punished in public, which just goes to show there is no respect any more and never will be again. We were so upset about this that we could not even talk about it, both of us thinking that sooner or later we would have to suffer something similar because we do not want to obey any man just because he is a man. How dare they do this to us!

A long time after that when we were asleep, we were woken up by an awful screaming in the distance and knew a cougar had killed a llama. We lay there shaking even though we were in no danger, and I wondered if it was Brindle who had died. That was enough to get me out of bed and we went to see. It was another one, not Brindle. The killed llama was not there, only a big bloody patch, so the cougar has dragged it away into the forest. This has never happened before, a cougar coming so close to church lands. When they attack livestock it is at the furthest farms, not so close to the village, so this is something new, like everything else since the change. The llamas were very nervous and came crowding around us even though we had nothing to feed them, so we made a fuss over each one with lots of petting until they seemed to calm down a little and began drifting off to graze again, searching for something green among the dried grass. If I see Chad I will ask him to kill the cougar before we lose another llama from the field of Selene.

29

More awful things have been done by the village men. Grover Styles came to the church in a very bad mood and went directly to the hospice to look at sister Ursula, still alive despite not having eaten for a long time or even drunk any water. He and three other men crowded around her bed, peering closely at her lined old face and wanting to know why this woman had not died yet, which of course I could not answer, being puzzled myself about this. They blamed her for the sun still being where it is in the sky, blazing down constantly and making everything bone dry, like the village well. They made me leave the room while they talked about the problem. Willa was nowhere around, hiding from Grover Styles as usual. She is really scared of him but will not say why, only that he is horrible, which is true. I waited outside, then they all came out carrying sister Ursula completely hidden in a blanket.

'Where are you taking her?'

'Her last resting place,' said one of the men, and another one laughed.

'She just now died,' Grover Styles told me. 'We'll give her a decent burial, don't you worry.'

'She has to be burned…'

'And start a fire that burns out the whole valley? She'll be buried like anyone else.'

'But that's not what she would have wanted…'

'If she sits up and complains, we'll do it her way,' one of the men joked.

They carried sister Ursula to a wagon and put her in, but they did this clumsily and the blanket fell open at one end, where her head was, and I could tell by the way sister Ursula's head hung sideways that they had broken her neck. This frightened me very much and I could not say anything as they covered her again. Grover Styles said to me, 'You did a good job looking after her, but that's all over now. Soon as Sol knows she's gone he'll do the same, go to rest and then come up tomorrow morning same as usual. She just hung on too long is all. When Sol comes up again, you and that other one better get yourselves ready for moving to the village. There's some good people been arguing who gets you, so that's a good sign you'll be with folks that'll look after you and bring you up right.'

'We want to stay here.'

'Well, you can't, not two young girls alone. Might be a bear comes out of the woods and eats you.' He laughed, feeling good about things now that he had killed the person he thought was keeping the sun in the sky.

'If Sol doesn't go down can we stay here?'

'He'll be going down.'

'But if he doesn't.'

'Now look, here's the truth of the matter. There's nobody wants to take you in, only the other girl. You, you're too strange for most folk, but there'll be someone that'll do the right thing and take you in, only it won't be with any of them sister friends of yours. All of you need to be kept separate till you get over this Selene shit and act like other folk, then we can all be happy. You want to be happy, don't you?'

'I want to stay here.'

'That won't happen, so stop thinking it.' He climbed into the wagon, saying, 'When you see old Sol drop down behind the trees again like before, you start getting ready for a new kind of life. Me or someone else'll be here in the morning to take you away, got that?'

They drove slowly away with dust rising from the wheels and horse's hooves. It stayed hanging in the air for a long time. I felt sick at the thought of being taken to live with anyone from the village. They do not want me anyhow, I believed him about that, and it would make things much worse to be with someone who took me in out of obligation and not love. So I will not go. I will not go and Willa will not go either, even if they want her to. We will stay here and live somehow. And I have just this moment thought of something clever! I will tell them we want to live with Chad! He is the one grown-up I trust in the whole valley, and he does not have a home so he will come here to the church and take care of Willa and me and we will take care of him, fixing him meals that are better than he makes himself and we will all be happy by ourselves. And he will be very handy for keeping cougars away from the sacred herd. Having lost sister Ursula I do not want to lose Brindle also. It is the best idea I have had in a long time. I do not know where Chad lives exactly, nobody does, but our paths will cross as they always do and I will tell him my wonderful plan, which he will see the sense of and come here to live!

I ran to find Willa and tell her, but she would not come out from hiding until I finally found her in the tower. She was not using the instrument, was curled in a ball beside it and would not uncurl until I made her, and she did not say anything while I explained about the plan. We have been wanting one of these for the longest time and now we have one that is perfect, but Willa did not cheer up at all. I asked her what was wrong but she only shook her head, looking very sad, which upset me because I was feeling so good about the plan. Then I remembered about sister Ursula and told how the men had come and broken her neck and taken her away with them, which made her look even more fearful.

'Now they'll take us away too.'

'No, because we'll have Chad here, I just told you.'

She shook her head. 'He won't come.'

'You don't know that,' I said, annoyed because she is not being the way I want her to be, but then, she is the Seer, so maybe she does know what Chad will or will not do. And thinking this, I realized my secret is safe now because sister Ursula will never be able to tell Willa about that. Now I can love her as much as I want because she will not be placed over me. Really, things are looking better than they have for a long time. Chad can have sister Ursula's bed, which he will appreciate after living like a creature in the forest for so long, and we will keep him company like a pair of daughters that he can love and take care of. I would like to see old whiskerface Grover Styles try to tell someone like Chad what to do. Hah!

'It's him,' said Willa.

'Who?'

'Grover Styles.'

'What about him?'

'He'll be the one.'

Her mouth was turned down, her eyes fearful, not like the Willa that used to be at all, and talking in riddles.

'What one?'

'The one that kills me.'

'No he won't. Why would he do that? He shouts at people but he doesn't kill them.'

'Yes he will. I *know*...'

'How do you know?'

'Because I *do*. I just *know*...'

Looking at her face all twisted with pain on the inside, I felt a shiver come over me. Sister Luka had said Willa knew when sister Belinda would die, and she had died when Willa said. But that was not the same as seeing her own death. How could she know such a thing?

'That's silly. He's awful, and a thief, but he isn't a murderer.'

'He will. I *know*. You don't understand. I got into trouble about this.'

'About what?'

'People dying, back home. I saw this one man with death on his face, and the next day he drowned, all tangled up in his own fishing net. I told someone before it happened and they told everyone else when he drowned, and I got in trouble. It happened again later, and I told, and when the woman died they all said I had to have a whipping so I won't do it any more… Then they whipped me… but I still see things. I know it's him…'

There were tears leaking from her eyes now. I went to her and put my arms around her shoulders to stop them from shaking, and told her she was wrong about Grover Styles even if she had been right about those other people, because seeing her own death was a different thing and she had got that part wrong, but her shoulders kept on shaking and her tears would not stop.

30

The sun has not gone down like Grover Styles said it would, which proves how stupid he is, and he said himself he will come back for Willa and me tomorrow morning, which will not happen now or ever again, so we are safe for the moment until I can find Chad and have him come here. It is so hot. A breeze has come through the valley but it brings no relief because it is also hot and making things even drier. We bring water from the creek now in our last bucket that has not been stolen. We are almost out of food, but Chad will kill us something to eat when he comes.

31

Grover Styles has come back with sister Amanda and sister Loren and the oldest of his boys. They came to take away the sisters' weaving looms and all of the spun llama wool and sister Ursula's bed. Everything else has been taken. I did not like it that the sisters acted like they were in charge of getting these things onto the wagon. Willa would not show herself and they asked where she was, but I said I did not know. Then they wanted to look at the llamas and I could not say no because when they were the church weavers sister Amanda and sister Loren were always fussing over the sacred herd, so I know they have as much affection for the llamas as I do. We went to the field and they were upset that one of the herd was missing, but glad that the rest are all right. While we watched them several came over for treats but were disappointed as usual now that the kitchen garden is almost gone.

I asked sister Loren if they were happy being married, and she said, 'It isn't like we thought it would be.'

Her sister said, 'He isn't mean to us. He doesn't hit us or anything like that.'

'The worst thing is him trying to make us pregnant.'

'We don't like that. We think he probably isn't very good at it.'

'But it doesn't hurt or anything. He wants lots more children so he can have the biggest family in the valley and own more things that way.'

'We think he wanted us for wives because we can weave. He can trade what we make for other things. That's the only reason he picked us.'

They looked at each other for the blink of an eye, then Loren said, 'Grover says he can take you or Willa into his house. He's planning to build an extension, so there'll be room.'

'But only for one of you,' said sister Amanda.

I told them, 'We're staying here.'

'But you can't, you're too young.'

'I don't care. We're staying.'

'They'll come and take you away.'

'Chad won't let them.'

'Chad? What's he got to do with it?'

'He's coming to live with us and take care of us.'

That made them look at each other again, then sister Loren said, 'I don't think Grover will like that idea.'

'Well, that's too bad, because Chad won't let him take us away.'

'You don't have to be nasty about it. It's Willa he wants anyway, so his oldest boy can marry her.'

'She doesn't want to get married. She wants to stay here with me, me and Chad.'

'Rory, you're acting like you're the one in charge of everything.'

'I am the Scribe,' I said. 'There's no one left now that's above me.'

'The Seer is above the Scribe.'

'Well, sister Luka never got around to saying who that was, so whichever one was supposed to be the Seer, she's gone away and gotten married and isn't a real sister any more, so she doesn't count.'

'We heard it was Willa.'

A red curtain came down over my eyes. 'Who told you that?'

'Sister Briony says sister Luka told her.'

'She's a liar!'

'I think that's insulting to sister Briony.'

Sister Loren said, 'We think you're jealous.'

'I am not!'

'Anyway, it doesn't matter any more who the Seer is because the church is empty.'

'No it isn't. We still live there, and soon Chad will come live with us.'

'Chad lives with the squirrels. You're making it up, Rory.'

'I am not!'

They began walking back to the church and I came along a little way behind, furious that they would not believe me. If sister Briony has told them, then some of the other sisters will know too. Sister Luka should not have told anyone before she told the Seer herself, who should have been me. In a way I wanted what sister Loren said to be true, that it did not matter any more who the Seer is because the church of Selene is gone now, with just the building left behind. If being the Seer still mattered, it should be me, but if it does not matter, then Willa can be the Seer for all I care. And they did not believe me about Chad either, so I was glad to see them returning to their wagon. They only came out to steal what was left from the church along with their awful husband, who they did not seem to hate very much at all, so really, everything they said is wrong and I wished they had not come.

Their husband and stepson were waiting on the wagon seat. It did not hurt that Grover Styles wanted Willa to marry his oldest boy, not me. The thought of either of us being married to anyone is so stupid it almost made me laugh. It will never happen. Willa will not let them separate us, I know this. If Willa marries anyone it should be me, but that would never be allowed. Now that the church has gone it will not be allowed for sisters to be bedfriends even, let alone married.

'Where's that other one?' he asked me.

'Hiding,' I said, hating him.

'From what?'

'From you because she doesn't like you.'

'Is that so? Well, when you see her, you tell her she can come live in my house.'

'She doesn't want to.'

'You didn't tell her yet.'

He was smirking, not caring that I was being rude. He thinks I am rude all the time anyway, just because I do not like him and do not care if he knows. I was also thinking how wrong Willa is to be afraid of him. Why would he kill her if he wants her to marry his son? Then I had to ask myself if Willa should be told this to make her stop being afraid, but I decided not to, because being told she was supposed to get married against her will like all the others would upset her almost as much, and this was something real that might actually happen, not some vision.

Sister Loren said, 'She thinks Chad is going to live with them.'

'Chad? He wouldn't set foot inside any man's house.'

'He's coming here to take care of us, so we don't need anyone else.'

'You're not the one says what'll happen around here, so bite your lip, girlie.'

'Go away. You took everything so you don't need to come back.'

I heard the sisters make a little sound of alarm, and knew that backtalk was something that does not happen in Grover Styles's house. He wagged a finger at me. 'Anything taken from here will be put to good use, from the women on down to the furniture and bits and pieces. You don't own none of it, so quit acting like you do. There'll be no Chad and no home here for you and her, so get used to that.'

He was so smug, talking to me that way. I decided to poke him with a thorn that he could not shrug off. 'The sun hasn't gone down,' I reminded him, putting a little smile on my face to irritate him. 'You said it would when sister Ursula died, but it didn't, so you don't know everything.'

His face darkened. 'And I guess you know why that is.'

I did not know, but that would not win an argument, so I said to him, 'The sisters of Selene are still powerful. The sun won't set until *we* say so, not you.'

The sisters wanted me to shut up. 'Rory, you're being silly.'

'No I am not. Why do you think the sun won't set if it isn't the sisters of Selene?'

Of course they could not answer that, any more than I could, but I had won the argument, I could see it in Grover Styles's face. I was very pleased I had upset him because he has been upsetting me a lot so it is only fair. He said, 'The people hereabouts won't think so. They'll say it's your fault seeing as you're the one keeping Sol waiting in the sky, if it's true. You and her both, or just you?'

I did not want them to think Willa has any power, not after telling the sisters she is not the Seer, so I answered, 'Me, and you can't stop me.'

He jerked his thumb at the wagon seat and the sisters climbed aboard, neither one looking at me, like they were ashamed or embarrassed to know me at all. Well, I do not care about that. They are not sisters any more, just wives that will not cross their stupid husband, so I do not need to respect them now. The reins were slapped and the wagon began moving away with nobody on the seat looking at me, maybe because they are scared now because I have so much power to keep the sun standing still all this time. Of course it is not me, and not Willa either, but that does not matter. I could have told them the world has tipped over and nobody did it, not Selene and not Sol, nobody at all, but he would not believe that. Grover Styles has done everything he has done in the name of Sol, all the stealing and taking the sisters away and telling me what to do, so if the sun stays where it is that means Sol has no power, not as much as Selene anyway, which will make Grover Styles even angrier, but what can he do? Nothing, hah!

When I told Willa what happened I left out any mention of who is the Seer, just told her the villagers were making plans for us that had nothing to do with Chad coming here. I did not mention her marrying the oldest boy, which might have upset her. She nodded after I finished telling but did not say anything, as if it did not matter. Willa has been very quiet lately. I gave her a hug but it made no difference. I am getting worried about her. Willa used to make jokes and be funny, but not now. I miss the old Willa, but she will come back after Chad gets here to take care of us. But I have not seen Chad since I made the plan. I want Chad to be here before Grover Styles comes again.

32

We have not rowed the boat for a long time, and I am worried about Willa. She will not talk and does not eat even the little bit of food we have left. When I ask what is wrong she just says that it is too hot, but I know it is because she still believes Grover Styles is going to kill her. I thought again about telling her she was to be his son's intended bride, but said nothing because it would make no difference, she would keep on believing what she knows, or thinks she knows. Willa is just not herself any more, and it is all Grover Styles's fault, but he will not do what she thinks because that just does not make sense.

Another seventh night has come and gone, although it should be called seventh day now, and I will do that, call it seventh day from now on. Sister Frieda's bees have not come back and more birds have fallen from the sky, the smaller birds like sparrows mostly, but several crows also and one owl. The owls must be very unhappy because they like to hunt at night, and never will again. We hear the cicadas all the time. They fill our ears when we go to sleep and are still rasping away when we wake up again later. There is no sense at all of time passing. We take our water from the creek now that the yard well has run completely dry, and it is a long walk there and longer coming back with a full bucket carried between us. There is not enough water to keep ourselves clean any more and our smocks are smelly with sweat. Sometimes I think I sweat more than I drink. And still no sign of Chad, so I had to do what I did not want to do and go to the village to ask if anyone has seen him.

Willa would not come with me. I think she has been afraid of the villagers ever since we saw what they did to poor sister Nell. I went to Franklin Lee the butcher first, but he said he has not seen Chad since the change, then he asked me if I have been getting enough to eat out there at the church of our lady. I told him I had but he did not believe me and offered me a strip of dried beef. 'I don't have anything to trade,' I told him, but he said it did not matter, it is just a little piece of meat, so I ate it, almost crying because it tastes so good and he was a good man to be giving me food like this without a trade, and this reminded me that not everyone in the village is against us, even some of the men like Franklin Lee. I thanked him and left, hoping to see one of our sisters in the street, but there were very few people around. I should have saved half the beef for Willa but had not done that, which made me ashamed. I knew I would not mention it when I got home, and that made me feel like a coward, but I was so hungry when I tasted it I just could not stop. Even while walking around the village I could still taste it and felt even hungrier than before now that my stomach has been woken up with just a tiny bit of food. I would not have felt this way if the village thief had not come and taken away so very much. I hope Grover Styles falls under his grinding wheel and is squashed so flat he could be used for a carpet.

Then I saw sister Briony walking a little way ahead of me and ran to catch up. I was very annoyed with her for telling sister Amanda and sister Loren about Willa being the Seer, but that is sister Luka's fault for telling her in the first place. When she saw me she smiled, so I forgave her and asked if she had seen Chad anywhere, but she had not. 'I don't see many people at all, not in this heat. Everyone's staying under cover as much as they can. Is Willa all right?'

'Yes, but we need Chad to take care of us.'

'Chad couldn't do that even if he wanted to. Chad's mind is simple.'

'We don't want him to be clever, we just want him to be there.'

'Maybe I could ask Vern, that's my husband, if you and Willa could come live with us.' The way she said it told me it was an offer made from goodness of heart but with no expectation that it might happen.

'We want to stay with the church.'

Sister Briony looked relieved. 'He probably wouldn't allow it anyway. He's a cranky old man most of the time. His first wife left him and took up with some farmer. He hates her still, even though it happened years ago. He complains a lot too, so I don't know what I was thinking. He'd never let two girls into the place. I worry about you and Willa.'

'We'll be fine when we get Chad.'

'Rory, listen to me. Stop thinking about Chad. He isn't going to come live with you. Sooner or later you and Willa are going to have to move in with a village family so you can be cared for properly, but you're going to have to change your ways to fit in. A little bit of gratitude and humility is all folks are asking, but you seem determined to put them off with your… your way of speaking and carrying yourself. Be a little bit humble, and let people know you're able to make yourself useful to them, so they'll want to take you in. Everything is different now, so you need to be different too.'

She would not see that my plan is better, just like the other grown-ups, even though she is a sister of Selene. It was disappointing to find she thought this way, and I suspect the other sisters I might bump into would all say the same thing, that I have to change my ways and accept being adopted into some family or other. Well, I will not do that, and neither will Willa, even if Grover Styles wants her for his son. Willa getting married to someone like that is like a beautiful hawk getting married to a stupid chicken. She is so much more than that.

I had to ask, just could not stop myself. 'How many people did you tell that Willa is the Seer?'

She gave me a sorrowful look. 'Did you think it was you, Rory?'

'No, why would I think that?'

'No reason, but you might think it anyway, knowing you.'

'What does that mean?'

'It means that from now on you'd better stop thinking about things that don't mean anything any more. The church is gone, and nobody who was a sister should do or say anything to try and bring it back.'

'If the world goes back to day and night the sisters could come back too...'

'No, Rory. Listen, being away from the church you get to see how other people think, and nobody had respect any more for the sisters, especially sister Luka. There'll never be another High Sister, and you and Willa better not go around talking about the Seer, because folks don't want to hear any of that. Some of them are blaming us for the sun burning everything up. They're saying we won't go back to the way it was before until every part of the church has been burned out.'

'We didn't do anything wrong. The sisters kept Selene in the sky all this time...'

'Did we? The rooster thinks he commands the sun to rise, but he's fooling himself.'

'We *did*!'

'You mean the Scribe did. Let go of that, Rory, and tell Willa not to let on she was chosen as Seer, it's just too dangerous now. You saw what happened to sister Nell. Her husband told her to admit the church was nothing but a bunch of women fooling themselves into thinking they're something special, and she wouldn't. It's a different world now. All this heat is making people crazy, and crazy people do crazy things.'

'Willa was mischosen anyway.'

'There, that's what I mean about your way of conducting yourself. Seers and Scribes are about as much use now as wings on a fish. Just you be careful.'

Sister Briony stopped outside a house. 'This is where I live. You can come in and drink some water, we still have half a barrel.'

'No thank you, sister, I have to find Chad.'

She sighed and wished me well, then went inside. An old man was watching me through the open window, and I felt sorry for sister Briony having to live with him and not with her sisters any more. She has changed since going away, just like the sister-sisters. It made me sad to know she had come to the same kind of thinking I have, that the moon does not listen to us and our lady is not there, and not anywhere else either. I do not know why I will not say this out loud even though I am thinking it, but it is so awful to think that if I am not the Scribe for the sisters of Selene then I am nothing, and if Willa is not the Seer then she is nothing too, and our rightful place is to be with the rest of the sisters, split up and divided among the unmarried men, or with families wanting another pair of hands around the place to do boring work that a person of low intelligence could do.

I could not find Chad anywhere in the village and ended up sitting in the shade of the stocks where sister Nell was humiliated. Now I am very worried that everything sister Briony said is true, and that we will never be able to keep ourselves separate from the village and the farms, never be together as bedfriends, about as special as a rock in the road. I thought about going into the forest to look for Chad, but he could be anywhere at all and I would never find him, and there are bears and wolves and cougars that will find me instead. So I have come back home to an empty well and all these rooms crowded with silence and heat.

33

We were woken up by a strange sound, a kind of soft roaring, and went outside to see what it was. The sky, whichever direction we looked, was filled with tiny brown dots all heaving this way and that before they fell to the ground. Grasshoppers! A million million million of them! They clung to our hair and clothing before realizing they could not eat these and jumped away, falling at our feet to eat the grass from the yard, and millions more were swarming in the elm tree. Above us the sky, usually too bright to look at, was filled with so many grasshoppers they blocked the sun, wave after wave of them, and our ears were filled with the droning of their wings. The air itself seemed alive, crammed with darting insects wanting just one thing, to drop down from their flight and begin eating whatever their tiny jaws could grind, every leaf of every plant, and every blade of grass. It was useless trying to swat them away from our faces, they were replaced right away by more, and we could not open our mouths even a little bit or they would have climbed inside to look for food.

I wanted to see if the grasshoppers were covering the whole valley, and went up to the tower. They were all over the floor up there and covering the instrument entirely with their tiny bodies. I cleared them away and peered at the village, where every house appeared to be covered with grasshoppers, then I swung the instrument to see the trading field, which was one huge mass of squirming brown. I could not see any of the closer farms, but it was plain they would be swarming too. The last plague of grasshoppers happened long before I was born. I remember sister Ursula telling us how they ate everything in sight and the valley starved for almost a year. In the other direction our orchard's apple trees were shifting and bleeding into the air as every branch and limb was attacked, the white apple blossom already gone down those greedy little throats. The trees were already suffering from lack of water, and this would finish them off. I went back downstairs through corridors rustling with grasshoppers that had flown in through all the open windows, so many I could not help squashing them underfoot with every step. Sister Ursula never said they came inside, so this must be an even bigger swarm than the one she saw as a girl.

Willa was in our room with the door and window shut, but not before thousands had flown inside. She was squatting on her bed under a blanket that must have been very hot, but she would not come out from beneath it, yelling, 'Noooo!' when I told her to stop being silly. I did not want to stay there when something so interesting was taking place, so I left her and went to find sister Frieda's big hat with the fine netting that kept the bees from her face, and put it on to go outside again. I did not mind the grasshoppers tickling my arms and legs as long as they could be kept from my face. Then I set off for the village.

All of the roadside grass and flowers had been buried under grasshoppers, and the nearest field of wheat looked how I have often imagined the ocean looks, its surface moving and tossing, only brown, not blue. Every single stalk was hugged along its length by grasshoppers, every head of grain a thick cluster of munching jaws and gripping legs. I could not see very clearly because grasshoppers kept clinging to the mesh around my head before dropping off. The humming and buzzing their wings made covered every other sound, filling my ears with a steady droning that I liked because I had never heard it before. There were grasshoppers filling the tops of my moccasins but they did not bite, just tickled. I could not see another person anywhere. If some farmer had come out of his house to try and sweep away the swarms from his crop it would have been almost funny, because there are too many to stop, so many that the only sensible way to look at them was to accept their presence all across the valley and filling the air above, the way you would walk through a rainstorm without trying to avoid the raindrops.

In the village I walked alone. Every shutter had been dropped, every door closed against the swarm, every person hiding away until it passed, except me. They were all afraid and I was not, because these are only little creatures driven by hunger and nothing to be afraid of, but nobody else would come out to walk among them, only me, and that made me fear them less, the villagers I mean, because they are filled with fear. Somehow I was expecting to find Chad loping through the swarm, unafraid like me, searching for me the way I have been searching for him. Chad would not let insects drive him indoors. He would come walking out from a buzzing cloud with grasshoppers clinging to every hair and whisker on his head and every filthy part of his shaggy wolfskin shirt and along his bowstring and every feathered arrow. He would see me and come to me, knowing my need for a protector, and we would return to the church to tell Willa she does not need to be fearful now. But no matter how many times I walked up and down through the village, Chad never came, and after a while I gave up hope and went home again to find Willa still hiding, still fearful.

I coaxed her out from under the blanket, red-faced and sweating, and we sat holding each other while grasshoppers examined us closely. I swear I saw some of them drinking the drops of sweat on Willa's forehead! The one good thing about this plague is it will keep Grover Styles away. We sat together for the longest time, or maybe it was not so long, and only left our room to find some food in the kitchen, the very last heel of bread from the last loaf we baked before the last of our flour was stolen from us by the evil man who milled it. Sister Kim traded spun wool for that flour and he has gone and taken it back without any payment, just a thief. How I hate him! That did not take long to eat, then we went outside and found the elm tree has been completely stripped of leaves, which is something sister Ursula did not say about the last plague, only that the crops were eaten, so this is much worse. I think it is because the world has fallen over and the top part facing Sol has gotten too hot now and is driving the grasshoppers crazy as well as making birds fall from the sky and making the bees fly away somewhere else, or maybe they died.

I made Willa put on sister Frieda's bee hat and we went crunching through grasshoppers to the field of Selene, where the llamas were standing together and trying to understand what this swarm of insects was. They could not graze because every little bit of the field was covered by grasshoppers. The herd could only stand and watch as their fodder was eaten before their eyes, flicking their ears to keep the grasshoppers from crawling inside and looking very disapproving of this calamity. What will they eat when the swarm goes away? I did not think of this earlier, so now I am worried about what will happen. And the valley's cattle and goats will face the same problem. And the people will starve again if the livestock dies like they did when sister Ursula was young, so this is a terrible thing. Willa looked so strange with the bee hat on it made me want to laugh, but those other things stopped me. What I am thinking now is, will the villagers blame Willa and me for this, the way they blame the sisters for having made the sun stand still? Now I am afraid. I was not afraid of the grasshoppers, but I am afraid of the situation they will leave behind when they go.

34

The grasshoppers have gone. It happened while we slept. The wind blew them away, and it was the sound of the wind, or maybe its difference to the sound of the grasshoppers, that woke us and drew us outside. Everything green was gone completely. They ate it all except for the pine trees surrounding the valley, so these must not taste good because of the resin. The wind was hot and blowing from the direction of the sun. It picked up dust from the yard and dust from the road and blew it away just like it blew away the grasshoppers. From the tower our instrument could barely see the village, there was so much dust in the air. It is a good thing to be rid of the grasshoppers, but too late because they already ate everything, and now this wind will dry the land even more. The sweat on our skin was soon covered in dust as we went around the church closing windows before more dust could blow inside to cover the piles of dead grasshoppers everywhere that were too stupid to fly out again and eat while there was still something left to eat. Sister Luka would throw up her hands in horror if she could see the state of the church now. When that was done we sat in the kitchen, listening to the steady moaning of the wind outside. I held Willa's hand but she would not squeeze my fingers. My beautiful hawk is sad beyond sadness. I love her so much, although it is hard to say this. But I think she knows.

35

Now the wind has gone wherever the grasshoppers went and the air is still again, but so very hot. We do not know how long it blew, but we slept and woke up several times before it finally stopped. Dust that was not blown away began settling quietly over everything, turning the whole valley a pale brown. We did not have even a single scrap of food left, and decided we must go to the village and ask sister Briony or one of the others for help. We did not want to, but it hurts to be hungry this way.

Walking along the road, we raised dust that rose to ankle height and hung in the air before settling. Fields of wheat had been stripped to nothing but stubby stalks by the grasshoppers, and the wind had blown the soil away from their roots, leaving them exposed. Cattle had their noses in the dust, looking for grass that is not there. This is going to be very bad for everyone.

As we walked through the village we saw people, not like when the grasshoppers were there, but they did not talk to us, just stared as we went by. I knocked on the door of sister Briony's house and she opened it. One look at Willa and me was enough to tell her why we had come. 'Wait,' she said, and went to fetch something, food we hoped, but it was a mug of water to share, which was almost as welcome. 'I can't give you anything to eat,' she said, 'he won't let me. And I can't invite you in because the council has put a ban on you entering any house in the village or the valley. I'm sorry…'

She was almost in tears so I believed her. I asked, 'What did I do?'

'It's both of you. People have been saying things.'

'What things?'

She looked very uncomfortable. 'Silly things… They say you're responsible for the crops being eaten and the soil blowing away… and Sol staying where he is. They took a vote just a little while ago.'

'But we didn't do anything.'

'I know that, Rory, but… they've decided. There's nothing I can do, or any of the other sisters. We're all under suspicion because of everything that's happened, but you and Willa are the ones they blame, because you're still there, still living in the church.' She lowered her voice. 'You've got to offer yourselves up for adoption, and you've got to tell them you've given up believing in our lady…'

There was a kind of roaring from inside the house, her husband saying to get rid of us. Sister Briony jumped, then started closing the door. 'Talk to Grover Styles,' she said, 'and be humble…'

The door shut. We stared at it, then walked away, our stomachs crying for food. Willa said, 'What should we do?'

'Go to him and ask for something to eat. He's the one that took all our food.'

'I don't like him. I won't go there!'

'I don't like him either, I hate him, but he's got food and we're hungry.'

'No!'

There was no telling her, she is just too scared of him, so I told Willa to wait by the stocks while I went to Grover Styles's house to get us something to eat. When I knocked on his door it was the oldest boy who opened it. He was very surprised to see me there and asked what did I want, so I told him I wanted food and he went away to fetch his father, who took his time coming to the door. 'Well, well,' he said, 'look who's here.'

'I want my food back.'

'What food would that be? Food's in short supply hereabouts.'

'My food that you stole.'

He looked around behind me. 'Where's your friend?'

'She's sick because we're so hungry.'

'Is she now? You can come in.'

He stepped aside to allow me through, being very polite so I was on my guard. In the main room there were two girls about my age and his son, also sister Amanda and sister Loren, who were weaving, their looms set up opposite each other so they could talk while they worked, the same as back at the weaving room in our church. The girls stared at me but the sisters would only glance in my direction as they worked their shuttles back and forth. One of the girls was sent to fetch something to eat, and I was invited to sit on a nice chair. The girl came back with some cold soup with little bits of meat in it. The moment this was put in my hands I spooned it into my mouth so fast I spilled some. Everyone watched me eat, but those shuttles were kept working. I licked the bowl clean, not caring, then the spoon, and handed them back. 'Thank you,' I said, and those words to this man almost made me vomit the soup back up.

Grover Styles had a smile on his face but it was fake. 'You girls having a hard time out there?'

'Yes.' I almost added Because you took everything, but did not.

'I'm guessing you pray to Selene for comfort and assistance.'

We had not. Our lady hardly ever passes through my thoughts any more, and Willa was not there long enough to become a true sister of Selene before the change came. But to say this would give him pleasure, so I told him we prayed all the time to have our food brought back. His smile got wider when he heard that, and he said, 'You and me need to talk in private.'

I followed him to another room, much smaller with two beds, so this was the bedroom of his girls. There was a framed picture on the wall of some kind of bird we do not have around here, but the glass was cracked. He sat on one bed and pointed at the other. I sat down, not wanting to talk, wanting more soup to take to Willa. He stroked his beard and said, 'Folks are upset.' I did not say anything. He said, 'Selene has got more power than we thought. It was Selene sent the grasshoppers and the wind.'

'No.'

'No?'

'Those things just happened.'

'You think? I'd say things like that, things that ruin the best efforts of everyone in the valley, they don't just happen, they get told to happen, for punishment against the ones that don't believe in Selene.'

'Well, that would be their fault for not believing.'

He cackled even though what I said was not funny, then he said, 'The reason I'm talking to you, I want you to ask your lady Selene pretty please to quit all this now, before she kills us.'

'It's Sol that's killing everything with too much heat.'

'But he'd like to go down and bring back the night. Wouldn't that be something, nice cool darkness to lay down our heads and sleep like we're supposed to? But that would take a powerful prayer to make that happen, a powerful prayer to Selene to back off and let Sol go down like he wants.'

'If you give us back what you took I could offer a prayer.'

'You can make Selene let Sol go down?'

'I can pray to our lady, but that kind of prayer takes a long time, and I keep fainting.'

'So you'll do it for food.'

'Yes.'

'You've got yourself a deal, but I expect results. How soon?'

'I don't know.'

'But not a real long time.'

'No.'

He stood up. 'You better not be lying. We got folks going crazy from all this.'

'I want a basket of food, a big basket.'

He told his daughters to do that, and I was handed exactly what I wanted. At the door he told me, 'This better work out fine or I'll want to know the reason why.'

I said nothing. I had spoken enough words to this evil man. The smell of bread and meat rising from the basket almost made me swoon. He closed the door and I hurried to the trading field where Willa stood waiting. Her face when she saw the basket made everything I had to suffer in Grover Styles's house worthwhile. She clawed off a hunk of bread and rushed it to her mouth, and her eyes closed in pleasure as she ate. If it was not so hot I think she might have cried. Through a mouthful of bread she asked me, 'How did you make him give you all this?'

'I told him I can make the sun go down.'

Her eyebrows shot up. 'Can you?'

There was such hope in her face I wanted to say I could, but Sol is as far away from me as Selene. The important thing was to get the food. 'Can you?' she said again.

'I'll try.'

We picked up the basket between us and carried it home. After eating some more I took my secret book from the room of names and went up to the tower where at least there is a breath of air, and have set this down. I have made a promise I cannot keep. Something bad will happen from that, but what can I do?

36

A long time passed after we were given the food. We did not go to the village again, and the villagers stayed away from us until the basket was almost empty. Then they came, almost all of them, but no sisters at all, so those were kept away so they would not see what happened and maybe try to stop it.

Grover Styles marched us both outside, where the milky arc of Selene's sunward side was cradled in a blue sky. Seventh day has come again. There was a lot of murmuring and muttering as we were brought out into the yard. Men were going into the room of names and bringing out the books of names, and others were going into the room of numbers and bringing out sister Ursula's books of numbers. All of these were being piled around the trunk of the naked elm, and I thought to myself how lucky I am that my secret book is not among them. I hoped no one would go to the tower to steal the instrument, because I left my book up there, and for some reason it seemed like the most important thing in the world to know it was safe. Grover Styles pointed at the sky. 'Tell me what you see up there.'

'Selene...'

'What else?'

'Sol...'

'That's right, he's still there, which is not what you said would happen. Did you pray?'

'Yes…'

'Pray real hard, did you?'

I nodded, feeling a very urgent need to pee. Everyone in the crowd was staring at us with hatred in their faces. More books were carried out and dumped around the elm, their covers falling off and ancient pages tumbling out, they were handled so roughly. Sister Luka would have cried to see such a thing.

'Seems like your prayers weren't good enough, or maybe the wrong girl was doing the praying.' He pointed at Willa. 'You, are you the Seer?'

Willa was confused. For all that sister Luka's choosing of her had been passed around among the sisters, nobody had said anything to her, especially me. She looked into Grover Styles's angry face, understanding nothing, knowing only that she feared him. He gave her a shake to get an answer from her, but Willa could say nothing because she knew nothing. He said, 'All those sisters, they're saying the same thing, that you're the one, not this other.' He glared at me, daring me to deny I have been lying. 'So which is it?'

I found my tongue and yelled, 'It doesn't matter which one!'

'Why wouldn't it matter when there's all this happening?' I had never seen him so angry. His eyes were popping and spit flew from his lips into my face. 'Why the fuck wouldn't it matter?' There were shouts from some of the others, encouraging him to find out the truth. More books joined the pile, books whose covers had not been open for generations. I watched as a million names of Selene were tossed onto the ground, unable to explain myself. I had lied and they had believed me, and now this was happening. It was all my fault.

'Why wouldn't it matter, you little cunt?'

'Because she isn't there! She isn't there…!'

'Who isn't there?'

'Selene!'

That made him pause. He seemed as confused as Willa.

'And neither is Sol! They're not there!'

He took me by the scruff of the neck and made me look into the sky. 'Not there? Not there? A blind man could see they're both there! Look! See them? See them both? Tell me you can see them both!'

His fingers were hurting, my eyes dazzled with light. 'I see them… but…'

'But what!'

'They're just *things*…'

His anger became confusion again. 'Things?'

'Things in the *sky*… not Selene, not Sol… just things that are *there*…'

The crowd had gone silent. Even the men bringing books from the rooms of names and numbers became aware that something strange was taking place. It seemed that every eye in the world was watching me, waiting for more peculiar talk to come spilling from my lips. I saw this and felt an enormous rage inside myself. It rose from the deepest part of me, the secret part I do not share. It came rushing up my gullet and spewed like bile from my mouth into the air. I could not stop myself.

'They don't mean anything! They're just things that don't even know we're here! Stop praying to them! Stop it! They don't hear anything! They're too far away! They don't care about us! Stop praying to them… and Willa is the Seer! I wanted to be but I'm not! I'm not and I don't care! It doesn't *mean* anything! Nobody made anything happen! It just happened… You're stupid stupid *stupid*…!'

My lungs ran out of air at the same time my mouth ran out of words. I had told them the truth. And I had also told myself the truth, the full truth for the first time. It was such a simple thing really. Suddenly I felt light enough to rise above the ground, rise like thistledown and be blown away, far away to some other place, some new place where I could sink to earth and find peace. And it came into my mind that I am truly the Seer after all, but what I have seen is not what anyone would wish to hear, because it hurts them to follow me into the fire of truth. I am the Seer and I have seen the simple thing that is there to see. I see that the creatures of the forest and the beasts of the field have more wisdom because they do not look up and offer prayers to what is not there. They do not imagine things and hurt each other in the name of imaginary things. We are cursed with imagining. We are blinded by nothing at all. I have told them what I have seen. I have told them the truth and now they will kill me.

Grover Styles could not believe his ears. For him, as for the rest of them, the truth – *my* truth – was invisible, just not there at all. He even had a silly little smile on his face, as if he felt sorry for me. His hand fell from my neck. He seemed not to know what to do next. Someone in the crowd called out, 'Which one?' and that brought him back to the task at hand – finding blame and punishing the guilty one. That would be me.

Very slowly, he said, 'Are you speaking the truth?'

'Yes…'

I did not care now. He could never make me take back those words, this truth that I have finally accepted into my mind. He might kill me, but he could never kill my words that too many people already heard. Words cannot be crammed back into anyone's mouth, not even the mouth of a truthteller. I watched my words entering their heads, unwelcome words that gave no comfort. The villagers were confused and angry.

'Which one?'

He pointed at Willa. 'That one.'

Two men took hold of her and began dragging her toward the elm tree. I could not move, too surprised to understand what had happened. Willa gave a little cry that flew straight to my heart. I took a single step before being smacked so hard across the face I fell over. Willa's voice made me spring up again, but Grover Styles grabbed me and held me tight. I kicked at his shins and he punched the side of my head so hard I stopped hearing anything for a moment and could only watch, stunned, as Willa was bound to the elm with a length of old harness, her wrists tied with a leather belt. Her mouth was open with fear but no sound came from her, no sound that I could hear inside my ringing head. There was distant shouting, a moving mass of people, waving arms, and then a flame. I heaved and pushed but could not break free. More flame as someone ran around the elm with a flint striker, setting fire to pages from the past. Willa's cries stabbed through my head like blades. Somehow I had fallen again. Legs rushed by, books spilling from arms too far above me to see. I heard my name called over and over as I lay there, blinded by sunlight, then came a roaring and crackling as all that paper, dry as autumn leaves, caught fire. Shouts and cheering, the smell of smoke. I heard my name again, coming from a faroff place, then a whooshing sound as the fire took hold and ran in a circle of flame around the elm. My name became an awful shrieking.

37

Sister Nell's face was very close to mine. She asked if I was all right, but I could not speak. I was trying to think of something important, a thing beside which all other things were nothing, but I could not see the thing. Sister Nell's face and voice were a distraction from my efforts at bringing the important thing to mind. And then it came, flooding my head so fast I sat upright. 'Where's Willa…'

'You worry about yourself now, there's nothing to be done.'

'Where's Willa…!'

She put her hands on my shoulders as if to press me down again onto the bed. I was in a strange room. 'Willa's walking with Selene, so you don't need to be worrying about her any more. Lie back now.'

'I want to see her…'

'You can't, not until your time. She's gone from this place, and lucky to be away from hardship and evil.'

Her strong hands pushed me down. I stared at the ceiling, remembering.

'Is she dead?'

'There's nothing left of her in this world. Her pain too, that's gone. Rest easy, Rory, there's nothing to be done. She's gone to Selene and you have to be strong now.'

The bed beneath me seemed to fall away, leaving me suspended in a great void, a howling emptiness that could never be filled, a place echoing with her name. She is gone from here and I will never see her again, never touch her face or hear her voice, never hold her hand in mine and walk among the pines together. Everything that brought me joy has been taken, destroyed by fire, and my world can never be the same. I am without her. I am suspended between earth and sky and crushed by both. I am a wound impossible to heal. I told them. I told them Willa was the Seer and they killed her. I spoke the truth and killed my love. How stupid that I am alive after a betrayal so great, while innocent Willa has been made to suffer for my foolishness. They have burned the wrong one, they are so stupid. I am the one for burning, but they chose another because of my words. There could be no greater folly, and I am its cause.

'Are you hungry? We have a little food.'

The window shutter was wide open, a square of brightness. This must be where sister Nell lives now, with her husband who put her in the stocks to be pelted and ridiculed for disobeying him. Her face is the saddest I have ever seen, but she is concerned for me, not for herself, because she is good. I am not good. I have never been good. I am selfish and vain. I am unworthy. I am alone with my unworthiness. That will be my punishment and I have earned it.

'You must be thirsty at least. It's been a long time. I worried you might not come back to us. Drink, Rory.'

Her hand behind my head lifted me. A mug of water was under my nose, pressed against my lips. I drank it down, warm and tasting of wood, the last of someone's rainbarrel water. It flowed down my throat, then realized it was inside a worthless betrayer and came up again, pushed out by a wailing sound that became a scream that died away to sobbing, none of it intended by me. Sister Nell's big arms folded about me for comfort and I wetted her breast with tears I could not stop. The door opened and a man's voice demanded,

'Make her quit or she goes,' then the door slammed shut again. Sister Nell stroked my hair and made soothing sounds. This is how my mother must have held me when I was small. I stopped crying, suddenly very tired and wanting very much to sleep, so I could forget who I am, forget I am the one who aimed a finger at my love and told them to take her in my place, take her and kill her. I want that gone, every part of it, and only sleep can give me release.

Sister Nell eased me back onto the pillow. 'He's letting me keep you here for a little while, but you'll have to be quiet now.'

'The sun hasn't gone down.'

'No, and it's had plenty of time to make up its mind, so there'll be certain people asking themselves if they did the wrong thing, but don't be expecting apologies.'

'Now they'll come to kill me too.'

'Nobody's going to be doing that, don't fret yourself.'

'They'll say I lied and I'm the Seer, so now they'll kill me to make the sun go down.'

'Not a bit of it. There's been enough foolishness about Sol.'

'But they should. It might work. I might really be the Seer and sister Luka made a mistake, so now they should kill me instead and make the sun go down.'

'They've done what they did and there's no taking it back. Not everyone was in favour of what they did, Rory. There's people that aren't like that, and they won't allow another mistake.'

'But they should try, just to see if it works.'

'What kind of talk is this? I'm told you were singing a different tune before, telling everyone it's all nonsense, Sol and Selene, but I'm thinking you said those things to try and save Willa. People don't want to hear such talk, not when they need deliverance from this everlasting heat. There's some that have died for no particular reason, and they're saying it's because the world is an unnatural place now, with all this sunshine making everyone tired and weak and going

265

crazy, some of them. It was never meant to be this way, so we need to be asking what we did wrong.'

'I did wrong, nobody else. I'm the one…'

'Just you hush. Older heads will figure it out by and by, and likely the answer'll be something nobody knew. That's not your concern. You just have to get well again. Now I'll leave this bite of food here for when you're ready to eat, and the water. Do you want the window closed for a bit of dark to sleep in?'

'No.'

She stood up, gave me a grim smile and left. Sister Nell is such a good sister. Alone, I drank the water down, then ate the food, a bowl of mush gone cold but it tasted good anyway. Then I got out of bed and put on my moccasins and climbed out through the window. I have walked away from the village and gone back to the church because I must see the place where Willa died. There were people walking about, but they did not stop me or speak to me, and some of them seemed not even to notice me at all, as if they have gone blind, so maybe this is the craziness sister Nell spoke of.

The elm tree was a low pile of ash around a smoking stump. I could not get close without burning my soles. Somewhere under the ash are Willa's bones, if the fire did not turn them to powder. I went to the tower and cleaned the instrument of dust, then aimed it at the village. Nobody was coming along the road after me. They did not care. One killing was enough. I picked up my book and quill and opened my ink pot. All of this must be set down. My secret book is the last book in all the world now, so it is a precious thing. And I have another precious thing too. When I lay down on Willa's bed I found her whale tooth under the pillow. I had not seen it since she became a sister of Selene and was told not to wear this any more. I slipped it over my head. Now it hangs on my chest, on the outside of my smock, and on the inside is my moon pendant that used to be sister Luka's.

38

The sacred herd is starving. They came crowding about me when I visited, eager for the things I could not bring. All I could offer was their freedom. If they roam in the forest they might find some grass, since the grasshoppers seemed to avoid the pines. They risk being attacked by the beasts of prey, but that is better than slow starvation in the field of Selene. I opened the gate and they came out hesitantly, curious and willing to trust me. I walked toward the forest and they followed, led by Brindle, who trusted me more than the rest. Among the pines they spread out to find grass that has not been smothered by old blankets of fallen needles, and paid me no further attention, desperate for food. I said goodbye to Brindle but she ignored me, nose to the ground tearing up grass that to my eye looks dead, but at least it is there and not eaten by grasshoppers, so their lot has improved, but mine has not and never will again.

I know that I have come back to the church to die. We are all going to die soon because this is an unnatural world, as sister Nell said. Strange to say, I do not care. I have been asking myself if death will bring me to Willa's side in the gardens of Selene, or simply bring release from hunger and this awful sunshine. I think most likely that this will be all. I can never see Willa again because there is no garden of Selene and never was. That is the cruellest part of the truth, the part that offers no consolation as death comes plodding down the road toward us all. He will stop beside me with a smile and open a doorway in the air, and invite me to step through into welcoming darkness. How I wish I could return to the day I first saw Willa with the sea traders. If I had known then what was to come I could have thought of a way to avoid all this calamity because I am cleverer than most. But even my cleverness is useless now. Death takes the clever and the stupid into his embrace without favour or preference. She is gone and soon I will be gone too. My only purpose now is to remain faithful to my truth and set this down as I see it, even though no one will ever read the last book in the world and it will turn as everything else to dust after I am dead.

39

I have gone to the village to beg for food. I went to every door, but even those houses where a sister lives would not welcome me. I did not go to Grover Styles's house or to the blacksmith's because I do not want Grover Styles or Buford to see me begging. They would not give me anything anyhow. I have been told by some people I am not to be fed. They will not kill me the way they killed Willa, but they will not offer me food to stay alive. One man told me to kill a llama and eat it. He would be very surprised to learn that I have already thought of this, but do not know how to slaughter a creature, especially anything so friendly and pretty as a llama. So I will starve after all. I am very weak and very sad. I cry sometimes but my tears are very few. The last house I went to was sister Nell's. Her husband answered the door and screamed at me to go away. I went as far as the road and waited there. Soon sister Nell came out with a small package tied up with twine, but the man came out after her, yelling that I am bad luck and cursed and not to be helped. She did not care and gave me the package, a very light amount of food, and then said to him that if he did not stop she would give him a smack, and if he tried to punish her by having her put in the stocks again she would kill him with the biggest knife in his kitchen. That made him shut up. Sister Nell said, 'Our lady protect you, Rory,' and went inside.

I ate my food in the shadow of the stocks, just some stale cornbread and a little salt fish, probably the last of what the traders brought. I ate that raw, for the salt as much as for the flesh, and felt a little better. There was very little activity in the village. I think people have gone inside to escape from the sun and to slowly die there. Loose cattle roam in the trading field looking for grass. Their flanks are hollowed, their ribs showing. They will have to be slaughtered soon if their meat is to be kept. I smell like a dead animal myself and am ashamed to be so unclean, but I am not alone in this.

40

Sister Frieda came to visit. Her husband Roy allowed it, she says, because he is a good man. She came to tell me the village council has made a decision. They have decided that nothing will make Sol go down below the horizon. They have said this falling over of the world is the worst thing to have happened since the great stone hit Selene and then the earth, and there is nothing anyone can do about it. Sister Frieda was very pleased that they have all let go of their new faith in Sol as their god. Sol is killing them and they did nothing to deserve it, so they do not love Sol any more and there will be no more blood sacrifices to him. And the biggest decision the council has made is to leave the valley. This surprised me very much. So far as we have known for a longlong time there are people in the valley and another bunch of people by the sea, with a long mountain trail in between. Everything else is wilderness where nobody lives. They have decided to leave everything behind that cannot be carried and to drive their herds before them in a journey away from the sun. They will go as far as they can, hoping to reach a place at last where the sun sits lower in the sky and does not burn everything the way it does here, a place cool enough to grow things. The last of the seed corn and wheat will be taken along to begin new crops in a new place, if the sun will allow it. Some of the old people will not go with the travellers, knowing they would never survive such a long journey. They will stay here and die while the younger ones turn their backs to the sun and go searching for a cooler world. Sister Frieda and Roy are going. She says she hopes to find wild bees along the way that have grown used to a standing sun, and Roy will make beehives for her to begin again. She says the new place, if they find it, will be called Honeyland. She is very hopeful, and wants me to go with them. I told her No.

'But Rory, everything here is dying from the heat. You can't stay. How will you feed yourself?'

'I'll find something.'

'You're just being silly. You can't stay here.'

'Yes I can.' I took sister Luka's moon pendant from inside my smock and let it rest on the outside, next to Willa's whale tooth. 'I am the last High Sister, and no one can tell me what to do.'

Her face got very sad. 'Rory, you can't.'

'Yes I can. I will. You can't stop me. Nobody can.'

'Think about everything that's happened here, how everything went bad, all the dying... and what happened to your friend. How can you bear to stay here surrounded by all that misery? You're young, you can start over...'

'No.'

She shook her head. I could tell she had given up. She said, 'If you change your mind, come to the village, but don't wait too long, everyone is already packing up and gathering the herds. Sister Amanda and sister Loren will be in charge of the llamas, and you could help them.'

'I let them go. You'll never find them.'

'You... you let them go? The sacred herd? Oh, Rory, how could you? I thought you loved them.'

'I do, so I let them go, so they could find some grass.'

She was not happy about this. 'They would have been a special part of the journey, something to remind all the sisters who are going of what we're leaving behind. We can't take the church, but we could have taken our lady's llamas.'

'They're not our lady's, they're mine, and I let them go.'

Her face got hard. I had offended her. 'There are some who've lost their minds in all this, and I see now that you're among them.'

'Yes.'

'Goodbye, Rory.'

'Goodbye.'

She went away. I went up into the tower and watched her dragging her feet through the dust back to the village. The trading field had a lot of cattle in it, so they have been bringing in herds from all over the valley. My llamas will not be joining them. I will not go away from the sun with the people who have always hated me, the people who killed my Willa. They can never go far enough away from here to suit me. They are leaving behind everything that means something to them, their houses and farms and their elderly grandparents who will not survive for long. It must be very hard for them, and I almost feel sorry for what they have lost, but I have lost everything too.

41

nother visitor, the last person I would have expected, and very unwelcome. He found me in the orchard among the sunblasted apple trees that will never blossom again. As soon as I saw him I felt a terrible sense of foreboding, because nothing to do with Buford can ever be good. I wanted to run away, but I am the last High Sister and must be dignified. The moon pendant on my breast would ward off evil. He came right up to me, smiling his lopsided smile that I hate. I told my legs not to run, not to run.

He showed me his teeth. 'Heard you don't want to come along, is that right?'

'Go away.'

'You can't stay here, a girl like you.'

'Go away.'

'I'm going away, everyone else too that can walk. You can't stay.'

'Yes I can.'

He fidgeted with his belt buckle, pulling up his pants that were baggy around the middle, so he has got skinny like most people. I am a stick inside a smock.

'Well, here's the thing you should know, Spooky. What it is, I'm asking you to be my bride. There, I said it.'

I could not believe my ears. There is only one person I hate more than Buford, and that is Grover Styles. I could never be any man's bride, but least of all Buford's. Just looking at him makes my skin crawl. I have seen him as a threat ever since he began hinting at a union between us of a sexual kind, and now he stands before me suggesting marriage, looking awkward as a little boy, so now I am not only afraid of him, I despise him for his pathetic request. His face had rearranged itself into what he thinks is a look of love, but it is the face of a wolf who says to a calf, Hello, I'm your friend who will show you the way through the dark woods and you will come out the other side safe and sound. I almost laughed at the ridiculous thing he had done, asking me to marry him.

'No.'

He looked surprised. He actually thought I might say yes. This man is so stupid.

'Well now, think about it first. On a long trip like we're taking, you'll be needing a strong man to take care of you.'

'Go away.'

'You told me that. I'm saying you need to think again about this.' He looked around, at the apple trees, at the ground, at the sky, then said, 'I love you.'

I could not stop myself. I laughed. It was not loud or long, but it must have sounded mocking to Buford. His face changed back to its normal self, like a mongrel that wants you to feed it but will bite your hand anyway because that is its nature. 'You don't talk to me like that, not a little nothing bitch like you…' He struggled with himself, really wanting to persuade me, really thinking it might be possible if he just smiled a little wider and did not start shouting. 'Now listen, you think I'm some kind of rough person, but I'm not, not on the inside. What I'm saying, you should reconsider about this. Pretty soon there'll just be dying old people and you left here. You don't want that. You come with me and we can be happy somewheres else away from here. You want to be happy, don't you?'

'No.'

That puzzled him for a moment, then he stopped trying to understand or to persuade. Not able to think what he might do to change things, he turned slowly in a circle, as if giving me time to think again while he turned and rearranged his face yet again into something like friendliness, an awful sight. He finished his circle and grinned at me with yellow teeth.

'Last chance, Spooky.'

'Go away.'

He unbuckled his belt and let his pants fall around his ankles. He stepped out of them and took himself in his hand. 'This is what you been missing in your life, you and the sisters. You don't want it, you better run.'

He stroked himself, squeezing it, making it hard. I could not move until he took a step toward me, then I fled, all my weakness gone, my legs filled with strength, heart pumping fear throughout my body that made me run faster and faster through the orchard with his feet pounding behind me and his voice making little whoops of joy. My lungs burned with heated air, my hair flew out behind me. I ranranran but his panting followed close behind all the way across the orchard and then the herb garden. I wanted to reach the church, why I do not know because there are no locks on the doors, nothing to place between him and me. He was getting closer, then I heard him stumble and fall. Looking over my shoulder, I saw him on the ground, but already getting to his feet again, still grinning with happiness to be chasing me like a boy chasing a squirrel that he will stone to death if he catches it.

I ran inside the church, trying to stop the awful sounds of fear coming from my mouth. He would catch me and hurt me if I did not do something to stop him, but he is stronger than me. In the whole church there was only one weapon, the secret weapon used by sister Winona to kill Ranger. I ran upstairs to sister Luka's room and took the weapon from her desk. It was so heavy I had to pick it up with both hands. I ran along the corridor, hearing Buford call for me as he came inside, making a joke of my name by saying it over and over in a silly voice and laughing. He thinks I will not be able to get away from him. He thinks he will do to me what I do not want. The thing that would save me was in my own hands, an evil thing that had already killed, but sister Winona would not have done that to a good man, only someone evil like Buford, so it was as if our lady placed it there for me to use, but it was a club, not a bow and arrow, and could only be used when you are close by someone, not far away. I did not want to be close to Buford to kill him, wanted him to die far enough away for me to see him fall, but not close enough for him to grab at me.

'I know you're in here! I don't want to hurt you, just love you...'

I turned the corner and went down the stairs, making no noise, hoping he would be unable to find me in so big a place and go away, but he came running along the upstairs corridor very fast, I could hear his feet slapping the floor, so I had to think of a place to hide. The stairway to the tower was only a little way off, and I ran to it with my weapon clutched tightly against my chest and began climbing. He saw me because I was too slow, only halfway up the stairs when he came in sight. His face was horrible, split side to side with a grin and his eyes shining. He called for me to stop but I ran to the top of the staircase and then to the smaller stairs leading to the tower. He was already at the bottom when I reached the top and came into the open space where the instrument stood with its glass eye staring at the village. There was nothing to hide behind and no way to climb down the outside of the tower. I had not been clever in my flight. He was coming up the stairs slowly, slapping his feet against the stone, cooing my name softly over and over, knowing this would frighten me. I had been hunted down and was about to be used like a wife by this awful thing coming slowly up the stairs.

There was a weapon in my hands but I barely had the strength to lift it. In between taking in a long breath and letting it out again, I knew that whatever strength still lived inside me would have to be called upon. I stood beside the square hole in the floor where the stairs come up into the open room where the instrument stands. I stood on the side of the hole that Buford would have his back to when he came up those last few steps, and I raised the weapon over my head.

'I know you're up here, Spooky, I saw you. You don't have to be afraid, not of me, I only want to love you…'

I saw the back of his head come into sight, still too far below me to strike. I should have been kneeling by the hole in the floor, not standing, but if I moved now he would hear me. I waited, and he began coming up those last few steps that would lift him closer to my weapon. But then he sensed me behind him and turned his head while still too far away. He saw me with arms raised, but because he was below me he could not see what was hidden behind my head. His grin got wider. 'There you are…'

I could not strike him with my club, so I threw it with every part of my strength. I threw it straight into his smiling face. The weapon struck him in the forehead with a sound like someone's knuckles rapping sharply, just once, on wood. Heavy though it was, the weapon actually bounced back from his forehead and fell down the staircase with a loud clattering. Buford's stupid face did not change for the longest time, then his eyes slid up toward the roof above us and his body simply dropped where it stood, collapsed into a heap of limbs that could not support it and so went tumbling down the staircase. When he came to rest at the bottom I looked over the lip of the hole in the floor. Buford lay sprawled at the bottom of the stairs, my weapon beside him. I waited, to be sure he was dead, but he stirred, moving just a little, and groaned. So I had to go down and stand beside him. If I did not, he might have recovered and picked up my club to do the same to me. Going back down the stairs was very hard, and I could only make myself approach Buford by thinking about what might happen if I did not.

I picked up the thing that had saved me, sister Winona's weapon, and waited some more, surprised at the hammering in my chest because inside my head there was a strange kind of calm, like the silence and stillness that happen before a storm. Buford opened his eyes and slowly raised a hand to touch his forehead. He made a sound of pain, a gasp that became a whimper. He could see me beside him, would not take his eyes from mine, but seemed unable to move his body apart from one arm. The still place inside my head knew he could not be allowed to rise. He had not caught me and hurt me the way he wanted, and now was helpless. I could kill him if I wanted, and I did want to do that, kill him dead. There was nothing to stop me, and yet I did not step forward to hit him again, even though I knew he might get up after a while and begin chasing me, this time without any grinning because I had hurt him and made him look foolish. If he was able to chase me again, and catch me this time, he would not just hurt me, he would kill me to get back his pride. I knew this as surely as I knew his name. And yet I did nothing, just watched him moving his arm and moaning while he stared at me, unable to make his mouth work. He had lost, but was still a threat to me. His eyes wandered from mine and seemed to find something in the air to stare at. Blood began leaking from his nostril. There was only a small wound to his forehead. He looked like a drunk man who has fallen down and can only lie there with a peculiar look on his face. I watched him, not knowing what to do. And then he found the strength to get up on one elbow. He paused then, looked at me and grinned, to show me he was not defeated. For as long as he lay like a drunk man I could not kill him, but once he was able to get even a little way off the floor it was as if someone else commanded my arm to lift the weapon again and bring it down very hard on the top of his head where his sweating scalp showed through the hair. I did it again and he slumped back down. Buford was still breathing but I did not want him to because he did not deserve it. And so I killed him. I killed the thing that would have killed me. I am the rabbit who has slain the wolf. I do not care, and I do not care that I do not care. I am beyond caring now. I do not care that I am the last sister, nor do I care that I will never know love again. I do not care that our lady is dead, as dead as Buford. I care nothing for what his father or any of the villagers might do now. Let them come, I do not care.

42

I have been waiting for Buford's father, but he has not come. I am also waiting for my own father. Yes, I have thought about this and the truth is plain. It is Chad. He is my father. Why else would he have brought a deer to my door? He is my father, not the murderer that killed my mother. It makes perfect sense now that I know what I did not know before. I know many things now. Even if they sometimes change around and I do not know them for a little while, they come back to me and I know them again and find strength in what I know. Chad is my father, and he will come for me. I am so lonely. Where is he? I keep watch through the instrument. It is a sad old instrument all covered in dust because it lives in the tower all the time. I have dragged my mattress up here to sleep on, and taken jars and jugs to the creek and filled them and brought them up into the tower so I can stay here for a long time. If Buford's father comes to kill me he will have to come up the tower stairs and I will be waiting with my weapon to kill him the same way. I have dragged Buford away from the tower and into a corner of the herb garden because he smells very bad. It took a long time to drag him that far because I am very weak now and so hungry.

43

They have all gone. The trading field is empty. I have swept the instrument back and forth across the village looking for anything alive, and there is nothing. Has my father gone with the rest of them? He is so independent it is hard to imagine him trudging along with the villagers, herding cattle and sharing their food if they have any. If they do not he will kill some for them. No, he will kill something for me to eat, not them, they do not deserve it, except for the sisters. But he is not with them anyway. He is somewhere near to me, watching, but he will not reveal himself. Chad has his reasons.

I have gone to the village. It is a strange place now with no one there. I have gone into the houses looking for food but there is nothing, they have taken it all. I have seen five old people, one of them very old and lying in her bed. The dead ones were in bed too, so I thought this one was dead also until she turned her head to look at me. She looked for a long time and then looked at the ceiling again and I went away. Going back to the church I saw two llamas a long way off, over at the edge of the forest, but they did not see me. I am glad I set them free, even if soon they will be eaten by beasts. And the pine needles are turning brown. It is a brown forest now, not green any more, so that is dying too. Everything is dying but I am not. I am waiting. I am running out of ink.

I have seen deer and elk coming from the forest and walking through the village. They are walking away from the sun, going the same direction the villagers went, and for the same reason. There have been bears too, three of them. I have not seen any wolves but I know they are walking away from the sun too. Everything that is alive is walking away from the sun. There are no more birds. All the birds have flown away from the sun. I went into the herb garden and something has been eating Buford. He is in pieces and scattered all over with much of his meat gone. I do not care but I am glad something was able to feed its hunger that way. I am starving now and very weak.

I have seen a cougar down in the yard, so that is what has been eating Buford. It was looking all around and sniffing the air, but it could not smell me because I am so high up. It was a very beautiful creature although dangerous. It went away after a little while, going the same way as the rest. My father has not come yet but he will. My ink is almost gone.

44

Our lady has cast her shadow over the earth on seventh day, making the air cooler and bringing a little welcome darkness. I have never seen anything so lovely. For a moment our lady moved over Sol, a big circle of wonderful blackness surrounded by sunfire. I cried when I saw this. The village looked like it used to at night with everyone sleeping, but there are only old dead people there. I went down and stood in the yard to stare at our lady, wishing I could send a prayer that would make her stay where she is, but prayers are empty things, as empty as my stomach. The moon moved aside after just a little while and Sol began pouring fire over the world again and I could not look into the sky without going blind. The sky is so bright, when I hold up my hand to shield my face I can almost see the bones through my flesh. Chad is not coming. I think I am beginning to die, but somehow I do not care. It is painful to be alive now.

My blood has come! I have real moonblood along my thighs. I have scraped it off with my fingers and let it drip into my ink bottle. Now my words are red not black. I am not so hungry now. My stomach has been hurting for the longest time from hunger, but that has gone away. Now I know I am truly dying.

45

I saw him coming through the open gates from my perch in the tower. I do not know if he came from the forest or the village, only that he has come. He stood looking at the pile of ash that once was an elm tree. I knew I must be asleep and dreaming, but he came further into the yard and looked up. When I saw that he had seen me, I fell down right where I stood. I think I could not bear to believe I had seen something real, in case I had not. I waited, lying beside the instrument, hoping to hear his footsteps on the staircase leading up to my hideaway, and when they came, when it was made clear to me I was not to die alone, I allowed my eyes to close as if overcome suddenly by sleep.

What caused my return to the world was the wonderful smell of cooking meat. It came curling into my nostrils, reminding me I am alive, and I sat up. He had taken me downstairs to the kitchen and propped me against the wall like a sack of flour. Sister Kath's stove was crackling with fire and Chad stood over it poking at something that gave out that best of all smells. All the pots and pans had been stolen, so the meat sat directly on the stovetop, hissing merrily. He was no different than before, still wearing animal hides and with his wild hair tied back with a leather band. He looked like some peculiar creature that has come inside to pretend it is human. This was my father, come to save me from my fate, and yet I could think of nothing to say, could only stare at his narrow shoulders made broad by matted fur and feel grateful that now I might live. The smell of meat made me drool like a dog and twisted my insides painfully. He turned and saw me watching. I was expecting a smile, maybe even some words, but all he did was turn back to the pan while scratching idly at his ribs, unapproachable as ever. My father is a man of mystery with a strange gift for survival, and it is this that will protect me from further harm. I have been delivered from the arms of our lady to those of Chad, whose arms are real, with strength and purpose.

When he was ready, Chad brought the meat to me on the end of his knife and dropped it onto the table, since there are no more plates. I made myself allow it to cool a little before snatching it up and cramming it into my mouth. My lips were burned as I bit into that slab of sizzling delight. Chewing was easy, swallowing was hard. I ate it all, then was sick. Chad prepared more meat without a word. I asked what kind it was and he put his hands on top of his head to make llama ears and made a snooty llama face that made me laugh it was so clever. But then I felt awful because he had killed one of the sacred herd, and more awful still because I wanted the next batch to hurry up and be ready for eating. I wanted to apologize to our lady but then remembered she is not near, which made me even more sad. Chad poked at the pan, watched it sizzle. I stared at the table top and wondered if our lady had left an actual hole inside me, or if that was only the hunger.

46

He will not talk. My own father, and he refuses to make conversation, even though there is so much to talk about. I showed him Buford's remains and told how I came to kill him, but all Chad would do was nod his head understandingly, as if such things were to be expected. I wanted him to praise me, but Chad is content to feed me. I told him the story of the elm tree and its end, and the murdering of Willa, which made him shake his head with sadness but did not produce any words. I wanted him to say the villagers were evil and stupid, but he offered no judgement or opinion. I wanted him to step inside the emptiness left in my heart by Willa's absence, but he chose not to. I asked him if the world would one day tip back to its usual position and all he did was shrug, as if this most important question was none of his concern. Chad is most certainly a presence, but he is not a person, not really. I think my father is even more different than people allowed, but I do not condemn him. I went so far as to ask if he knew he is my father, but all he did was look thoughtful for a moment, then wander away. The villagers always said he was touched in the head, and it may be that they were right, but I am proud of him anyway because he has rescued me and made me whole again. I showed him my secret book and have begun reading to him from it after every meal. He gives the impression of listening closely, but his face tells me little, his mouth even less. I want him to say how well I have told the tale in this, the only book in the world, but apart from listening as I read, he makes no comment, as if what I tell him is a made-up story for passing the time. He is not who I thought he was, but that does not matter.

Brindle has returned! I found her in the remains of the kitchen garden, nosing through the baked soil in search of something green. She is very thin but does not seem to be sick in any way, and is very affectionate, nuzzling and huffing to say how lonely she has been. I gave her neck the longest hug and cried a little. I should be hugging my father and crying against his chest, but that has not been possible. I am the last High Sister, leader of a broken church, and my fellow sisters are a silent man and a llama. I think this is very funny, but it does not make me laugh. I explained this to Chad and he did not laugh either, but I did not expect him to.

Having Brindle with us has changed my father. He has made a rough packsaddle for Brindle and shown me how our few possessions can be carried by her. Carried where? When I asked him, Chad pointed away from the sun, the direction taken by the villagers, the only place it makes sense to go, but I do not want to catch up with them, those killers and hypocrites. We will travel slowly, following the streams for as long as these continue to flow. One day they will stop because the sun will have melted every stretch of snow in the high mountains and there will be no more runoff to feed them. That is when the top of the world will start to become a desert. I have heard about these places where nothing can survive for lack of water and everything that ever grew there turns to dust. The top of the world will soon be dust and the bottom of the world will be covered in snow. Somewhere in between the two we will find a place to live. The sun will be high enough in the sky to grow things, but not so high it drives us mad. There will be clouds in the sky there, and rain will fall to sustain us on the cool earth. We may find other people who have done this, people not from our valley who I do not want to see again. Willa's people may sail their boats away down the coast in search of cooler waters to fish. But there must be more than just these because the world, half baked and half frozen, is a very big place. We are leaving soon.

My red ink keeps drying out in its bottle and I must spit into it to make it flow while I set down these last words. Everything I ever loved will be left behind – an old stone building filled with ghosts – a faith entwined with things I no longer believe – and a loving soul buried under cold ash that is slowly being borne away on the wind. My companions on this journey to a new life will be silent, but I know they care for me just as I care for them. Caring is the invisible baggage we take with us that must not be lost along the way. It does not depend on prayer, and it may remain unspoken between us, but we will carry this precious burden to a new place on this new earth, where it will grow as it must. There will be little I take with me, my two necklaces to signify lost obligation and lost love, and my battered book, the last in all this ancient world. This is our small history, flawed but true, and must be kept for reading to the children who will follow in our footsteps, so they might know where they have come from, and where they may go.